PIPI HOT

SUSAN MILLER

To Hugh –

'Happy we've been together'

Love, Susan

Published in 2019 by Lozenge Books

ISBN Paperback: 978-1-9160923-0-3
Ebook: 978-1-9160923-1-0

A CIP catalogue copy of this book can be found in the British Library.

Published with the help of Indie Authors World
www.indieauthorsworld.com

To the memory of Bobby,
who rated the pipes one better
than the vacuum cleaner
and put up with both.

ACKNOWLEDGEMENTS

My grateful thanks go to all my fellow band members, without whose forbearing this book would never have been written and particularly to Barbara Scott Emmett, who taught me a lot about writing. Thanks also go to Indie Authors World for their assistance in publishing this book.

CHAPTER 1

Old Ewan's death and subsequent obsequies gave Auchentullum its biggest laugh for years.

For a start, he had been found lying by the Tullum Water which ran through the village and his aversion to water, both internally and externally, was well known. It was charitably assumed that he had fallen and knocked himself out, but when efforts to bring him round failed, an ambulance was called. He was removed to hospital in Dunfermline where it was found that he had died of a heart attack.

His death and his manner of meeting it were the main topic of conversation the following evening in the public bar of The Stag's Head, from whence he had set out on his final and unaccomplished journey home. The pub's name referred to the crest of the Earls of Tullum, but the establishment was known locally as The Coo's Heid.

Some wag remarked, 'Ewan must've known that he was about to meet his maker.'

'How so?'

'Well, they say that cleanliness is next to godliness and as Ewan McDougal was no' one of the godly, why else would you be finding him so close to water?'

'Aye, and the last time he was near water would have been at his christening. I pity whoever had to lay him out.'

At that point, the group by the bar was joined by Duncan Mackenzie. He was in his early fifties, a little under six feet and his dark straight hair flopped over his forehead. His face was long and lugubrious and admirably suited to his occupation: he was the village joiner and undertaker. However, his looks belied his nature as he had a well-developed, if somewhat dry sense of humour.

''Evening Duncan. The usual?'

Without waiting for a reply, the barman drew a pint of bitter and put it in front of his customer, who downed it eagerly. Duncan was also the pipe major of the Strathtullum Pipe Band and he had just come from a practice session.

Someone enquired, 'Are you seeing to Ewan's funeral?'

'Aye. He has a sister in Glasgow, she's all the family he had. She used to live here afore she married and she phoned me this afternoon and asked me to make the arrangements.'

'It must have been an awful shock for the poor woman.'

'Och, I don't think so. She was surprised that he'd lasted so long.'

The customer who had made the remark about cleanliness and godliness asked, 'D'you know what it was that Ewan died of?'

'Heart attack.'

'That so? I would've thought it would be cirrhosis of the liver.'

'The doctor's lassie plays the side drum and that's what she overheard her dad saying. Apparently he'd been treating Ewan for some years.'

In view of Duncan's activities it was an accepted fact of village life that one went to the library and consulted *The Piping Times* before approaching him to deal with the last remains of one's nearest and dearest. Any mourner who insisted on a Saturday funeral, particularly in the summer months when the majority of pipe band competitions occurred, was not offered much in the way of condolences.

Old Ewan's sister was not up-to-date with local customs.

Band practices took place on Monday and Thursday evenings in the village hall and on the Thursday after Ewan's death, Duncan announced that Neil, the pipe sergeant, would have to take over the band on Saturday morning as he would be otherwise engaged.

'Why did the silly bitch have to arrange it for a Saturday?' asked Neil.

'Husband said he wasnae wasting a day's wages on a brother-in-law he hadnae seen in twenty years.'

'Well, I suppose that's as good a reason as any.'

'You will be able to take the band out?' enquired Duncan as an afterthought.

‘Oh aye. The shops can mind themselves.’ Neil Dunn owned the butcher’s shops in Auchentullum and the neighbouring mining village of Brankstone and it was in the main square of the latter that the band was due to play in order to raise funds, something which they did round the neighbourhood two or three times a year.

Alan Lindsay, one of the younger pipers, watched them as he tuned up. The two men always reminded him of a couple of dogs. Duncan was a bloodhound and Neil a terrier, being stocky, with close-cropped grey hair, bushy eyebrows and a short moustache.

After about fifteen minutes cacophony, with nine pipers all playing different tunes in various corners of the hall, the lobby, the kitchen and cloakrooms, Duncan called them into a circle and went round tuning their chanters against his own. Alan found himself with a piece of insulation tape partly covering one of the holes as the note sounded slightly flat against the pipe major’s instrument.

While Duncan was doing this, Alan’s neighbour, Big Sandy, complained, ‘Duncan can ye no’ get us better reeds? Thae new yins is rubbish, nae volume in them.’ Anyone other than a piper would have heartily disagreed with this statement, but there was a general rumble of assent from the other band members.

‘That’s just what the judges wrote on the score sheets the other week at Scotstoun,’ said old Willie. Willie Simpson was the former pipe major, who had stood down some three years previously and was now in charge of the beginners’ class. He was in his early sixties and had a pithead job at Brankstone Colliery.

The recollection of their performance at the Glasgow Highland Gathering at Scotstoun cast a pall of gloom over the band. Piping competitions work on similar lines to the football league, with four adult grades. Strathtullum had been playing at grade three for several years, but this summer they were hoping to do well enough to earn promotion and in some competitions were going to play up a grade.

The band played for about a quarter of an hour, drones corked, until the chanters had settled down, then Duncan went round, tuning the drones and they began to practice their competition medley.

'That wasnae too bad,' he said. 'Now we'd better have a run-through what we're going to play on Saturday. We'll start with last year's competition set.'

A few minutes later it was quite obvious that several members of the band had been so sick of the sound of that particular march, strathspey and reel that they hadn't practiced it since the end of the previous summer, but after going through it a couple of times, they found that they could put their fingers onto automatic pilot again.

Duncan then leered round the circle. 'And now we'll have a run-through the family favourites.'

There was a chorus of groans and protests.

'Aw Jeez, Duncan!'

'We're not playing that lot, surely?'

'Do we have to play yon rubbish?'

'Lads and lassies of the band –' there were three girls: two pipers and a drummer, '– if you want the public to fill the collecting tins, you've got to play the occasional tune that they recognise and like and as far as folk are concerned, *The Flower of Scotland* and *Amazing Grace* are God's gift to pipers, even if pipers are no' of the same opinion. However, we'll liven things up at the finish with *The Drunken Piper* and *The Black Bear Hornpipe.*'

Bob Rennie, a metal work apprentice at Rosyth dockyard and son of local shopkeepers, muttered to Alan '*The Drunken Piper,* that's Sandy's signature tune.' Sandy Henderson's thirst was well known, but despite his large frame, he did not have a good head for alcohol and it was a standing order that at competition outings he was to be kept away from the beer tent until after the band had played. He worked as a plumber for a local builder and was the occasional butt for jokes about "pipes".

After a short practice, Duncan looked at his watch. 'Alan, go and get the drummers from the committee room, we've just time for a quick run-through a few of the sets for Saturday.'

Alan returned shortly with Jimmy Gourlay, the leading drummer, and both had long faces. 'Ron says he's no' coming out on Saturday,' announced the latter.

Ron Findlay was the bass drummer and ran the local garage. He liked to think that he also owned it, but as his wife reminded him occasionally, Dad had left the business to her. As Peggy Findlay, née Jamieson, was built on Junoesque lines and knew her way around the insides of a car as well as her husband used to know his way round not a few of the local girls, he did not argue the point too often.

'What's got into the bugger the noo?' growled Duncan.

Neil groaned and clapped a hand to his head. 'What's got into the bugger is that he's mad at me for shifting my account along to Lang's at Brankstone.'

Willie looked at him in exasperation. 'Now why would ye be after doing a daft thing like that?'

'He was aye complaining that I never settled my accounts quick enough. I do my books the last week of the month and he does his the first and he didnae like it that his bill had to sit three weeks afore being paid, so last month I told him what he could do with his oil and petrol and the van's now dealt with at Lang's.' He glared round the others. 'And I'm no' going back to him just to keep youse yins happy.'

The band practice ended in an uproar.

'Hell! We cannae play on Saturday if we've no bass drummer.'

'Borrow the lad from the colliery brass band.'

'He's nae use. Doesnae know a two-four beating from a six-eight one.'

'Jimmy, is that youngster no' ready to play yet?'

The leading drummer shook his head. 'Ron said that if we got a substitute, he'd go elsewhere.' He held up his hands to silence the reaction. 'He's good enough for grade one, so I'm for keeping him sweet.'

'Bloody drummers!' muttered Bob, 'Who needs 'em anyhow?'

Willie's comment was pithily succinct: 'Nae drummers, nae competitions, ye sumph!'

Alan edged out of the circle of gesticulating musicians and packed his pipes into their case. He pulled a face at Ian McLellan, the band secretary, who had been writing in a corner of the hall and on his way out said, 'If I don't hear from you by tomorrow evening, I'll assume that we're not playing on Saturday. OK?'

Ian nodded and wished him goodnight.

*

Auchentullum was situated on the north bank of the River Forth, between Alloa and Dunfermline. Castle Tullum, the seat of the former Earls of Tullum, was perched above the village and the Tullum Water cascaded down the hillside, forming part of the castle's original defences. The community had grown up on each side of the burn, on the flatter ground at the base of the approaches to the castle.

This oldest part of the village was called Burnside and was something of a local showpiece. It was about two hundred yards long and the rivulet was flanked on each side by a wide stretch of grass, a road and a row of cottages, including the pub. The village had evolved in the approximate form of an H, with Burnside forming the crosspiece. The long arm on the southern side of the village was formed by Brankstone Road, and Castle Lane made up the shorter one, petering out in a field at its east end. There was another crosspiece, Oakley Avenue, which ran through a small, modern housing estate. At the western end, the two arms of the H merged and the village hall was in the triangle of land at this junction.

The earldom had become extinct during the war. What was left of the estate after death duties had been turned into the Strathtullum Trust and the castle now housed a sixth form college.

Alan Lindsay lived at the opposite end of the village from the hall. The cottage where he and his mother and brother lived was nearly the last house on the road. The three-quarter mile walk was no hardship on a May evening, but he would have enjoyed it more if he had had company for part of the way. The vivacious seventeen-year-old daughter of Dr. Angus Grant was a side drummer and the previous winter Alan had suddenly realised that Sheila was a pretty lass. There had been no sign of her when he left the hall and thanks to the row over Ron Findlay, he had not even had time for a quick chat during the practice.

As he opened the garden gate, Alan reflected that "Forthview" might have been a suitable name for the cottage when it was built in the previous century, but "Petrochemical Works View" would be more appropriate now as Grangemouth was on the other side of the river. However, it was far enough away to be ignored, unless the wind blew in a certain direction.

He paused in the small hallway. The furious clacking of a typewriter was coming from the sitting room to his left, so he turned right and went into the kitchen-dining room. His brother was sitting at the table, watching a small, portable black-and-white television set.

'Oy! Shouldn't you be swotting?'

Gregor scowled at him. 'Just because you've finished your exams and left school, there's no need to gloat. Anyhow, I've only got Technical Drawing tomorrow and Art on Monday and you can hardly swot them.'

Alan grunted his agreement and sat down by his brother. Apart from a slight similarity in facial features, they didn't resemble each other. The former was already beginning to fill out and had red hair, whereas his sibling was tall and skinny with black hair. They watched until the pop concert finished and then simultaneously reached for the "off" button when a party political broadcast was announced.

The sound of the typewriter was still audible.

'Is Mum doing her monthly letter to Dad?'

'I guess so.' The boys looked at each other. 'D'you think he'll ever come back?' said Gregor.

'Dunno… Ten years in a labour camp is a helluva long time… I wonder if he ever gets Mum's letters?'

'Well, we never get any direct news from him. When was the last letter from the consulate?'

Alan thought for a few moments. 'Just after New Year.'

'If he didn't return, d'you think Mum would marry again?'

'Paul?'

Gregor nodded.

'I've wondered about it, but he does keep saying that he's sure Dad'll survive. After all, he knows what it's like, he was in one.'

'Yeah, but he escaped after only a few months and he was a good bit younger than Dad then.'

Alan shrugged and sighed. 'Y'know, there are times when I can't even remember what he looks like and I have to go and look at the photo on Mum's dressing ta–'

The door opened. 'Hello. I didn't hear you get back.'

The boys looked up as their mother came into the kitchen. Jill Lindsay was a tall, slender woman, neither pretty nor plain, with light brown hair cut in a short, layered style. She had an oval face, large brown eyes, a thin, straight nose and a wide mouth. She was normally an outgoing person, but with the recent advent of her fortieth birthday, reading glasses and some grey hairs, she was feeling low. This was not helped by trying to write a cheerful, newsy letter to a husband who she had not seen for nearly five years and who, at times, she wondered if she would ever see again.

'Good band practice? Are you out with them on Saturday morning?'

'It was OK until the last five minutes, but I left them in the middle of an almighty row.'

'What was it about this time?'

'Pipers versus drummers, as usual. Neil and Ron have fallen out. Duncan can't come because of a funeral and Ron is refusing to play under Neil's leadership and as he's the bass drummer, it puts us on the spot.'

'Is that the funeral of the smelly old chap who lived in Castle Lane?' asked Gregor.

'S'right. Some of the band were talking about him and apparently he used to be a piper. He was a founder member, along with Duncan's father, just after the war.'

'I'm going along to the post with this letter, before it gets dark,' announced Jill as she went out. This was followed by an angry exclamation from the hall. She came back into the kitchen, tight-lipped. 'How often do I have to tell you not to leave things lying in the middle of the floor? And you might at least look after other folk's property.' The kitchen door, followed by the front doors, banged after her.

'You twit!' commented Gregor as his brother went and retrieved his pipes, which were on loan from the band, 'You know Mum's always got a short fuse on letter-writing days. Why can't you be a bit tidier? Anyhow, what's happening about the band's outing?'

'Oh, I expect things'll sort themselves out, as usual.'

*

The following evening when the phone went, Jill half got up from her chair in the sun room and sat down again.

Gregor answered. 'Alan, it's for you.'

'I'm roosting,' replied his brother from the bathroom. 'Shove it in, the door's not locked.'

The phone, which was situated in the hall, was fitted with a cable long enough to reach into either the sitting room or kitchen and the bathroom was between the two.

'Evening Ian. What's happening about tomorrow? … Pipers only… Yes, that's a help… And be down there for nine-fifteen… Full dress? Ah well, I suppose if we're togged up like Christmas trees, the public feels it's getting better value for money. Thanks. 'Bye.'

A few minutes later Alan went through to the sunroom which had been added to the back of the cottage. 'Mum, d'you know where my spats are?'

'No idea. Probably where you threw them down the last time you wore them.' Alan pulled a face. 'When you do find them, there's a new tube of white canvas cleaner in the cupboard in the utility room. I thought I'd better get some.'

'Thanks.'

When Gregor later went up to the room which he shared with his brother, he had to pick his way over items of band uniform which Alan was frantically excavating from the wardrobe.

'Have you seen my spats anywhere?' enquired a muffled voice.

Gregor dodged a shoe which came flying out. 'Try looking in the bottom of the airing cupboard. You threw them in there the last time you wore them, but you'll have to wait, Mum's having a shower.' He picked up a jacket which was lying on the floor. 'Some of the braid's coming off this cuff.'

A dishevelled Alan backed out of the wardrobe, grabbed the jacket and went and banged on the door of the shower room, a small compartment between the two bedrooms. 'Mum, my jacket needs mending.'

A damp, towel-wrapped Jill stuck her head round the door. 'What's the matter now?' The garment was thrust at her. 'It can wait till I've got some clothes on – and this time you can press your kilt and plaid yourself, then perhaps you'll learn to put them away more carefully in future.'

Ten minutes later, the Lindsays had congregated in the kitchen, Jill with her sewing box, Alan with the iron and ironing board and Gregor with the whitener and an old sponge. The lights in the cottage did not go out until late.

At half past eight the following morning, Jill banged on the kitchen ceiling with a broom handle to signal that breakfast was ready. Alan appeared first, wearing band uniform on his lower half, with a tee-shirt above. A scowling Gregor followed a few minutes later. 'Mum, it's not fair! His stuff's all over the place. The room's like a pigsty.'

'Not fair? I like that!' exploded his brother. 'You've got your workshop at the end of the garage, so I reckon I'm entitled to a bit more floor space upstairs.'

'A bit more? The whole bl–'

Jill thumped the table. 'That's enough! End of argument!' An argument which had been going on for nearly four years, even since they had moved to the cottage from a Victorian terrace house in the west end of Glasgow. She sighed. 'Gregor, I know we're short of space and you were used to a room each, but do try and put up with each other for just a bit longer. All being well, he'll be away to college in the autumn and his untidiness'll be someone else's problem in term time. Alan, I've got to go into Alloa this morning. D'you want me to give you a lift along to Brankstone and collect you on the way back?'

Alan shook his head and swallowed a mouthful of porridge. 'Sorry, I meant to tell you last night, Ian said that Paul was taking some of the kids into Alloa in the school mini-bus and that there'd be room for a few of the band. I expect they could squeeze you in if you want. He's picking folk up at the lower end of Burnside at nine-fifteen.'

'Thanks, I'll take up the offer and save petrol. Gregor, are you coming?'

'No. Duncan dropped off the timber for the garden seat yesterday afternoon and I want to get on with it.' Gregor Lindsay's main interest was woodwork and he had recently told his mother that he wanted to be a cabinet maker. Unlike his brother, he was not academically inclined and she had been worrying about his future.

At about nine-twenty a white mini-bus, with "Castle Tullum College" painted on the sides in red, drew up at the meeting place and Jill and Alan got in. The latter's appearance, in full band uniform with his feather bonnet hanging from the hook on his belt, drew some admiring looks and comments from the foreign students. Secretly, he was rather pleased, though would have sooner died than admit it.

The driver called out, ''Morning, Jill. I wondered if you'd be joining us. There's room up here for you.' Only a slight liquidness in the pronunciation of the letter "l" indicated that he was not speaking his native tongue: Paul Holland had started life some thirty-eight years previously in Czechoslovakia as Pavel Holandov. He had fled the country in the short-lived "Prague Spring" and had taken up British nationality as soon as he was eligible to do so. For the last five years he had taught Russian and German at the college as he was bi-lingual in the former and spoke the latter fluently. He was over six feet tall, broad shouldered, slim-hipped, with wavy fair hair which brushed his collar. His face was triangular, with a wide forehead, blue-grey eyes set above flat, high cheekbones and a short, pointed chin.

Before setting off, he took out a pipe, gestured at Jill, who smiled and nodded, so he proceeded to light it. She watched with a slightly amused expression as he tilted his head back, half shut his eyes and extinguished the match with a long exhalation. It seemed such an odd, almost sensuous way of doing it, most men would have either waved the match about or given a quick puff.

At the end of the village, near the hall, they stopped at Rennie's Mini Market and picked up Bob. As they moved off again he and Alan jeered and gave brief V-signs in the direction of the garage, a few yards down the road on the other side. Fortunately, Ron Findlay had his head under the bonnet of a customer's car as they went past.

The two pipers were dropped off in the square in Brankstone and while they were getting out Jill looked around and wondered why Fife villages were either picturesque or ugly, with no intermediate types. The village had grown up round the colliery during the last century and even though the rows of cottages flanking the main street were similar to those in Auchentullum, they had a drab, dismal look about them. However, initial impressions could be deceptive and as Jill had learnt, the community was a close-knit one, with many kind folk.

Neil was already there and when the two lads went up to him, said, 'It'll just be pipers this morning, but some of the drummers are coming to shake a collecting can.' Alan hoped Sheila would be among them.

Paul stuck his head out of the window. 'I told my students I would only take them shopping on condition that they did a bit of collecting on the way home. See you later.'

Neil laughed and said to the boys, 'He certainly takes his duties seriously as band president,' a post to which Paul had been elected the previous year.

As the others arrived, Alan came to the conclusion that the only time Big Sandy looked presentable was when he was in band uniform. He had thinning fair hair, a straggling moustache and usually wore faded jeans, a tee-shirt and a tatty pullover. At the moment, his kilt was acting as a corset, but normally his belt buckle was concealed under an overhang of flesh.

Before they started to play, Neil warned them, 'You may curse the drummers, but just remember, they cover up a multitude of sins – and wrong notes – so take things easy. We'll start with the four-four set: *Scotland the Brave* and so on…'

*

Jill was one of the last to return to the bus after doing her shopping and as she apologised for keeping them waiting, she noticed that Paul had been to the barber. She had gone off men with long hair years ago and was still able to impose a shortish cut on the boys, even if it did involve an occasional wrestling match in the bathroom and a compromise on what the two parties considered to be "short". Paul's hair was still a bit long by her standards, but he looked a lot better than earlier on.

The bus arrived back in Brankstone at about eleven-thirty and its occupants took over the collecting tins for the last half hour of the band's recital. After Neil had dismissed the pipers and thanked them for their attendance, Paul produced a carrier bag and handed round tins of lager and cola which were downed eagerly.

There were some extra passengers for the last leg of the outing and Alan was delighted to be able to persuade Sheila to sit on his knee. He was much less pleased when she spent the entire journey talking over his shoulder to one of the male students.

After dropping Bob Rennie at the entrance to the village, they proceeded along Castle Lane and Paul drew up at the bottom of the drive up to the castle, which was opposite the churchyard. As some of the passengers disembarked, a small cortège emerged from the church and made its way over to a freshly dug grave. The rest of them got out, stood respectfully by the wall and some of the students crossed themselves. They saw Duncan step forward and say something to the large, grey-haired matron who was following the coffin. She looked towards the spectators and nodded. Duncan broke away from the group and came over to them.

'Alan, Mrs Lawson would like to hear *Flowers of the Forest*. Get your pipes out lad and I'll give your drones a quick tuning.'

After Alan played the lament, he stepped back from the graveside and the committal started.

A shrill voice suddenly interrupted the proceedings. 'Yon's no' Father's headstone!'

The minister stopped in mid peroration and gave the deceased's sister a startled look.

'Yon's no' the white marble Mother saved up for.' She gave her diminutive spouse a hefty nudge with her elbow. 'Alec, awa' and read me the inscription, I forgot ma glasses.'

Mr Lawson stepped round the pile of earth, bent down and read out the inscription, running his finger under the words. 'To the memory of John McDougal and his wife Agnes Ballin–'

'Mother's name was Annie. Yon's ma Aunty Aggie. Ewan couldnae stand the silly woman and he'd no' rest in peace beside her.' She swung round and pointed an accusing finger at Duncan. 'Where's Father's headstone?'

Duncan stood there, looking like a very unhappy bloodhound. After opening and shutting his mouth several times, he managed to stammer, 'Mrs Lawson… I …I'm terribly sorry… There seems to have been some awful mistake. What were your parents' names?'

'John McDougal and Anne Ballingall. Father and his cousin had the same names and they married sisters. It was a wee bitty muddling at times.'

Alan heard a snort coming from the direction of the wall and turned round in time to see Sheila duck down behind it with both hands clamped over her mouth. Those of the spectators who understood the local accent did likewise, but the foreign students stood there, looking puzzled. They realised something was wrong, but weren't sure what had happened. At the other side of the bus, Jill and Paul were leaning against each other, ribs aching as they tried to contain their mirth.

Paul recovered first. 'Poor Duncan, how very embarrassing for him.'

Jill wiped her eyes. 'But what a marvellous story it'll make to tell in the pub.'

'It would be unkind of you to make fun of the poor man's discomfiture.'

'I'm afraid the rest of the village won't be so eager to spare his feelings. The story'll soon be part of local folklore.'

When Duncan recovered his composure, he oversaw the removal of the coffin back to the church, the correct plot was located, the grave digger and his assistant agreed to some overtime, the minister said he could recycle an old sermon for tomorrow – the one about the drunkenness of Noah would do very nicely under the circumstances – and it was arranged that the burial would recommence at three o'clock. The undertaker then said to Mr and Mrs Lawson that The Stag's Head did very good bar lunches and he would be pleased if they would be his guests.

Once Mrs Lawson's ruffled feathers had been smoothed by a stiff whisky and a large plateful of food, she said she would like to visit her brother's home before the funeral recommenced. The three of them wandered up Burnside and continued right down Castle Lane.

Old Ewan's abode was a cottage at the far end of the lane, next to the field, and had been rented from the village trust. The gate hung half off its hinges and the overgrown garden was enhanced with a variety of junk in the undergrowth. Duncan felt behind a stone by the door, located the key and let them in. They were greeted by a smell compounded of several kinds of rot, stale cooking, unwashed clothing and general dirt. The chaos and squalor was indescribable. Mrs Lawson took one look at it and her face crumpled into tears. After a hasty glance at the seating accommodation, Duncan steered her outside and helped her to sit down on the doorstep.

As her husband patted her on the shoulder, Duncan said, 'This must be a very distressing day for you Mrs Lawson, but I assure you, there'll be no more hitches.'

She shook off her husband's hand, rummaged in her bag and trumpeted into a handkerchief which struck

Duncan as being on the small side for a funeral. 'I'm no' upset. I'm fair blazing! If yon brother o' mine were no' dead already, he would be the noo.' She looked up at the two men and said indignantly, 'We may ha' been poor, but we were aye clean. Mother kept the place spotless and it breaks ma heart to see it the noo.' She drummed her heels on the ground. 'Oh, the scoundrel! I should ha' left him to lie beside Aunty Aggie!'

Duncan gazed heavenwards.

Once Mrs Lawson had calmed down, her husband enquired, 'Is there no' anything ye'd be wanting from the house?'

She snorted angrily as she struggled to her feet. 'It can all go to the local coup, it's all it's fit for.'

Duncan made a move to depart and stopped. 'There's at least one thing that it would be a pity to send to the dump.' He went back inside. A few minutes later he came out with a long wooden box. 'Would you allow me to buy these from your brother's estate?'

'What's that?'

He opened the box and took out a very tatty set of pipes. 'I've a promising young lad in the band who's looking for some and if you're no' wanting your brother's set, I'd be glad to take then off your hands.'

'Oh aye. They're nae use tae us.'

'How much would you be wanting for them?' As the Lawsons looked enquiringly at each other, he gave the pipes a cursory examination. 'The bag's rotten…there's a crack in the chanter, that'd have to be replaced…and he'd also need a new mouthpiece.'

'Fifty pounds?' said Mr Lawson.

'Done!' replied Duncan with an alacrity which made the others wonder if they should have asked for more. 'I'll get my wife to take it off the account for the funeral when she does the books.' He looked at his watch. 'Now I think it's time we were getting back to the church.'

When Jill answered the doorbell that evening, she found Duncan on the step with a pipe case in his hand. ''Evening Mrs Lindsay. Is Alan at home?'

'Yes, both boys are in the garage.'

Duncan went round the side of the cottage to where a modern, prefabricated garage was set well back from the road. 'Hello lads. How's the seat coming on, Gregor?'

'I've got all the pieces cut to size and I've just started to plane and sand them.'

Alan had been eyeing the box. 'Those aren't your pipes.'

'No, they were Old Ewan's. I bought them off his sister this afternoon as I though mebbe they'd do for you.'

Alan's eyes went round with excitement, but when Duncan opened the box and removed the contents, his face fell.

Duncan laughed at his expression. 'Don't be so hasty to condemn them, lad. Come outside and have a good look at them.'

The ivory mounts were discoloured. The woodwork was dull and some bits were growing mould. The drone cords and bag cover were rotten and smelt horrible. The bag was like a board. Alan's face fell even further.

‘Look at the drones, lad.’

‘That’s funny, they seem to be lined with metal.’

‘Exactly. They were made by McDougal of Aberfeldy. Ewan was a relation and they’ve just about the finest tone of any drones I’ve ever heard and once set up, they’ll stay in tune longer than most. Don’t worry about the chanter, it was no’ a good make. I’ve got an old spare which is better and I’ll fit your ivory sole onto it. It’ll do for when you’re playing solo, but otherwise you’ll continue to use the band’s one. The next time your mum’s in Edinburgh or Glasgow, get her to buy you a new bag and I’ll tie it on for you. And get a new mouthpiece as well.’

‘What sort of bag?’

‘Sheepskin’s the traditional material, but as you’re a wet blower, you’d be better with hide. And get a large one, plenty of wind under your elbow’ll steady your blowing. Meanwhile you can oil the wood, clean the ivory with lemon juice and renew the hemp on all the joints. Bring them along to band practice when you’ve got the bag and in the meantime, I’ll take the chanter.’ The stammered, grateful thanks were brushed aside. ‘Och away lad, they’re going to a good home.’ He looked in the bottom of the box. ‘And as a bonus, you’ve got a book of pibroch settings.’

As he turned to leave, Alan said anxiously, ‘What do I owe you? They’re obviously a valuable set and I may not have saved up enough to pay for them.’

‘How much have you put by?’

‘About two hundred pounds.’

There was a pause. ‘Well, I think a hundred and fifty would be a fair price and I’ll include the chanter with it.’

‘Wow! Thanks! That’s terrific!’ And as Duncan departed, he heard Alan calling out excitedly, ‘Mum! Mum! I’ve got my own pipes!’

At the pub that evening, Duncan was the object of a good deal of ribaldry, but he merely smiled into his pint and commented that he had ended the day in profit.

CHAPTER 2

The passenger woke with a start when the air hostess touched him on the shoulder and asked him to fasten his seat belt. Despite having rinsed his mouth after being sick, a sour taste lingered, but there wasn't enough time left to ask for a drink. In confirmation, there was a thump under his feet as the landing gear was lowered. He looked out of the window and a sprawling grey mass resolved itself into the familiar outline of Windsor Castle. A bright spot of colour over the Round Tower indicated the Queen was in residence. He gazed avidly at the symbol, still unable to take in the events of the last twenty-four hours.

Unlike the rest of the passengers, he didn't relax after the plane landed, but sat tensed in his seat as they taxied to the terminal building. As soon as the warning lights went off, he was on his feet, heading for the exit. Others got there first and he was obliged to queue patiently, his back muscles quivering in anticipation of the detaining hand that would prevent him from stepping onto blessed British soil once more. All that happened was that the hostess smiled, thanked him in accented English for travelling with the airline and hoped to see him again soon – which was the last thing he wanted.

He wanted to kneel down and kiss the ground at the bottom of the steps. Looking around, he saw no sign of the media, nobody appeared to be taking any interest in him. With a sigh of relief he followed the signs to passport control, where the officer didn't appear to notice the photo was no longer a good likeness, nor that the newest stamp was nearly five years old.

Such was his luggage that he had no hesitation in going through the "green" customs channel and after negotiating what seemed like endless corridors and staircases, found himself in the domestic departures section of the terminal. His ticket had been made out for Glasgow and at the Shuttle desk, he was told a flight would be boarding in half an hour, so he booked onto it. That would give him time to phone home and announce his arrival. Where were the phones?

A policeman was standing nearby, so he picked up his plastic carrier bag and shoddy little suitcase and went over to him. 'Excuse me, could you tell me where the phones are, please?'

'Certainly, sir. Over there, sir.'

It was then that he was hit by the realisation that he was home again. A policeman had called him "sir". He really was home! He shut his eyes as he was overcome by a wave of emotion.

The constable made a move to support him. 'You alright sir? You don't look too good.'

The man opened his eyes and smiled. 'Oh yes, I'm definitely alright thanks. It's just…it's so marvellous to be home again.'

'Been away long, sir?'

'I've rather lost count of time, but I think it's about five years. Thanks for your help.'

When the passenger got to the kiosk, which looked as though a large mushroom had sprouted from the floor, bearing four phones, he remembered he had no change. He went across to a newsagents, picked up a copy of *The Guardian* and passed over a five pound note. He received back a handful of coins and looked at them suspiciously as there were two which he didn't recognise. He poked at them. 'Er, excuse me…'

The woman leant over the counter and said loudly and slowly, 'Them's the new coins, ducks. That's twenny pee and that's a quid, a pahnd. New. Coins. Y'unnerstan'? Give yer pahnd notes if yer want?'

He shook his head and walked slowly back to the phones, scanning the paper. 'Inflation down again… The Prime Minister said in her speech to the Commons…' *Her* speech? He read a bit further and wondered what Social Democrats were. He looked at another headline. What on earth was an Ayatollah? The front page carried a photo of a tall, pretty, fair-haired young woman with a group of children and the caption said something about the Princess of Wales. Who had Charles married? It didn't look like the Wellesley girl, she was dark…

Back at the phone, he put in fifty pence, dialled the familiar number and listened to it ringing with his heart thumping. A strange woman's voice answered. Jill must have got a new daily. 'Hello. Could I speak to Mrs Lindsay, please?'

'I'm sorry, you've got the wrong number, there's nobody of that name here.'

'That is eleven Buckingham Crescent?'

'Yes. Oh! You want the family that used to live here?'

'Yes please. Have you any idea where they went?'

'Let me see now… The neighbours were talking about them other day… Something happened to the husband… I think they moved to Fife.'

Fife? Then perhaps they'd gone to the cottage? 'Thanks very much. Sorry to have bothered you.'

There had been no phone at the place when they used it for holidays, but if the family was now living there, surely they would have installed one? He went back to the newsagent to buy something to write with. Directory Enquiries eventually found the number, after he had twice spelt out Auchentullum and convinced the operator that it was in Fife, in the Dunfermline area.

By the time the phone was answered again, he was feeling sick with excitement.

A man answered.

His stomach knotted. A man! Oh dear God! Had she divorced him? He swallowed hard in an effort not to vomit again. 'Is that the Lindsay household?'

'Yes.'

'Could I speak to Mrs Lindsay, please?'

'Sorry, she's at work. Can I give her a message?'

‘I’d rather speak to her myself. Can I get hold of her there?’ He didn’t want to embark on explanations to this stranger.

‘Sure, I’ll give you the number.’

It was another Auchentullum one and he scribbled it on a corner of the newspaper. ‘Thanks very much.’ He started to put down the receiver.

‘Hey! Don’t ring off! You’ve a funny sort of accent. Are you from Russia?’ The voice went up half an octave. ‘Have you news of Dad?’

He dropped the receiver with a clatter and had to hold onto the kiosk as his knees went weak with relief. What a fool he was! The boys’ voices would have broken years ago.

He took several deep breaths to steady himself and with a shaking hand dialled the number he’d been given. After two rings, the phone was answered by the voice he’d been longing to hear.

‘Hello, Auchentullum Library.’

‘Jill?’

There was a gasp, then a very shaky, ‘Who’s that?’

‘Steven. It’s me, Steven.’

‘Steve! Where are you?’

‘Heathrow.’

‘You mean, they’ve freed you?’

‘Yes, I still can’t believe it.’

‘When did it happen?’

‘Today. They flew me to Moscow from the camp yesterday, gave me back my passport, tidied me up a bit and put me on a flight to London early this morning. Not a word of explanation. I think I must be dreaming.’

'Well for God's sake, don't wake up till you get home.'

The phone began to bleep at them. He fed it another coin. 'I'm running out of change. I'm coming up to Glasgow on the Shuttle that gets in at twelve-thirty. Can you meet me there?'

'Edinburgh would have been nearer. I'll try, but it depends–'

They were cut off.

Less than two hours later, Steven hurried along the corridor from the Shuttle gate at Glasgow airport and looked round the concourse… But there was nobody there who resembled Jill… His shoulders slumped. Where was she? A tall, well-built youth in a scruffy denim jacket and jeans, who reminded him vaguely of someone, was leaning against one of the mushroom-like phone booths and scanning the emerging passengers. He had greasy red hair, spots and a single earring.

They glanced at each other. Like a pair of opposing compass needles, their eyes swung away, hesitated, then returned and locked on each other. They said simultaneously, 'My God, you've changed!' and stood staring in slack-jawed disbelief and dismay.

Alan was the first to recover. He shuffled from one foot to the other and asked, 'Is that all your luggage?'

'Yes.'

'Then we'd better be off. I'm supposed to be at work at two, but I phoned the manager and said I'd be late.' He swung round and headed rapidly for the stairs.

Steven called after him sharply, 'Would you please slow down? I've been travelling for over twenty-four hours and it'd help if you took my luggage.'

Alan stopped and waited for his father to catch up, then grabbed the case and carrier bag from him. They went down to the exit in silence, both in a state of shock at the other's appearance.

As they crossed the car park, Steven suddenly said, 'Who's the Princess of Wales?'

Alan gave him a startled look. 'Lady Di.'

'Lady Who?'

'Lady Diana Spencer. She married Prince Charles in the summer of eighty-one.'

'There's no need to say it in that tone of voice. I've been cut off from world news for nearly five years.'

'Sorry.'

Alan stopped by a small red car, opened the doors and threw the luggage onto the back seat.

'What's this?'

'Mini Metro. They came out in 'eighty.'

'What happened to the Rover?'

'Mum sold it as soon as you were sentenced. She kept the Fiesta until last year, then got this, not new, but a low mileage demo model. Belt up.'

'I beg your pardon?'

'Seat belt.'

Steven made a gesture of irritation.

'You gotta wear 'em. It's the law now.' As an afterthought, he added, 'Sorry, d'you want to drive?'

'Heavens, no! I daren't risk it till I've seen an eye specialist.'

'Why?'

'At one stage, I suffered from night blindness.' In answer to Alan's horrified look of enquiry, he went on,

'Vitamin deficiency, we all had it to various degrees. It hasn't bothered me recently, but I want to be on the safe side. How long have you been driving?'

'I passed my test about six months ago.' He glanced at his father, 'I'm eighteen now, you know.'

'You mentioned work. What are you doing?'

Alan negotiated a sharp left-hand turn onto the motorway slip road. 'I'll tell you later. D'you mind not talking? I haven't done much motorway driving and I need to concentrate.'

Steven soon nodded off, only waking when the car stopped. He looked round eagerly, but it was a service station. He peered at the price above the pumps and reached into his pocket. 'Here, you'd better fill up,' and put a couple of the pound coins into Alan's outstretched hand.

The hand remained outstretched.

Steven gestured indignantly in the direction of the price. 'How much more d'you want?'

Alan said witheringly, 'Wake up, Dad van Winkle! That's the price in litres and there are nearly five to the gallon.'

Steven did some mental arithmetic. 'Good God!' A five pound note joined the two coins.

He dozed off again and came to as they were crossing the Kincardine Bridge. As he sat up and began to look round expectantly, he remarked, 'That didn't take very long.'

'It's dual carriageway or motorway all the way now, makes a big difference.'

'You mentioned a job earlier on.'

'Yeah. I'm working at the local Co-op. I did it full-time last summer and then on Saturdays in term-time. I'm only part-time at the moment, but it'll be full-time again once the staff start taking their holidays.'

'Oh, I thought you meant a proper job.'

'Lord, no! Exam results permitting, I'm hoping to do dentistry in Glasgow, I've had a conditional acceptance. But surely Mum told you in her letters?'

Steven said with feeling, 'The only letter I've had was the one telling me of Mother's death.'

'Jeez-oh! But Granny died four years ago… Well, don't blame Mum, she's written you a monthly volume of family news ever since you were sentenced.' There was a pause and he went on thoughtfully, 'I think we're all going to be doing a lot of catching up.'

'What are Gregor's plans?'

'Says he's had enough of school and wants to be a cabinet maker.'

'That's not very ambitious.'

It wasn't long before they arrived in the village and Steven noticed that the building site next to the hall and shop was now a housing estate and was already losing its new, raw look. And the little square was new, too…

'Here we are,' said Alan, 'Home, sweet home at last.' He parked in front of the house and strode off to unlock the doors, leaving his father to bring up the rear with his luggage. Steven got out slowly and stood looking around him.

It was recognisably the same, but a lot had been done in his absence. The porch was new… So was the garage… The place had been painted. He liked the white walls, black window surrounds and bright yellow front door.

He stopped again when he got into the hall. Surely the hall and stair carpets were from his parents' house? The sitting room was next for inspection. It had changed completely, and for the better. Steven moved further into the room and looked around, something nagging. The bureau and hi-fi unit between the door and window, they were old friends, as was the bookcase between the door and the French window. The French window! Of course, that was new.

'I'm going to do bacon, eggs and fried bread for my lunch. D'you want some too?'

Steven jumped as his son's enquiry cut into his thoughts. 'That sounds marvellous.'

'Two eggs and three rashers?

'Er, no. One of each will do. I think I'd better go canny on food for the next few days. I made a pig of myself on the plane and was sick afterwards, my stomach couldn't cope. Oh, and don't make the bacon too crisp. My teeth are a mess, that's something else I'll have to see to as soon as possible.'

Alan looked interested at the mention of teeth. 'What's wrong with them?'

'Scurvy.'

'Whaaat!'

Steven gave a wry grin at his son's expression. 'It softens your gums and your teeth fall out.'

'But…but I thought that was something which happened to ancient mariners?'

'It can happen to modern land lubbers if you have to exist on a starvation diet for months on end.'

Alan stood staring at his father, lost for words.

Steven continued in the same wry tone. 'Mind you, my teeth were never very great, one of the penalties of being a red-head – or former red-head,' and he turned to the mirror over the fireplace and ran a hand over his grey stubble.

'Mum's going to get a helluva shock when she sees you. When I saw you at the airport, you reminded me of Granddad just before he died.'

'I'm not surprised, I got a shock too when I looked in a mirror last night for the first time in ages. However, a few weeks of home cooking will work wonders. Now, what about that bacon and egg?'

Alan turned to go out, paused, then went back to give his father a quick pat on the shoulder before going to prepare lunch.

Steven stood looking after him for a few moments, then went over to the French window, slid back one of the panels and stepped down into the sunroom. Jill must have got hold of a good architect as it was a faithful realisation of the sketch they had made together on his last visit.

The appetising smell of frying bacon wafted past his nose and was shortly followed by a shout of, 'Grub's up, Dad.'

He went back through the sitting room and hall, then stopped in amazement on entering the kitchen.

He gazed round at the circular table and rush-seated, ladder-back chairs in some light wood; a dresser and an L-shaped run of pine units. The scullery window had been replaced by a door.

Alan was standing at the cooker and said, 'Please would you set the table?' The lack of movement in response to his request prompted him to turn round and he grinned when he saw his father's wondering expression. 'It's turned out well, hasn't it? Duncan did a good job.'

Steven realised he was still holding his luggage. He put it on one of the chairs and said, still gazing round, 'Who's Duncan?'

'Duncan Mackenzie, the local joiner. He's been a good friend to the family. Gregor thinks the world of him.'

'Oh.' Someone acting *in loco patris*? 'I'd better go and wash.' When he came back he remarked, 'It's marvellous to get back to proper facilities. Now, where's the cutlery kept?'

In the time it took Steven to eat one egg and one rasher, Alan demolished two eggs, three rashers and a slab of fried bread, then looked at his watch. 'Time I was off. Is there anything else you want? There's milk in the fridge and tea and coffee in the cupboard above.'

'Have you any white bread?'

Alan pointed to a wholemeal loaf on the table. 'Have some of this. Mum made it, it's jolly good.'

'I'd rather have some white.'

'That stuff Mum calls damp flannel?'

'Yes. I've had nothing but coarse rye bread for years and I fancy some white bread spread with unsalted butter and some raspberry jam, home-made if possible.'

'Hang on, there may be some in the freezer. I think Mum keeps a loaf for bread-and-butter puddings. How many slices?'

'One will do.'

Alan went out of the back door and returned with a slice which he put on top of the cooker to thaw, then went round peering into several cupboards before emerging with an unopened pot of jam.

'I see your mother still has to hide the raspberry jam.'

'Yeah, it's never put out for everyday use, even though she made quite a lot last summer. We went up to Blairgowrie and picked our own fruit. I drove there and back, good practice for me. Must be off now. Mum'll be home just after three. Can you do the dishes? I haven't time. 'Bye.'

After the doors banged behind Alan, Steven unashamedly picked up his plate and licked it, relishing every last flavoursome drop of the bacon juices. After months of black bread and thin vegetable stews, his body craved protein and fat. He picked up the thawed slice of commercial white loaf and spread it generously with butter, longing to feel the silky richness sliding over his tongue, but after consideration, scraped some off and replaced it on the dish: he didn't want to be sick again. He added a thin layer of jam and nibbled his treat very slowly, savouring it all to the final crumb. Once finished, he made himself some coffee and sat for a while with the mug in his hands, appreciating the luxury of being alone in warm, quiet, comfortable, civilized surroundings with a full stomach. He still couldn't take in the events of the last twenty-four hours and the reason for his sudden release was a complete mystery to him.

While his palate reacquainted itself with the aroma of real coffee, Steven acknowledged that his homecoming was nothing like he'd imagined it would be. There was no joyful family reunion at Glasgow airport with Jill hugging him and crying, with the boys dancing round, shouting in glee. Instead, there was only this unfamiliar, taciturn young man. They'd got off to a poor start, not that they'd ever done much in the way of blokeish things together, but by the end of the meal, he had the impression they were beginning to feel their way towards each other again.

Jill's reaction over the phone was a bit more welcoming, but why hadn't she come to meet him?

And what would Gregor be like? He'd always been the quiet one, never showed much emotion.

As for his own emotions, he'd learnt the hard way to keep them in check. To begin with, he'd responded eagerly to the slightest show of kindness or friendship from the other prisoners, only to be rendered bereft when they were moved elsewhere, or far worse, died. Kaiya's death had been the absolute nadir of his imprisonment, particularly as he felt partly responsible and once he'd hauled himself out of that particular Slough of Despond, he'd made a point of keeping everyone else at arm's length. Now, he would have to learn to open up to people again.

And home? He'd expected to return to a large house in his native city and here he was in a cottage on the other side of the country.

Oh for heaven's sake man, stop moaning, Steven admonished himself. It may not have turned out as you occasionally dared to hope for when you lay shivering in your bunk with aching muscles and an empty stomach, but you're a billion times better off than when you woke up yesterday morning.

He washed and dried the dishes, but left them on the worktop as he didn't know where to put them. The clock on the cooker said two-thirty, so there was still time to kill before Jill got back. He did a tour of inspection upstairs and it took him several minutes to work out that a dormer, running the length of the back of the cottage, had created the extra space in the two bedrooms and a small shower room between them. Even so, it was obvious that the boys found it difficult to share and he shut the door on the disorder.

He opened the door to Jill's room – their room – and the faint waft of her perfume brought back a host of memories which he had tried hard to suppress during the last five years… He stood for a while, looking out of the new window into the garden. It was a fine afternoon, so he might as well wait outside.

Steven went out of the back door into a utility room. There was a movement at the edge of his vision and he turned his head just in time to see the tail of a cat disappearing through a hatch in the bottom of the door leading to the garden. A cat! That was something he hadn't bargained for: snooty, supercilious animals.

He returned to his luggage, got his paper, then from the sunroom collected a folding chaise longue, which he recognised as having been his mother's favourite, and took it out into the garden. Someone had put in many back-breaking hours since he had last walked here and a wilderness had been transformed.

He placed the seat on the grass, adjusted it to his satisfaction, settled himself and began to read. After a few minutes, the print went out of focus. The sooner he got glasses, the better. He put down the paper and as he did so, the cat which he had seen earlier trotted towards him, tail held high. It was a seal point Siamese. The animal sat down suddenly and washed the inside of one paw very thoroughly. Once finished, it squinted at him with bright blue eyes, then jumped onto his knees and started to knead, but soon discovered there was very little to work on. It turned round a couple of times and settled itself with its head on his chest and promptly went to sleep. He stroked it for a few minutes and followed its example.

CHAPTER 3

After the phone call had been cut off, Jill stood staring into the distance, unable to think or move. An impatient cough released her from her trance. She put down the receiver and turned round to meet the inquisitive gaze of Mrs Oliphant.

The old woman was the biggest gossip in the neighbourhood and well-positioned to "take an intelligent interest in her neighbours", as she put it: her niece Elspeth ran the village post office and the latter's husband Johnny was one of the postmen. The faded blue eyes scrutinised Jill. 'You're looking a bit pale dearie, I hope it was no' bad news?'

Jill pulled herself together. If Old Elephant Ears got wind of Steven's return, it would be round the village within the hour and she wanted time to get used to the idea before it became public knowledge. She said briskly, 'No, it wasn't bad news,' and started to look for the tickets for the books which Mrs Oliphant was returning.

'Would it be good news, then?'

Damn the old nosey parker! She gave a conspiratorial grin. 'We've just taken delivery of a new batch of Mills and Boon. I haven't yet had time to put them on the shelves, but if you like to have a look round, I'll get a couple out of the office for you.' That should put her off the scent.

The prospect of being first in the queue for some of her favourite literature made Mrs Oliphant forget about the librarian's odd reaction to her phone call.

As soon as the old woman left, Jill grabbed the phone and dialled one of her co-librarians. The number had rung half-a-dozen times before she remembered Anne had gone up to St Andrews for the day. There was no reply from Flora and she knew Kathy had gone into Dunfermline to the dentist, but had assured her that she would be back in time to take over at three. She wrung her hands in frustration. Oh why did they all have to be unavailable the one time she urgently needed someone to take over? She phoned home and after a long wait, Alan answered. 'You took your time,' she said.

'I'd only just gone back to bed after the last disturbance.'

'At this hour?'

'Well, a chap needs a bit of rest after all those exams.'

'Oh…rattlesnakes! You should go to bed a bit earlier. Look, you'll have to go to the airport for me, I can't get away and his plane's due at twelve-thirty.'

'Whose plane?'

'Dad's, of course.'

There was a pause. 'So that's who it was.'

'Did he phone you first? Anyhow, he's just phoned me from Heathrow to say he's been freed and he's on his way home. He's coming up on the Shuttle. You'd better get moving, otherwise you won't get there in time.'

'It doesn't take that long.'

'Well it takes me nearly an hour and a half.'

'What? Oh, he's going to Glasgow?'

'Sorry, didn't I say that?'

'No. But that means I'll be late for work.'

'Damn your work! This is far more important!'

'OK, OK, keep your hair on. I'll go and get him.'

Jill gave vent to her frustration by slamming together a pile of books and despite a steady flow of customers, time crawled. She tried to stop her eyes from straying to the clock every few minutes, but it was impossible. Now he should be boarding the plane... He should have been airborne for ten minutes by now... What if the plane crashed? Oh shut up, you fool! By now he would be over Yorkshire…the Borders…starting to approach Glasgow...landing. She should have told Alan to phone her once they met. He hadn't had much experience of motorway driving… What if they were involved in an accident? Stoppit! They should be coming through the village by now… Oh why did the library have to be designed with a blank wall on that side so she couldn't watch the road? The minute hand on the clock seemed to have an invisible weight attached which prevented it from climbing up the hill towards the hour. Come on Kathy! What's keeping you? The minute hand was starting to descend the hill when Kathy finally arrived.

'Hello, sorry I'm a wee bit late, but he found a second–'

'Here's the keys. I'm off.'

Jill had grabbed her bag from under the counter from where she had put it in readiness and was accelerating towards the door before an astonished Kathy asked, 'What's up? Is the house on fire?'

'No. Steve's back, they've freed him.'

'Steve? Your– ? My dear, how marvellous.'

Jill slammed the door on her congratulations and took off down the street as though determined to set a world record for the half mile distance between library and cottage. She arrived at the gate with her lungs burning and a stitch in her side, oblivious of startled looks from passers by. In succession she flung open the gate, the porch door and the house door and once indoors she gasped, 'Steve, I'm back. Where are you?'

She was greeted by silence.

Her stomach knotted. Surely he must be home by now? She hadn't dreamed the phone call...? A quick glance showed that he wasn't in the sitting room or sunroom. Nor in the bathroom. He wasn't in the kitchen. What had happened? Then she caught sight of the bag with Cyrillic lettering and went weak with relief. He really was home, but where? Not in the bedrooms. The garden? She raced downstairs and through the kitchen, then from the utility room, caught sight of the figure in the chaise longue.

She made herself slow down to a walk and took several deep breaths to steady herself as she crossed the terrace and approached him, but as she took in the details of his appearance, she came to a halt several feet away, biting the back of her knuckles, appalled. The haggard, emaciated, grey-haired man asleep in front of her bore very little resemblance to the well-built redhead who was just beginning to acquire the suggestion of a jowl and paunch.

The cat blinked and yawned, sat up and stretched, then jumped down and came and rubbed against her legs.

The removal of the warm weight from his chest woke Steven and like the cat, he yawned, then blinked hard. It took him several seconds to equate the neatly-coiffed, willowy brunette with the mental image he'd been carrying for so long: the last time he'd seen his wife she had been comfortably plump with shoulder length fair hair. He said dazedly, 'I'd forgotten you were a bottle-blonde.'

Jill came over and knelt down beside him, put her arms round his waist, her head on his chest and burst into tears.

He held her tightly until she gave only the occasional shuddering sob, then he said shakily, 'My shirt's wet. Have you a hankie?'

She shook her head, gave a long sniff, wiped her face on her sleeve and nuzzled the side of his neck.

'Your feet are twitching,' Steven said.

'Pleasure.' She let go of him briefly, stood up with a grunt of discomfort, then sat down on his knees. The old chaise longue groaned at the extra load and collapsed under them.

As they extricated themselves, flailing round on the grass, Jill's laugh developed a slightly hysterical tone.

Steven sat up, pulled her onto his knees and rocked her gently in a tight embrace, tears trickling down his lined cheeks.

Once they'd recovered a degree of composure, Jill moved onto the grass, sat back on her heels and gave him a lengthy scrutiny. She shook her head and said through pursed lips, 'What in God's name have the bastards done to you?'

'Overworked and underfed me.'

'And how! You're nothing but skin and bone.'

'Don't worry, I'll soon put on weight with your cooking.' He reached over and patted her hand. 'I haven't been like this all the time. After I was moved to Kazakhstan I was reasonably well fed, but we got a new camp commandant about three months ago and he decided the old one had been molly-coddling us.'

He'd been far worse at the end of his Siberian sojourn… He'd expected to die when chronic malnourishment had left him with no reserves to fight pneumonia. But this wasn't the time to give her the details. Steven thought back to the morning when he dragged himself out of his bunk, only to collapse on the floor, shaking with fever and struggling to breathe. Before losing consciousness, he remembered the concerned cries of his companions as they tried to haul him to his feet. He had a vague recollection of being bumped around in a vehicle. When he woke up in a hospital ward, lying on clean sheets in a proper bed, for a few seconds he thought he'd died and gone to heaven… And now he really was in heaven, sitting in a Scottish garden, looking at his wife.

Jill rubbed her knees and got up. Steven pushed himself off the ground, staggering slightly. She moved to support him and they clung to each other, scarcely able to take in the events of the last few hours. After a few moments, he took a deep breath and said shakily, 'I think we could both do with a good, strong cuppa… with plenty of sugar. You go and see to that and I'll get out chairs and a table.' On the way, he gathered up the chaise longue and leant it against the garage wall.

When Jill put the tray in front of him, he observed, 'Plain chocolate digestives, the stuff dreams are made of!' In reply to her startled expression, he went on, 'I had a craving for them at one point, but soon learnt not to think about food too much.' He ate a biscuit rather more quickly than the bread and jam at lunch. 'I gather from what Alan said, you wrote regularly.'

'Of course I did,' she said indignantly. 'Why? Didn't you get my letters?'

'Only the one telling me of Mother's death.'

After a long pause, Jill echoed her son's comment about catching up. 'It's just as well I kept carbon copies. I didn't expect you to get them all, but it never entered my head the swine would censor the lot. Did you get any of the parcels?'

'Yes, about two per year. How did you manage that?'

'I sent money to the consulate. It was no use me trying to post anything from here and in any case, someone on the spot would have had a better idea of what was needed most. Were they OK?'

'They were marvellous. Not much in the way of food, but the clothing was a godsend even if I didn't always wear it myself.'

'What d'you mean?'

'I used it on occasions to bribe the overseers into giving me a less arduous job. It was worth a woollen pullover to be taken off potato picking to be put in charge of hen feed, even if they are horrible things.'

'What are?'

'Hens. Vicious creatures. The expression "pecking order" isn't just a figure of speech. Still, the occasional raw egg was more palatable than a raw spud.'

'But surely you could have eaten all the eggs you wanted?'

'Oh no, we had to be very careful, if the production norms went below what they were supposed to be, there was trouble.'

'Have another biscuit.'

'No thanks, my stomach isn't used to all this bounty, and I must get to a dentist and ophthalmic surgeon as soon as–'

'Wahoo! No more exams!' The exultant yell preceded a schoolbag skidding across the grass and Gregor's cartwheeling body. He ended up in an untidy heap at Jill's feet, flushed and grinning. 'Mum, can we have a celebration tonight? You promised us a special meal once exams were over.'

'Oh yes, we're going to have a celebration alright.'

Something in his mother's voice made Gregor look at her enquiringly and she indicated the person sitting beside her. As he took in the occupant of the other chair, the flush and grin faded and he sat staring, slack-mouthed and eyes bulging in astonishment.

Steven stared back. The chubby eleven-year-old had been transformed into a skinny youth, a dark-haired version of his mother. The two of them got to their feet and it was then Steven's turn to gape. 'Good heavens! Has your mother been feeding you on fertilizer?' When Gregor finally unfolded himself, Steven had to look up to his son.

Jill laughed, 'He's shot up in the last few months. He even tops Alan now and I hope he'll soon start growing outwards instead of upwards.'

Gregor said huskily to his father, 'You look as though you've been fed nothing.' He turned abruptly and loped off to the garage, from where there issued furious hammering noises for the next few minutes.

Steven sat down and gave his wife an apologetic look. 'I realise that my appearance – and sudden reappearance – must be an awful shock for you all, but I'd no way of giving you advance warning, I didn't even have any myself… I suddenly seemed to become a hot property and they couldn't get rid of me quickly enough.' He shook his head. 'I still feel I'm dreaming.'

'Well you're not! And don't apologise for anything. You're the last person who should be doing that,' she added fiercely. After holding his hand for a few minutes, she asked, 'How did the meeting with Alan go?'

Steven pulled a face.

She laughed. 'I know what you mean. They're both at the uncouth youth stage. Mind you, some of it's camouflage, they can behave in a civilized manner, but I do get so heartily fed up with reminding them to say “please” and “thank you”, to wash their hands and brush their hair and teeth. However, Alan’s been a bit better in that respect since he’s woken up to the existence of girls.’

‘Spots apart, I suppose he’s not bad-looking, but that earring…’

She laughed again, leant over and began to run a finger over his face. ‘He’s very like you. His eyes may be green instead of dark brown, but they turn down at the corners in the same way. His nose is still developing, but he’s got your square jaw with a dimple in the chin.’ She stroked him. ‘But I hope that your weight gains stop short of a jowl and paunch.’

He looked at her indignantly. ‘When did I even have a jowl or paunch?’

‘Just before you…you were taken away from me.’

‘Rubbish! That was simply my muscular development.’

She raised an eyebrow, pulled her chair closer and kissed him.

They drew apart when they heard Gregor come out of the garage. The cat was now draped round his shoulders.

‘Is that your animal?’ enquired Steven.

‘Ming? Yes, isn’t she super. Mum gave her to me the first Christmas we were here, she’s more like a dog than a cat.’

‘Surely Ming’s a Chinese rather than a Siamese name?’

'I know, but I wanted something oriental and easy to say and Ming seemed to suit her.' He ate the last chocolate biscuit. 'Mum, I'm hungry. What's for tea?'

'Go and get some bread,' said Jill.

'Aren't there any more biscuits?'

'Not today.'

Steven coughed and remarked that he'd opened a pot of raspberry jam at lunch. After Gregor had gone into the kitchen he went on, 'Why on earth did you give the child a Siamese cat? Surely a dog would have been more suitable?'

'He asked for one. When we moved here, Alan settled very quickly and made friends without any bother, but Gregor was more of a problem. He wasn't at all happy at school to begin with.'

'He always was the quiet one.'

'He still is. He doesn't have a lot of friends, but he seems quite content to potter on his own in his workshop.'

'Where's the school?'

'In Brankstone. It's a small comprehensive and there's talk of closing it and sending the children to Alloa or Dunfermline. Anyhow, he suddenly announced that he wanted a pet, something with a bit of character, but he couldn't be bothered to walk a dog. Cats were low maintenance and he'd heard that Siamese were dog-like, so could he have one? I was none too keen, animals are such a tie, but I gave in and managed to find Ming just in time for Christmas, but I've no regrets, they became instant soul mates and he settled down the following term.'

‘I gather he wants to be a cabinet maker.’

‘That’s what he’s told me. He’s not at all academically inclined, but loves working with his hands and the local joiner has given him a lot of encouragement.’

‘The one who did the kitchen?’

‘Yes, Duncan Mackenzie. He’s a nice chap and the boys like him.’ She gave a shiver. ‘Shall we move inside? I’m getting chilly.’ She picked up the tray and moved towards the back door.

After his experiences, the day was still pleasantly warm as far as Steven was concerned, but he followed her after collecting Gregor’s bag, which had been left lying in the middle of the grass. He had just put his luggage on the table with a view to unpacking what few possessions he had brought with him, when the door bell rang. Jill, who was piling the tea crockery into the sink, flapped a hand at Gregor to go and answer.

He returned with Paul, who beamed at the family. ‘My dear Jill, I’ve just heard your marvellous news. Dr Lindsay, I’m so glad to be able to meet you at last,’ and their visitor strode over to Steven and pumped his hand in both of his.

Steven looked Paul up and down and took an instant dislike to the newcomer. Just the sort of large, hearty type he detested and the Slavonic accent made his hackles rise even further, for all that he had acquired a trace of one himself.

Jill smiled at them both. ‘Darling, this is Paul Holland, he teaches at the college and he’s been a good friend to the family for several years.’

'How do you do?' said Steven stiffly. 'You don't sound as though you're British.'

There were gasps from Jill and Gregor, but Paul simply smiled and said, 'You have a quick ear. I really must make an effort to curl my tongue the other way when I say my "l's". But you can relax, I was born in Czechoslovakia and having left my homeland shortly after the Prague Spring, I feel about the Soviets the way you do.'

'How did you know Dad was back?'

'I would have thought that by now you would have realised this community has a very efficient grapevine.'

There was an awkward silence and to fill it, Steven started to unpack. He pulled a dirty, tattered garment from the plastic bag.

Jill came over and picked it up with a finger and thumb. 'Pooh! What's this disgusting thing?'

'That's my padded winter jacket. I couldn't have survived without it.'

'It looks fit for the dustbin.'

He considered it thoughtfully. 'No…I think I'll keep it. It'll do for gardening and as a reminder.'

'What for?' asked Gregor.

'Man's inhumanity to man,' said Paul quietly, before Steven could answer.

The latter's dislike lessened slightly. 'Not what I was going to say, but it'll do.' He looked round the others. 'If at any time I start bewailing my lot, just wave this at me.'

Jill lifted something out of the case. It looked like a sack, decorated with some coarse embroidery. Steven snatched it from her and hunched over it defensively. ‘That’s my pillowcase, it was made for me by a friend, a very dear friend.’

His wife was about to remark cattily that his “very dear friend” must have been female, when she remembered something. She gave Paul a quick glance, swallowed and said gently, ‘I’m glad you had friends to support you in your imprisonment. I hope you’ll tell me about them sometime. May I see it, please?’

Steven relaxed and passed back the thing he had snatched away. Jill spread it out on the table. It was indeed a sack, painstakingly embroidered with bits of thread unravelled from old garments. She stroked it and remarked, ‘I would never have had the patience to do anything like that and what a pity it couldn’t have been worked in silk on linen.’

Gregor picked up something else from the case. ‘What on earth’s this?’

Paul took the irregular dark lump and prodded it. ‘Unless I’m much mistaken, it’s a day’s bread ration.’ He rapped it with his knuckles. ‘And the quality hasn’t improved over the years.’

Steven looked at him sharply. ‘You mean, you were in one too?’

The other nodded. ‘Only for a few months and then I escaped to the West.’

The daily bread ration, doled out in the evening. But did you eat it all at once and sleep on a comparatively full stomach…or did you try and keep some back for the following morning and try to sleep on an unsatisfied hunger with the means to relieve it lying under your pillow?

The two men stared at each other in recognition of a shared hardship.

Steven gave himself a shake, pulled something else out of the case and thrust it at Jill. 'Here, I should have given you this earlier, even if it's a bit late for your birthday.'

'That doesn't look as though it came from a prison camp,' commented Gregor.

'No, I got it on the plane.'

Jill reached into the airline's plastic bag and pulled out a bottle of Marcel Rochas' perfume "Femme". She took one look at it and burst into tears again.

The men started to pat their pockets, but Gregor went over to the cooker, tore off a sheet of the kitchen paper hanging beside it and gave it to her with a laconic, 'Here, blow.'

When she had got herself under control, she sat down, clutching the perfume with one hand and Steven with the other. She smiled mistily at them all. 'Sorry about that, but it brings back such memories. You see, when we were in Paris on our honeymoon, he brought me a bottle of this, only I dropped it on the tiled bathroom floor and d'you know, he never said a word, simply went out and bought me another.'

Paul gave an indulgent laugh. 'Now that is what I call true love. Had Sonja done that, even on our honeymoon, I could never have been so forbearing.' He looked at the family group. 'Forgive me if I have intruded on a very special occasion, but knowing a little of what you've all gone through, I wanted to be one of the first to congratulate you. No, stay put, I'll see myself out,' he said as Steven let go his wife's hand and got up.

'It's alright, I want to heave this into the dustbin, wherever it is.' Steven tipped out the few remaining items of the case and picked it up. 'I never want to see it again.'

'Round the side of the garage,' said Gregor as the two men went out.

In the hall, Paul pointed to the case. 'Are you really going to throw it out?'

'Yes. Why?'

'Would you allow me to take it? You see, a lot of our students, particularly those who only go home once a year, find that during the course of their time with us that their luggage has "shrunk" considerably.'

Steven smiled. 'Take it then, but there's no key, anyone could get into it, not that it mattered to me. Thanks for calling.' As he watched Paul go down the path, he reflected that perhaps he had made too hasty a judgement on the visitor.

Back in the kitchen, Jill was unwrapping a parcel of meat. 'I got some steak for tonight, but there won't be enough for four of us. Gregor, pop along to Dunn's and get another piece.'

'What sort?'

'Fillet, for preference. If Neil's there, tell him why. He'll see you get a good bit.' She looked in the fridge.

'And get some cream for the chocolate mousse as well. I meant to get some at the Co-op on the way home, but my mind was on other things.' After the door closed behind Gregor, she went and put her arms round her husband and rubbed her head against his. 'Steve, darling Steve, I just can't believe I'm holding you again. It's all a blissful dream and the alarm's due to go off in a few seconds.'

He bit her ear gently. 'Does that convince you I'm real?' He went on musingly, 'It's funny being Steve again after being Stepan Gectorovich for so long.'

'Step-on Whatty-which?'

'Stepan Gectorovich – my name and patronymic.'

'I don't understand. Father's name was Hector.'

'Exactly, and for some odd reason it's Russianised to Gector, just as Harold becomes Garold.'

She giggled, 'It makes him sound like a lizard.'

A little later he drew away from her and looked at the kitchen clock. 'I think it would be a good idea to phone the family and tell them of my return before the mass media announces it. I asked the Russians to wait until mid-afternoon our time before notifying anyone of my release and they appear to have co-operated. Nobody took any notice of me at the airports.'

Jill's face fell. 'Oh damn! I'd forgotten about the press. I had more than enough of them five years ago, but I suppose it's inevitable and at least this time, it's good news. D'you want to phone Mum and Dad, or shall I? And Helen and Tony?'

'Och, you phone your parents and sister and I'll have a word with them when you've finished.'

CHAPTER 4

Memo from Oleg Sergeyevich Koshachin to his boss: 'The second part of "Operation Birdkill" has now started. When the English accomplish two deeds with a single act, they say they have killed two birds with one stone.'

CHAPTER 5

Alan arrived home in time to join the family in front of the television for the early evening news. They did not have long to wait for the expected item. 'As a good-will gesture, Moscow has just announced the release of Dr Steven Lindsay. Dr Lindsay, a university lecturer, was sentenced nearly five years ago to ten years in a labour camp for alleged charges of theft and drunken driving. It is understood that he is already back in this country. The leader of the National Union of–' Gregor switched off.

Steven said with feeling, 'God bless the Beeb for putting in "alleged", but I still don't know what happened that night and I've been over it a thousand times.' He looked at Jill, 'All I can remember is someone bumping into me in the foyer while I waited for you to collect your coat as we were leaving the theatre in Leningrad and the next thing I knew about was waking up in a cell with a splitting headache, to be told that I'd stolen a car and injured a street cleaner.'

'It must have been a put-up job!' said Alan, thumping the arm of his chair. 'It's just the sort of thing they'd do.'

'That's what most people said,' added Jill.

Steven looked at her with a raised eyebrow. 'Most people. But not quite everyone?'

'Ye-es.' She hesitated. 'There were one or two who seemed to take a delight in reminding me you'd been had up on a drunken driving charge once before and lost your licence for a year and I certainly wasn't sorry to move away from them.' She went on angrily, 'But for heaven's sake! That was ages ago when you were a student and ever since I've known you, you've been most careful about drinking and driving.'

'That's what I thought, until then.'

'You must have been doped. I've seen you quite cheerful on occasions, but never really drunk and certainly not in such a state that you couldn't remember the night before, the morning after. You must have been framed.'

'That's always been my feeling, once I was able to think rationally, but I can't really remember much about my first few weeks in Russia.' Steven rubbed his face. 'It was all a jumbled nightmare. I can't help wondering if I was drugged in some way, not just that first evening, but until after the trial, to keep me compliant.'

Jill nodded. 'The one thing which struck me the few times I saw you, was your dazed appearance… Mind you, I wasn't much better myself, a mixture of shock and drugs, though in my case it was Valium.'

'When we stayed with Granny during the trial,' said Gregor, 'she tried to keep the newspapers away from us, but I remember someone saying it was very low-key, not like the one for that American pilot.'

Jill nodded again. 'Yes, it seemed to be over and done with very quickly.' She gave herself a shake and straightened up. 'Anyhow, thank God, that's all in the past.' She hugged Steven and got up from the sofa where they had been sitting together. 'I'm going to see about dinner. How d'you fancy your potatoes?'

He thought for a few seconds. 'Mashed. With plenty of milk, a knob of butter and a pinch of nutmeg. Nice and smooth and creamy. It'll be a change from tasteless, soggy, grey lumps.'

By the time dinner was ready, the phone had been shoved into the cupboard under the stairs, with the receiver off and a coat wrapped round it.

They were enjoying their steaks when Steven noticed Jill staring at his hands. He smiled and grimaced. 'I know they're a mess, they'd never heard of rubber gloves in the camps and I expect that my table manners have deteriorated, too.'

She shook her head, 'No, it's not that… You're doing something different…'

He swapped over his knife and fork. 'Does that look better?'

'Yes, of course, but why the change?'

'They still correct corrie-fisted folk in the Soviet Union and everyone was so horrified to see me using my left hand that in the end, for the sake of peace, I learnt to be ambidextrous.'

And also in self-defence, he thought, remembering the guard at the lumber camp. The man watched him sawing with a puzzled expression and eventually came over, removed the tool and put it into his right hand. Steven smiled at him and transferred it back. The guard put it into his right hand again and when Steven started to move it, made a threatening gesture with his rifle. Steven did his best to explain and demonstrate that he worked better with his left hand. As a result, the offending limb was clubbed with the rifle butt, ensuring that he was right-handed for the next few days. To add insult to his injury, his rations were cut as he was not fulfilling his production norm. Thereafter he decided that he had better become ambidextrous.

He came out of his reverie to the unbelievable reality of steak on prettily-patterned porcelain and gave a short bark of laughter. 'Actually, I was regarded as something of a freak. You see, red-heads are pretty scarce there too and left-handed ones, even more so. However, they eventually sorted that on both counts, the Soviets don't like non-conformists.'

Alan enquired, 'Are you completely ambidextrous now? Can you write with the other hand?'

'I suppose I could, if I had to.'

'Can you read and write Russian?'

'Yes, I eventually learnt. Once I was moved to Kazakhstan, I was able to get tuition from some of the more educated prisoners in exchange for teaching them English and German, but Siberia was simply a case of trying to survive.' There were gasps of horror. 'I speak Russian fluently, but I suspect I have a pretty awful accent, not because I was a foreigner, but because of the type of person I often had to associate with.' He looked round his family and said airily, 'We criminals were the prison elite.' He grinned at their expressions and continued with his meal.

There was a short silence, then Gregor blurted out the question which was often in their minds, but nobody had ever dared to voice. 'Dad, did they torture you?'

'Good heavens, no!' He thought for a few moments then went on, 'Well, it depends on what you mean by torture. I was never hauled off to a dungeon and subjected to the modern equivalent of the rack and thumbscrew and by some miracle, I managed to avoid the solitary confinement cell... And the attention of the guard dogs... On the other hand, in Siberia I had to do hard manual labour on a starvation diet in sub-zero temperatures – Fahrenheit – and with inadequate clothing.' And the pain of returning circulation to frozen extremities was a form of daily torture in itself.

Jill stared at him, aghast. 'If you were one of the elite, what happened to the others?'

'The politicals and refusniks were liable to be sent to the gold or salt mines where they didn't last more than a couple of years, but enough of me, I want to hear about my family.' He looked at the others, but they had all been stunned into silence again. For the sake of conversation, Steven indicated the table. 'I don't remember seeing this before. What happened to the other one?'

'Oh, you mean the mahogany one, the old family one?' said Jill.

'Yes. The table which came from my grandparents, with the matching chairs and sideboard.'

‘We had to sell them and a lot more too. What was fine in a Victorian terrace house simply wouldn’t fit into a country cottage, but I got a good price for them.’

Steven looked at his wife’s choice. ‘I suppose it is more suitable. What sort of wood is it?’

‘Beech’, said Gregor. ‘We saw a gorgeous table in burr elm, but the price was way out. I tried to persuade Mum that it was a future antique, but no go.’ He stroked the surface. ‘It’s good, solid timber, and it simply laughs at spillages so we don’t have to make a mad rush for a dish cloth and duster like with the other one.’ He eyed his father’s plate. ‘Dad, if you aren’t going to eat any more of the mousse, can I have it?’

‘No, put it in the fridge and I’ll enjoy the rest tomorrow. I’m learning the hard way not to eat too much at once, my digestion can’t yet cope with all these goodies.’

After the washing up was finished, Alan collected his pipes and went into the sunroom where the others were having coffee. ‘I’m away to band practice now, I’ll be back at the usual time.’

‘Surely you could give it a miss tonight of all nights?’ said Jill.

‘I know Mum, but…you see…it’s the British Championships at Bathgate on Saturday and we want to put up a good show, particularly after the way we did at Scotstoun.’

Steven eyed the long wooden case. ‘Band practice? What d’you play? The trombone?’

‘Trombone? Of course not. I play the pipes.’

‘Bagpipes! What on earth induced you to take them up?’

‘I like ’em. And there’s good tuition available locally, more or less free, only twenty pence a lesson. I’ve been playing in the district band for the last year.’

Steven’s expressions ran the gamut of surprise, amusement and then respect. ‘Did you say something about a British Championship?’

‘Yeah… well… it’s only the grade three Pipe Band Championship.’

‘Then you certainly mustn’t miss your practice. I’m sure it’s the first time anyone in the family’s taken part in a British Championship of any sort. Off you go and we’ll bask in your reflected glory.’

After Alan had gone, Steven said to the others in an awed tone, ‘He must be jolly good.’

Jill laughed. ‘He’s a fair average, not that I’m any judge, but Duncan says he’s coming on well and has the makings of a good piper.’

‘Duncan? You mean the chap who…?’ He gestured in the direction of the kitchen.

‘Yes, he’s the local pipe major.’

‘And the undertaker’ added Gregor with a chuckle.

By the time Jill had told the story of Old Ewan’s funeral, Steven was laughing heartily with them and she reflected that it was the first time she’d seen him really let himself go since his return.

*

Alan was quite unprepared for his reception at band practice.

Sheila was hovering in the lobby. ‘It’s great about your Dad. I couldn’t believe it when Mum phoned from the library and we saw it on the news. Is he alright? Did you know he was coming home?'

He found himself at the centre of a hand-shaking, back-slapping throng.

'That's a rare bit o' news, lad.'

'Och, I'm awful glad for your mum.'

'Congratulations, son.'

'I hope thae bastards didnae treat him bad.'

A half bottle of whisky was produced from a pipe case and passed around. After joining the band, Alan learnt that anyone who takes up piping soon becomes inured to communal spit.

Once Steven's safe return was toasted, band practice returned to normal and they had a run-through the competition tunes. For the last half hour, Alan settled himself at a table beside Bob and took out his practice chanter and the music for the pibroch which Willie had recently given him to learn. His tutor was at a nearby table, listening to a girl of about eleven playing a scale on her chanter and gently correcting her mistakes.

Bob nudged Alan. 'If that'd been Old Duncan, she'd have been in tears by now. He was a good teacher, but a holy terror. He taught Sandy to play and once Sellotaped his fingers to the chanter 'cos he wasn't keeping them straight.'

'I've heard about him, he died just before we came here. I hope Duncan planted him in the right hole.'

Behind him the undertaker said pleasantly, 'Any more remarks like that and I'll make sure that the new reeds ye're all yammerin' for are strong enough to gie ye double hernias.'

Alan felt himself going red and thereafter applied himself to one of the variations of *Lament for Mary MacLeod*. He was going through it for the third time, when Willie left his young pupil and came over. 'Alan, ye're no' playing it the way I showed ye. Ye havenae got a good beat in it.'

'But you keep telling me that pibroch isn't played in tempo, like a march or jig.'

'Aye, but there are passages which do need a good strong rhythm. Now, try again.'

Alan did as he was told, but Willie gave an exasperated sigh. 'Look, laddie. Ye're standing in the prow of a boat with a stinking corpse and a following wind and ye want tae give the rowers a bit o' encouragement to get across the loch tae the clan burying ground. Again.'

Sod Mary MacLeod! thought Alan. Why did the silly old cow have to kick the bucket?

Willie eventually gave a small nod of approval. 'Ye're starting to get the hang of it, but just remember, it's a funeral and no' the bluidy Boat Race.'

As Alan repeated the passage yet again, Bob chanted *sotto voce*, 'In-out, one-out, two-ouch!'

*

When the doorbell rang for the third time in less than half an hour, Jill thought about ignoring it and staying snuggled up on the sofa with Steven. When it went again, she gave him a kiss and heaved a sigh. 'I'd better go and see who it is.' She opened the door a crack, then smiled at the figure who always reminded her of a smart version of a middle-aged Mexican bandit. 'Why hello, Angus. I though it was going to be yet another member of the press. What brings you here? Nobody's ill.'

'I had a call to make nearby and Kathy asked me to give you a message as she couldn't get through on the phone.'

'We had to take it off the hook, but come in.' She lowered her voice. 'I'm glad you've come, I don't think there's anything drastically wrong with Steve, but he's obviously had a bad time.' Her voice wobbled. 'They've turned him into an old man, he looks about seventy and he's only forty-four.' She led the doctor into the sitting room. 'Steve, d'you remember Angus Grant? You met him when he stitched up that gash in Gregor's leg the first time we stayed here.'

Steven got up and held out his hand. 'Yes, I remember. Nice to meet you again.'

'It's good to see you ho–' His mouth fell open in mid-sentence and he stood there with his hand following the angle of his jaw as he took in Steven's appearance. 'Good God, man! What have they done to you?'

'Overworked and underfed me.'

Dr Grant subsided onto the nearest chair, still staring at Steven. 'You look like a refugee from a famine.'

'I was worse than this at one point in Siberia. Kazakhstan suited me better, till we got a new commandant recently.'

Jill looked at her husband in round-eyed horror.

The doctor made a visible effort to collect himself and picked up his bag. 'I think it's just as well I called.

I'd like to have a look at you, Dr Lindsay. May we go upstairs, Jill?'

About ten minutes later the two men came back into the room and she looked up at them up with a questioning expression.

'Dr Grant wants me to go into hospital for a couple of days, nothing drastic, just a top-to-toe check-up.'

'Oh Angus, I've only just got him back.' Jill shoulders slumped. 'Please don't take him away from me again.'

Steven patted her. 'It's alright, I'll be home by the weekend. Come on, cheer up, I'm only going as far as Edinburgh, you can come and visit me if you want to.'

'Of course I want to.'

'I've made arrangements for your husband to be admitted tomorrow morning. I've got some elderly patients going in for day treatment, so the ambulance'll collect him as well, just before nine.' The doctor headed for the door, then stopped. 'Sorry, I nearly forgot Kathy's message. She says you're to take the rest of the week off. The three of them have rearranged the rota to cope at the library without you.'

'That's really kind of them. Tell Kathy I'll give her a ring in the morning.'

*

As they were getting ready for bed, Steven remarked, 'Hmm, you've certainly lost weight, not nearly as cuddlesome as you used to be.'

Jill was about to make a similar comment, but stopped herself. However, when he pulled off his socks she gave a horrified gasp. 'Your feet! What happened to them?'

'Frostbite. But it could have been worse, at least I didn't have to have toes amputated, not like Kaiya, poor girl.'

'Who's she?'

'Not is, was.' He remembered a slightly oriental little face, plain in repose, but transformed when she smiled…and the remains of her initial cheeky vivacity draining away in a haemorrhage… He jerked his attention back to his living wife. 'She was a ballet dancer… She was imprisoned for helping with a samizdat…an underground newspaper…and her case wasn't helped when her brother married a Jewess and they applied for exit visas.'

'But how awful…she'd never dance again.' Something in his expression prompted her to enquire, 'Was she the friend who made your pillowcase?'

He nodded, then frowned. 'Have you had your appendix out since I last saw you?'

She looked down at her abdomen and bit her lip. 'No, hysterectomy.'

'Surely you're a bit young for that?'

'I had an ovarian cyst…I – I couldn't understand why my tummy ballooned when I'd lost so much weight… and when they opened me up, I was full of fibroids as well.' She gave a shuddering intake of breath. 'So the surgeon did a hysterectomy…which was a helluva shock when he told me.'

'I'm not surprised.' He hugged her. 'And are you OK now?'

'Fine, particularly as I'm no longer anaemic. It was nail-biting till I got the results of the biopsy, but everything was benign. I had to be careful about lifting for a while…it was a bit of a nuisance as it was just before we moved here.' And before that there was his mother's death and house clearance and afterwards, her nervous breakdown… But that could wait... There was such a lot to catch up with… A large bruise on one of his shins caught her eye and she pointed at it. 'That looks sore, is it another souvenir of Russia?'

He rubbed it gingerly. 'Yes, but it's my own fault. I tripped over a suitcase this morning at the airport. The owner was most apologetic, picked me up and dusted me down, but still got an earful from the official who was escorting me. Now, is there any chance of a bath, not just a skimpy shower? I'm longing to wallow.'

When he came back, they stood looking at each other for a few seconds. She put her arms round his neck and caressed his head. 'I know I like you with a short back and sides, but this is excessive.'

'I agree, but it offers less cover for lurking lice.'

'Yuk!' She let go of him.

He pulled her back. 'I was properly deloused last night and I've just washed my hair again.'

She relaxed against him and said in mock indignation, 'Something's poking me.'

'Good, I didn't think I'd be able to get it up.'

'It must have been the steak.' She chuckled. 'Refreshes those parts which other foods cannot reach.'

'Eh?'

'I was paraphrasing a lager ad which was popular a year or two back.' She started to undo his pyjama buttons. 'Dr Lindsay, you are vastly overdressed for the sport which you are about to pursue...'

CHAPTER 6

The ambulance and a television crew drew up in front of the cottage at the same time. The occupants of the former were thrilled to be filmed, the male Lindsays less so and Jill, least of all.

No, she had no idea that her husband was going to be released.

Yes, it was a marvellous surprise.

Yes, they were both feeling absolutely great.

No, there was nothing seriously wrong with him, he was simply going into hospital for a check-up.

No, she bloody well wasn't going to kiss him goodbye on camera for the delectation of the great British viewing public.

With commendable restraint, she managed not to voice this last sentiment and the cameraman had to be content with a farewell smile and wave – cut to the reporter, with a view of the departing ambulance in the background.

Once everyone had gone, Jill found herself wandering round the cottage disconsolately, wondering if she had dreamed the events of the last twenty-four hours, but the sight of Steven's suit on the bedroom chair assured her it had been no dream. She picked the jacket up and buried her face in it, then pushed it away with an expression of disgust. It didn't smell of him. It didn't smell right at all.

She sat down on the bed, at a loss for something to do. Bed…? He'd complained that it was far too soft and in any case she'd been thinking about getting a new one. She might as well do some research before he returned. She got up, trotted downstairs and made some phone calls. She then went into the kitchen where the boys were washing the breakfast dishes, for once without having to be asked to do so. 'Have you any plans for today?'

They looked at each other and shrugged.

'Well unless you want to go on being pestered by the mass media, I suggest you go out for a bit. I'm going into Alloa to do a big shopping, then I've arranged to work this afternoon. I'll visit Dad this evening and spend the night with Nanna and Grandpa. We need a new bed so I'll look for that in Edinburgh tomorrow before seeing Dad again in the afternoon, then come back here. You can fend for yourselves in between. Oh, and you'd better finish off the remains of Dad's pudding from last night. OK?'

The boys nodded their agreement. Alan looked at Gregor. 'When d'you start school again?'

'Next Monday. Mum, do I have to go back? Why can't I leave now?'

‘I’ve told you before, we can’t make any decisions till your results are out and I expect Dad’ll want his say in the matter now.’

Gregor scowled at her. ‘I’m off to the workshop.’ He banged the door on his way out.

‘Go and do your teeth and your bed first,’ Jill yelled after him. Why did the boys either leave doors wide open or slam them shut? She sighed and turned to Alan, ‘Anyhow, d’you want to come to Alloa?’

‘Nah, nae money.’

‘For goodness’ sake, speak properly.’ She turned to go.

‘Mum, if you’re going into Edinburgh, please will you get me a pipe bag, some seasoning and a mouthpiece?’

‘I thought you said you’d no money? Alright then, write down exactly what you want and where I’m to get it.’

‘Thanks, and I’ll settle up with you when I’ve got the cash out of my savings account.’

Jill went back upstairs to get ready. She picked up Steven’s suit to put in the wardrobe, sniffed at it again and decided she’d leave it at the cleaners in Brankstone, together with her winter coat and a skirt. They should be ready to collect on the way home if the place wasn’t busy.

This proved to be the case and she was told they would be available by one o’clock. It was only when the car was moving away from the shopping precinct she remembered she hadn’t been through the suit pockets. She looked at her watch and her foot hovered between brake and accelerator. No, better get on, otherwise she wouldn't have time for everything. In any case, the girls could be relied on to check them.

*

Back in the shop, the assistant pinned the tickets to the garments and went through the pockets. Nothing in the coat or trousers, but her fingertips registered a lump in the breast pocket of the jacket. She removed a small wad of paper. She opened it out. It looked like a couple of lines of music, hand written. Nothing on the other side. She shrugged and put it by the till. Better keep it for the customer.

A few minutes later she called out to her colleague, 'Mary, will ye mind the shop a wee while? I'm awa' tae the Co-operative for a few messages. I'll no' be long.'

Mary had just put Jill's clothes into the machine when another customer arrived and dumped a kilt on the counter. 'Och, hello Jeanie, how's yersel'.'

'No' bad, thanks.'

'That Sandy's kilt?'

'Aye. There's stains doon the front I cannae shift.'

Mary opened out the kilt and scratched at the marks with a long fingernail from which the varnish was peeling. 'D'ye ken what it is?'

'Naw. Beer or whisky most like.'

'Och well, we'll do waur best.' She wrote out the ticket and handed over the receipt.

Jeanie put it in her purse, then started to hunt through her shopping bag. 'That's me come wi' oot ma list again. Ha' ye a wee bit o' paper?'

Mary looked around, saw the piece which had come out of Steven's pocket and pushed it over, blank side uppermost. 'That do ye?'

'Ta.' Jeanie wrote down several items, then paused. 'There was something Sandy wanted from the chemist. Now what was it? Oh aye, almond oil.'

'I've got some hand cream wi' that in. Good stuff.'

'It's no' for his hands, it's for his pipes.'

Mary gave her a startled look. 'Well I've heard o' folk mending leaks wi' chewing gum or sticking plaster, but almond oil's a new one on me.'

Jeanie looked equally startled, then gave a hoot of laughter. 'It's no' for that kind of pipe, it's for his bagpipes. He rubs the oil into the wooden bits two or three times a year to keep them from cracking and leaves a nice mess on the kitchen table. When'll yon be ready?'

'Tomorrow afternoon do ye? It'll need a fair bit o' pressing.'

'Oh aye, so long as he's got it for Saturday.'

'The band oot that day?'

'Aye, Bathgate. And as they've got a late draw, mebbe there's a chance of him coming home sober. Cheerio.'

When Jill returned for her clothes, the assistant who had served her was away for lunch and Mary assured her that nothing had been found in any of the pockets.

*

Jeanie Henderson was preparing tea when Sandy got home. She told him that his almond oil was still in her bag and to her annoyance, he located it by the simple means of tipping everything out onto the table. He was about to pick it up when he saw the shopping list. He swore at his wife for pinching his music and went out of the kitchen to put bottle and paper in his pipe case, leaving her glaring after him in innocent indignation.

*

It was early evening when Jill arrived at the hospital to visit Steven. He'd been put in a room of his own and she was surprised to discover he already had visitors: two men whom she'd never seen before. They got up as she entered and one of them put a cassette recorder into his briefcase.

'That was very enlightening, Dr Lindsay and thank you for your cooperation. If it's alright with the staff, we'll see you again tomorrow at about the same time. Mrs Lindsay, you must be very thankful to see your husband home at last. Goodbye.'

As Steven got out of bed and settled himself in one of the chairs, Jill enquired. 'Who were they?'

'Probably MI6. They were escorted in by Matron in person and they've been grilling me about my Russian experiences. Very polite, but extremely thorough.'

'MI6? Isn't that something to do with counter-espionage?'

He nodded. 'I think I've convinced them that I haven't been brainwashed and returned to spy for the Soviets.'

She gaped at him. 'But that's ridiculous!'

‘Not really. After all, there’s Grangemouth across the river and Rosyth practically next door. Plenty of potential material for a spy to work on.’ He laughed at her outraged expression. ‘It’s alright. I’m not going to be hauled off to another prison. I even offered to submit to a lie-detector, but they said rather huffily that it wouldn’t be necessary.’

She sat shaking her head in bewilderment.

‘Never mind them. Now, tell me what you’ve been up to since we made our television debut.’

‘It may have been your British debut, but it wasn’t mine. I got the full treatment when I came home after your trial.’

When she returned to the hospital late on Friday morning, Jill found Steven up and dressed, ready to leave. ‘Have they finished with you?’

‘I hope so. I’ve been to just about every department except obstetrics and gynaecology. That only leaves the dentist. I’ve seen an ophthalmic surgeon and got a prescription for glasses.’

‘I’ve made an appointment with the Glasgow practice for you next week. The receptionist nearly had a fit when I told her you’d been suffering from scurvy, but what did the surgeon say about your eyes?’

‘There’s no permanent damage, so providing you don’t starve me, they’ll be fine and I can drive once I’ve got glasses.’

‘We’ll stop in Dunfermline on the way back and you can go to an optician with your prescription. D’you want to look at beds too?’

'We might as well, but the orthopaedic surgeon told me to get a firm one as my back's suffered from heaving logs and sacks of potatoes and chicken feed. Sister said I was her first patient who'd ever complained about a bed being too soft. You should have seen her face when I told her that I was used to a thin straw palliasse on bare boards!'

'Have Laurel and Hardy finished with you?'

'Who?'

'The men from the ministry. Matron's blue-eyed boys. Your de-briefers.'

'Oh, them. Yes. They were here again yesterday and left me a phone number to ring in case I remembered anything else of interest. Remind me I put the card in one of the pockets of my sponge bag.'

On the way down in the lift, Jill said, 'If you need a firm mattress, there's a furniture shop not far away with an orthopaedic bed. It was a cancelled order. If you're feeling OK, d'you want to walk over and have a look at it?'

Which they duly did and as Steven said that it would suit him, they bought it and made arrangements to have it delivered. Jill reckoned the bed would be uncomfortable until she got used to it, but kept her reservations to herself. She was less reticent when he then suggested lunch at one of the more expensive restaurants in the city. 'Don't you think we've spent enough for one day? Just remember, my income's got to support four now, instead of three.'

His face fell. 'Oh help! I'd forgotten about that. I suppose we'd better go into the state of the family finances once we get home – and I'll have to start job-hunting.'

They settled for fish and chips at a nearby café.

When they got to Dunfermline, Jill left him at an optician and went to do some shopping, arranging to meet him at the entrance to the supermarket. When he didn't turn up, she waited for a few minutes, then went back to the optician and found him sitting there, looking exhausted.

'I hope you weren't getting worried, but I suddenly found I couldn't face the noise and bustle in the High Street, it all takes a bit of getting used to again.' He picked up a sample frame from the counter, 'How about these?'

She looked at him critically, 'The shape's OK, but I think you'd look better in a light-weight gold frame than academic horn-rims.'

'They're more expensive – and you turned down a good lunch because of the cost.'

'I know, but these'll last a lot longer than a meal.'

He grimaced at the optician. 'That's feminine logic for you, but I'd better do as the boss says. When will they be ready?'

On the way back to the car, Steven was surprised when Jill suddenly halted and tugged his arm. 'Next stop, dear.'

He looked in the direction of her pointing finger and read a sign which said "Employment Office".

'D'you want me to come in with you?'

He shook his head. 'I'll see you back at the car park.'

It was over half an hour later when he opened the door and slumped dejectedly into the passenger seat.

She put an arm round his shoulders. 'Was it that bad?'

'When I got off the plane, I thought all my troubles were over, but it looks as though they're just beginning. It never entered my head that I'd be joining the dole queue. Had I taught physics, maths or engineering, I could easily have got a job, but nobody seems to want a lecturer, or even a schoolteacher, in German. I gather that the universities have been cutting back on staff pretty severely in the last few years.'

''Fraid so.' She started the car. 'If it's any consolation, the chap who took over your old job was axed last year, so you might have found yourself in the same position, without having been to Russia. But cheer up, our finances are reasonably healthy and Alan should soon be off our hands. I wonder if he'll get a better grant if you have to sign on for a while?'

Steven gave her a bleak smile, 'I suppose it's an ill wind that blows nobody good.' He couldn't bring himself to tell her just then about the not so small matter of his backlog of National Insurance contributions.

He was surprised at the pile of letters waiting for him at home and took them into the sitting room while Jill started to prepare dinner. Alan came in shortly after and a few minutes later she heard his pipes start up overhead. She shrugged to herself and turned the radio on the worktop up to full volume. Two minutes later she was confronted by an irate husband.

'Stop that bloody row!'

She switched off the radio and said indignantly, 'It's not a row, it's Mozart.'

'That too,' he said, pointing to the ceiling.

'Tell him yourself, I'm busy.'

Her next interruption was from an angry son. 'Mum, it's not fair! Dad says I'm not to practice in the house and I need to.'

'But surely you've learnt all your tunes for tomorrow?'

'It's not that. Duncan gave us new reeds yesterday and I must get mine blown in for tomorrow.'

'Well, go down to the bottom of the garden, distance might lend enchantment.'

'It's raining.'

'The garage, then.'

'Oh, alright, and if Gregor objects, then it's his hard cheese.'

'Just a minute–'

'What now?' muttered Alan.

Jill pulled him back into the kitchen, shut the door and said quietly, 'I think it's going to be a case of "gang warily" until Dad's settled down. And his temper hasn't been sweetened by having to sign on for the dole this afternoon.'

The dial in Alan's internal pressure gauge rapidly returned to normal. 'Message received and understood, and I'll relay it to Gregor.'

Dinner was a subdued meal, but Jill was relieved to see that Steven looked thoughtful, rather than bad-tempered or upset and when they finished washing up, he announced, 'I want everyone back round the table so that we can discuss finances and future prospects. Gregor, you're the youngest, you go first.'

Gregor sat down and looked round the others uncertainly. 'How d'you mean? Where do I start?'

'I don't even know what O-grades you've just sat, or how you did in the prelims.'

'Woodwork, Technical Drawing, Art, Arithmetic and English. I did OK – apart from failing English.'

'And what are you proposing to do with that odd assortment?'

'I want to be a cabinet maker.'

'That's not very ambitious, surely you can do better than that?'

Gregor said sulkily, 'It's what I want to do, I like working with my hands and making things and I don't want to sit on my arse all day in an office.'

'There's no need to put it quite so crudely. Have you left school?'

'No. Mum says I've got to wait for my results, particularly English.' He looked appealingly at his father. 'Dad, please let me leave school, I'm sure that Duncan would take me on as an apprentice.'

'Has he made you a definite offer?'

Gregor dropped his eyes and shook his head.

'Then I think we'll continue your mother's policy of "wait and see". These days you need all the qualifications you can get.' Steven went on, half to himself, 'But that's no guarantee of employment, it seems.' After staring out of the window for a few moments, he shook himself and focused on Alan. ‘Anyhow, you next. Dentistry, isn’t it?’

‘Yeah. I’ve got a conditional acceptance from Glasgow and good marks in my prelims, so I should be OK, so long as I pass Higher English.’ He pulled a face. ‘I only got a Comp. O last year.’

‘What’s a compo?’

‘Complimentary O grade as I failed the Higher.’

Jill said apologetically, ‘English doesn’t seem to be their subject.’

‘It’s hardly surprising,’ snapped Steven. ‘The way they speak it, you’d think it was a foreign language and their accent and vocabulary have deteriorated in the last five years. They’d have done much better in all respects to have stayed at the Academy instead of going to a comprehensive. I really don’t know why you had to drag the family across Scotland to a cramped country cottage which was only supposed to be a holiday home.’

‘I dragged us here because I couldn’t afford their school fees, or the upkeep of a nice, big house.’ His wife leant forward, fists clenched and glared at him. ‘And it’s only thanks to your granny’s legacy that we’ve a roof over our heads. With. No. Mortgage.’ Jill punctuated each of the last three words with a thump on the table.

The boys jumped and exchanged alarmed looks.

Steven recoiled and held up his hands in an attitude of surrender. ‘Sorry.’ He rubbed his face and shook his head. ‘It’s just that… It’s just that when I got off the plane the other day…' His shoulders slumped. 'It's just that I wasn't expecting…' He gestured round him. '… this.'

Jill took a couple of slow, deep breaths and glanced at her sons. She patted Steven on the hand. 'It's OK, we understand.' She gave them all a reassuring smile. 'I did get some help from the family. I thought the boys would have to leave the Academy immediately, but your mother said she'd pay the fees. That did mean they had another year there, but after she died, it was impossible.'

'Gosh!' said Gregor. 'That was decent of Granny.'

Jill smiled at him. 'And brother-in-law Tony lent me money for the alterations here until our house in Glasgow was sold and I could invest the money for some income.'

Steven straightened up and returned to his original and hopefully less contentious topic. 'What exams have you just done, Alan?'

'I resat Higher English and did Sixth Year Studies in Chemistry and Physics with Higher Biology. If I pass English and get an A in the others, I'm in.'

'And I don't think that the sixth year has been wasted,' added Jill. 'Seventeen would have been a bit young to start dentistry and he seems to have enjoyed this last year. He was Deputy Captain,' she added proudly.

'Good for you, son. And d'you think you'll get a grant?'

'Should do,' said Jill. 'Though I don't know what difference your return will make. My job isn't full-time, but on the other hand, we have some investment income.'

‘If you’re going to talk finance, I’m going,’ said Gregor, scraping his chair away from the table.

His brother tugged at him. ‘Stay put and pin back your ears, you might learn something.’

Gregor slouched beside Alan with a bored expression.

Jill gave them an amused look and went on, ‘Our finances are now reasonably healthy, though they weren’t to begin with. The first year was a nightmare: no husband; no job; no income and on top of that, helping your mother to sort out your father’s estate; her final illness, then dealing with her estate. Thank God for Valium!’ But in the end, Valium hadn’t been enough.

‘What exactly happened to Mother?’ enquired Steven, ‘Your letter said something about a broken leg. That isn’t usually fatal.’

‘She slipped on the ice the February after you were imprisoned and was operated on to have her femur pinned. She was alright the first week and seemed to be making a good recovery, then quite suddenly, all the fight went out of her. She made no effort to get moving again and ended up with hypostatic pneumonia. I think she wanted to go, because she refused antibiotics.’ And she wasn’t the only one who wanted out of it all.

‘Poor old thing, except that she wasn’t all that old, only seventy-two, no age at all these days. I suppose the events of the previous year were too much for her. She was only just coming up for air after Father’s death when we went on that bloody Baltic cruise and I suppose the fracture was the final straw.’

‘I think she realised that she was only going to leave the hospital in her wooden kimono.’

‘Why was that?’ asked Alan.

‘Quite suddenly she gave me a cheque for a thousand pounds and said that it was for next term’s fees and a bit over for a holiday.’

The boys whistled.

‘And did you cash it?’ said Steven.

‘Not to begin with, but when it was obvious she was dying, I’m afraid I did. It was a godsend, even if I did feel guilty about taking it.’

Gregor sat up, looking less bored. ‘Don’t see why you should. It all came to you eventually, you only got your hands on some of it a bit sooner.’

Jill shook her head and explained how Mrs Lindsay’s estate had been divided up, including the boys as beneficiaries.

They looked at each other in astonishment. ‘Alan, did you know that?’ said Gregor.

His brother shook his head. ‘Well, you might have told us, Mum.’

‘I know we dealt with most things together,’ said Jill, ‘but you were a bit young then for such high finance.’

Steven laughed. ‘Your Granny was a canny old bird when it came to money and from the sound of it, you’ve nothing to complain about.’

Jill looked relieved. ‘Mother said that when you came home, she hoped you’d understand. There’s a letter for you from her in the deed box. Don’t let me forget to give it to you. There was only one legacy, to Miss Micklethwaite, her housekeeper.’

Steven clapped a hand over his mouth and looked contrite. 'Mickey! I'd forgotten all about her, I should have phoned my first evening back.'

'It's alright, I did, after you left for hospital. She sent her love and said she'd have a word with you when it was convenient.'

'Where is she now? Have you seen anything of her lately?'

'She moved in with us when Mother died and was a godsend after my operation. We felt it only fair to ask her if she wanted to come here, but she said she wasn't used to village life and she now lives with her widowed sister in Dewsbury… She came up to help when I was ill and we still keep in touch.' She saw the question starting to form itself and went on. 'Thanks to Mother's will being straightforward and you giving me power of attorney, our finances didn't take too long to sort out. At least, that's what I was told. Lawyers must work on a different time scale.'

Steven suddenly leant over and gave his wife a hug and a kiss, to the obvious embarrassment of the boys. 'Poor love, you've certainly had a time of it, but I'd like to think that the light at the end of the tunnel is a bit nearer. I know I've just signed on this afternoon, but I've already had a number of offers from various newspapers and publishers for my story. They all sound marvellous, but I think I'll use an agent, it'll be worth their commission to spare me the wheeling and dealing.'

'Are you going to write a book?' asked Alan. 'After all, it wouldn't be the first one.'

'Yes, but I suspect that there'll be quite a difference between an autobiography and a work on eighteenth century German poets.' He stood up and smiled round the family. 'End of meeting, let's have some coffee.' He started to fill the kettle then exclaimed, 'Oh hell!' as his trousers, which had been resurrected from a suitcase in the garage, slithered towards his hips. He grabbed them in one hand and stood there, feeling a fool, while the others roared with laughter. 'I don't care what our finances are like, I must get some properly fitting clothes.'

'There's no point in getting very much, you'll be putting on weight again,' said Jill reaching over to prod him in the ribs, 'In fact, you feel a bit less knobbly already.'

'Ouch! Well, I dare say, but it'll be a while before I return to normal, I was told at the hospital to put on weight gradually and I'm not going round in things several sizes too big. I can't even borrow the boys' clothes, they're quite differently proportioned and in any case, they aren't my style.'

'I know!' exclaimed Alan, 'The primary school's having a jumble sale tomorrow, there's a notice about it in the Co-op.'

'A jumble sale? I'm not dressing myself at a jumble sale,' said his father in outraged tones.

Jill got up and pirouetted round. 'How d'you like my trousers?'

Steven had already noticed them, in fact he could hardly fail to have done so as they were bright red and fitted very neatly. 'Hmm, people can certainly see you coming and they display the goods inside alright.'

She grinned at him: 'Jumble sale loot.'

CHAPTER 7

'Is it still OK for me to borrow the car to go over to Bathgate?' Alan asked as he liberally applied butter to a second slice of toast.

Jill gestured at Steven with her mug. 'Anything you want to do?'

'I don't think so, thanks. I just want to potter round here and generally get my bearings. After all, it is my first full day at home.'

'Yes, that's OK then, but I thought the band usually had a bus?'

'It depends on how far we're going. As Bathgate is fairly local, we agreed on cars.'

'When are you leaving?'

Alan looked at his watch. 'We're nearly the last to go in grade three, about one-fifteen. Duncan wants us there no later than midday, so better say eleven. Can I phone the others to tell them when?'

'Who're you taking?' asked Gregor.

'Sheila, Bob and Fiona.'

'Who's Fiona? Have I met her?' said Jill.

‘She’s one of the girl pipers. The fair one. The small dark, plump one’s Joan.’

‘Yes, I know her, she works in the hairdressers in Brankstone. Aren’t you taking her as well?’

‘She wouldn’t thank me for it, she’d far sooner go with Ron.’

Gregor raised a quizzical eyebrow at his brother, who gave him an “it’s none of my business” shrug.

Jill started to move dishes into the sink. ‘I suppose you’ll want a packed lunch. Get what you want out of the freezer. Did you remember to clean your spats?’

‘Don’t need ’em. It’s not full dress today, just black jackets with our Mackenzie kilts. Have you seen my cape anywhere?’

‘No. Try the cupboard under the stairs. Anyhow, it’s stopped raining and the forecast’s for a fine afternoon.’

‘I’d better have it, just in case.’

Steven went off to the bathroom. On his return he frowned. ‘The carpet sweeper and the vacuum cleaner are out in the hall. Is that intended as a hint to someone?’

Jill sighed. ‘No, it just means that Alan’s been looking for his cape and as usual, hasn’t bothered to put things back where he found them.’

‘I seem to remember as a child he was quite tidy.’

‘It must have been a passing phase as he certainly isn’t now. Gregor gets furious with him at times, but I suppose it isn’t easy for the two of them sharing a small room.’

When he had hung up the tea towel, Steven looked at the pile of dishes. ‘I suppose I’d better start learning where all these go. Anything else you want me to do afterwards?'

'I don't think so, thanks. I'm going to blow round the house and do a bit of cooking. If you come upstairs, I'll give you Mother's letter and also the copies of my letters to you. You can sit out in the sunroom while I'm busy.'

In the bedroom, she pulled out a thick file and a deed box from the bottom of one of the cupboards.

Steven noticed his suit hanging up. 'You can donate that thing to the jumble sale.'

Jill got up off her knees and handed him an envelope. 'There's Mother's letter. But there's nothing wrong with your suit, I've just had it cleaned and it'll eventually fit you again.'

'I want rid of the damned thing. Too many unpleasant associations. Give it to one of the boys.'

'I hardly think they'll thank you for navy blue with a chalk pinstripe. However, I'll enquire.' She took down the suit and put it on the bed. 'Look who's being inconsistent now. You throw out a perfectly good suit and keep an awful old jacket.'

'Alright then, throw them both out, but I don't want that suit!' He picked up the file and went downstairs, slamming the door behind him.

Steven's mood was not lightened by his reading matter. His mother's letter was a tired, elderly voice, resurrected through the medium of familiar writing distorted by a shaky hand. It conjured up quite a different person from the vigorous woman she had once been. Jill's letters weren't much better. She had done her best to be cheerful, but the strain and worry kept breaking through the veneer of light-heartedness.

He was quite glad when his arms became too short to keep the typed carbon copies in focus. He put down the file and stretched, wondering what to do next. After years of working from dawn till dusk, he wasn't used to having time on his hands. He gazed round, seeing familiar objects in a different setting, then got up abruptly and went out into the garden.

It was a warm, damp morning. Steven inhaled deeply. The air smelt of wood smoke from a neighbouring chimney, freshly cut grass and the sweet waft of some late spring flowers: quite different from Kazakhstan. After he'd recovered from pneumonia, he'd been moved to an agricultural area north of the Caspian Sea, where life was no longer a constant struggle to exist. Working as a farm labourer, he probably was no worse off than the local peasants…except for the last few months under the new commandant.

He wandered past the greenhouse down to the bottom of the garden and stood looking back up at the cottage. When he'd bought it with his grandmother's legacy, he'd had no thoughts of it ever becoming the family's main home…and what a change from the last time he'd been here…a dilapidated building viewed across a wilderness where sharp objects lurked in the undergrowth…as Gregor had found out the hard way.

Steven surveyed the vegetable patch. Last week – only last week? – he'd been digging *chyernozyom*, the rich "black earth" of the region. He bent down and ran some soil through his fingers. It was thin and gritty, but it was Scottish soil, which at times he'd never expected to set foot on again… He glanced round furtively, but there was no longer anybody standing guard over him. He pulled up a radish, wiped off the earth and munched it, relishing the peppery flavour. It was a treat after so much tasteless, subsistence food. After sampling a few more, he tossed the tops under the hedge.

The sudden movement disturbed a young blackbird. It gave a chatter of alarm and fluttered onto the greenhouse, but misjudged its landing on the ridge. It slowly slid down the roof, trying in vain to dig its claws into the glass, coming to a halt in the gutter, rump first. Steven burst out laughing. After sitting for a few moments, the fledgling shook its feathers and flew back into the hedge. What a joy to see and hear blackbirds, bluetits and robins again, instead of bluethroats and Siberian rubythroats – and it was a long time since he had spontaneously laughed out loud.

The garage and workshop were next in line for investigation. The car was out in the drive, where Alan was loading his pipe case and cape into the boot. 'Must go and get changed,' he said, looking at his watch and hurried inside.

Steven walked round the car, got into the driver's seat and sat for a few minutes, fiddling with the controls. He looked up to see Gregor grinning at him.

'D'you think you'll be able to drive it?'

'I don't see why not, once I get my glasses, but I'll take good care that the first few miles are over quiet roads until I get the feel of it again.' He got out and wandered into the garage, the back of which was fitted out as Gregor's workshop.

Ming was asleep in a box at the end of the bench. At Steven's approach, the Siamese cat opened an eye, blinked, yawned and stretched, before rubbing against him. He stroked her, enjoying the feel of her silky fur and the vibrations of her loud purr.

'Gosh, you're honoured,' remarked Gregor. 'She's pretty choosy who she makes friends with and when she sees Paul coming, she takes off in the opposite direction.'

Steven experienced an absurd feeling of satisfaction at this.

'Dad, how d'you like the new garden seat?'

'Very nice. Did you make it?'

'Yeah, and I designed it.' The seat was simple and sturdy, with pleasing proportions.

'Can I sit in it?'

'Not unless you want preservative on your clothes. Give it twenty-four hours, then you can christen it, weather permitting.'

The chaise longue was now propped up inside the garage. Steven indicated it. 'Would your skills run to mending that old family favourite?'

'Nah, it's got woodworm, s'only fit for firewood.'

Steven looked over the workbench. 'Hey! Isn't that mine?' He picked up a plane and made a few passes with it before putting it down again. 'A good one, too.'

'It won't be for long, the way you're treating it.'

'Eh?'

'If you put a plane down like that in the school workshop, you're liable to get a metal ruler across your knuckles. Lay it on its side so that you don't damage the blade.'

'Oh.' There was nothing like being put in your place by a child. 'I don't remember seeing that set of chisels before.'

'Nanna and Grandpa gave them to me for Christmas a couple of years ago,'

'You've got quite a good selection of tools there.'

'Christmases, birthdays and any spare pocket money, but there's one important thing missing.'

'What?'

'A lathe.'

'Is that a gentle hint?'

Gregor shrugged and gave his father a sideways look. 'Well…no, not really. They're kinda expensive. I've been using the school one and Duncan'll let me use one in his workshop if it isn't needed for something else. Dad, do I have to go back? Why can't I leave–?'

'Hi!' Alan's reappearance cut short the potential argument. 'That's me away now. Does anyone want a lift to the shops before I collect the others?' Hitherto, Steven had only seen his sons in jeans and tee-shirts and still thought of them as large, scruffy children. However, the sight of the smart young man in band uniform made him realise he was going to have to view them in a more adult light. Not an easy transition to make.

Jill came out, carrying Steven's suit. She showed it to the boys. 'Would either of you consider wearing this? Dad doesn't want it.'

In unison, they curled their lips.

'That's what I was afraid of.' She laid it over the back of the passenger seat. 'In that case, please would you leave it at the school on your way through the village, they can have it for this afternoon's sale.'

Gregor rummaged in his pockets. He tossed the suit onto the back seat and sat down. 'Drop me off at the post office, I fancy a Coke.'

After the boys had gone, Steven followed Jill into the kitchen. He straddled a chair and watched as she placed pieces of cold meat onto a row of buttered, sliced bread. 'Are we having a picnic?'

'No. They're for packed lunches for Gregor and me.'

'Doesn't he have school dinners?'

'Not any longer, it's too expensive, and some days I work over lunchtime.'

'D'you ever work on Saturdays?'

'Yes, evenings too, depending on the rota. The hours vary, but if one of the four of us is off for any reason, we swap round. I should have been on yesterday morning and now, but the others decided I needed some compassionate leave. They're a nice lot to work with.' She piled the cut sandwiches into a plastic box and after taking it out to the freezer, returned with a lump of dough which had been sitting on the boiler and started to knead it.

'What's that for?'

'Rolls, also for lunches.'

'But you swore you'd never work with yeast again after that time you tried to make hot crossed buns and ended up turning them into scones.

Jill grinned at the memory. 'I did, but then I saw someone making bread on a television cookery programme, it looked so easy that I gave it a try – and it worked. Now I make most of my own, it fills up the boys much better than the bought stuff.' She started to form balls of dough and placed them on a greased tray. 'But I'm no better at pastry. When Mickey was here, I watched her making it and copied her action for action. Result: one feather-weight tart and one leaden one.'

'And just why was Mickey here?'

She went on spacing out the dough balls.

'Come on, you've already ducked the issue once. What was wrong with you?'

She picked up the tray and put it on top of the cooker. Addressing the wall behind it, she said flatly, 'I had a nervous breakdown.'

After a few moments silence he got up and came over. 'Poor love,' he said, wrapping his arms round her. 'I'm not surprised. What exactly happened?'

She buried her face in his shoulder. 'It was like post-natal blues,' she said, her voice muffled, 'only far worse. Everything suddenly got on top of me, I couldn't sleep properly and I kept bursting into tears, I felt such a fool.' After a couple of steadying breaths, she continued, 'I signed on with Angus…after a bit of persuasion and he was such a help. He reckoned part of the trouble was the after-effects of my operation… on top of everything else.' She paused and sighed. 'He referred me to a psychiatrist, who put me on pills for several months. They made me very dopey till I got used to them…that's why Mickey came up. It was a bit of a squeeze and I slept in the sitting room…but we managed and it was marvellous to have her support.'

'And who persuaded you to go to the doctor? The boys? Your parents?'

She shook her head. 'Paul. And the butcher's assistant.'

'The butcher's assistant! What's he got to do with it?'

'She. Rose McGinty. Such a nice wee woman. You see, her husband had been in jail, so of all people, she knew how I was feeling. And Paul was in a prison camp before he escaped to the West.'

'Yes, I gathered that.' He led her over to the table and sat her down. 'Are you OK now?'

She smiled up at him. 'Yes. Honestly. Since I crawled out of the Slough of Despond I've been fine, particularly since the library opened. Getting that job made all the difference. I won't say that I don't get the odd moments of depression, but I can cope with them.'

'More pills?'

She laughed. 'No. Good quality plain chocolate! I read somewhere that it contains an anti-depressant and it seems to work. Anyhow, it's all in the past and

I want to forget the last five years, as I expect you do.' She got up. 'Coffee?'

To her relief, he nodded and did not pursue the subject which was just as well. She'd told him the truth, but not the whole truth, nor did she intend to if it could be avoided.

CHAPTER 8

As Jill sipped her coffee, she gazed into space and thought back to the wretched first few weeks in the cottage… The battles with tradesmen to get the alterations finished and the heating installed… Worrying about the boys at their new school… The interview at Rosyth Dockyard for a secretarial post and being shown the door when they learnt her husband was in a Russian prison… Her chronic insomnia… And her desire to slip into oblivion to escape the bouts of depression, her dreaded "Black Dog".

Before their world was shattered, Jill and Steven enjoyed going to the Scottish National Orchestra Concerts in Glasgow. She'd not had the heart to go on her own the previous winter, but her parents, who lived in South Queensferry, went to the Edinburgh series and persuaded her to join them for the current season. Her subscription was their advance Christmas present and she found the music helped to banish her miseries for a little while.

The tall, fair-haired, slightly foreign-looking man who was sitting near them at the first concert looked vaguely familiar. A few days later he was in front of her in the queue at Auchentullum post office. He nodded to her on the way out and asked her if she'd enjoyed the concert. The next time at the Usher Hall, he introduced himself and when he learnt that Jill lived in the village, he offered her a lift home, but she'd come by car.

It was her mother who suggested she shared transport with Mr Holland to save travelling costs. Jill rather diffidently agreed to this, provided she wasn't going to shop in Edinburgh earlier in the day. She felt guilty about leaving Alan and Gregor on their own, but at fourteen and twelve, they were no longer babies and a neighbour said she'd keep an eye on them.

She persuaded the initially reluctant boys to go on the school half term outing to London at the beginning of October and as she was going to be shopping in Alloa that week, she accepted Mr Holland's offer of a lift to the concert that weekend and said she would reciprocate at a later date.

Jill quickly felt she'd known him for ages as she found him an easy person to talk to and an attentive listener. Her enjoyment of their discussions about the various musical performances they'd been to made her realise just how much she'd missed regular adult conversation in the last year.

They were still chatting about that night's concert when they got back to the village. She wondered if she should ask him in for coffee, but on getting out of the car, she simply thanked him for the lift, wished him goodnight and gave a quick wave as she went inside.

As soon as Jill shut the front door, the "Black Dog" pounced before she'd even locked up and kept snapping at her heels as she got ready for bed.

She went into the kitchen, opened one of the top cupboards and took out a bottle of whisky. After gazing at it for a few moments, she replaced it. She'd had a swig one evening and had felt even more hellish the following morning.

Going back into the bathroom, she started to rummage through the medicine cabinet: surely there'd be something there which would help her to sleep? She pulled out a bottle of sleeping pills which she'd found during her mother-in-law's house clearance. They might give her a few hours respite…or even longer…? She'd tried to use them sparingly, but when she shook the bottle over her palm, nothing came out. She gave a wail of despair, dropped the bottle into the basin and started to cry.

Jill's racking sobs slowly drove her down until she was sitting on the floor, propped up against the bath panel. She hugged her knees and rocked from side to side, venting her misery.

She'd no idea how long she'd been like that when she thought she heard the door bell. She ignored it.

A few minutes later a voice in the hall called out, 'Hello there. It's Paul Holland. I've brought back the bag you left in the car. Is something wrong?'

She stifled her sobs, hoping he'd go away.

The voice got nearer. 'It's Paul Holland. I've brought back the bag from your mother's friend… The one with clothes for your sons… Can I help?'

'Go away, I don't want to see anyone.' She started to cry again.

He said firmly, 'There's obviously something wrong. I'm coming in.'

Jill put her head down and hunched over her knees as she sensed him come into the room.

After a brief silence, there was an explosive '*Bozhyeh moy!*' shortly followed by the sound of cupboard doors banging in the kitchen.

She looked up as Paul came back, holding a glass of cloudy, yellowish liquid. He hauled her to her feet, kicked up the toilet seat and thrust the glass at her.

'Quick, get this down!'

She stopped crying out of sheer surprise and looked at the glass in her hand. 'What's that?'

'It's a mustard emetic. It's to make you sick.

'But I don't want to be sick.'

He picked up the pill bottle out of the basin and waved it at her. 'With that lot inside you, the sooner you're sick, the better.'

She looked at him in bewilderment and began to laugh weakly. Some of the mustard solution slopped down her dressing gown. 'But I haven't taken any pills tonight… I was crying because there's none left… I wanted to take a whole bottle so that I could sleep and sleep.' She started to cry again. 'It's hell not being able to sleep properly… I don't know when I last had a decent night's sleep. Oh God! If only I could sleep.'

'Sorry *dushka*, but just to be on the safe side, you're going to be sick.' He took the glass from her, pinioned her hands in one of his and put to glass to her mouth. 'Drink it!'

She turned her head away, like a child.

'Drink it!'

'I don't need it.'

'If you won't drink it, I shall make you, even if I have to hurt you.'

Jill capitulated.

She knelt down, clamped her nose with finger and thumb and wordlessly held out the other hand for the glass.

Paul held her forehead until she had finished retching and checked that there were no pills bobbing around in what had come up. He cleaned out the glass and refilled it with tepid water. 'Here, rinse and spit.'

Jill used the mouthwash, flushed it away, then shut the lid, hauled herself onto the toilet and sat there shivering with her head in her hands. After a few moments, she got up slowly and started to spread toothpaste on her brush. Paul went out and while she washed her face, combed her hair and sponged her dressing gown, she heard him tidying the kitchen. He was waiting by the door when she emerged. He took her by the elbow and led her into the chilly sitting room, where she flopped onto the sofa, curled up in a ball and started to shiver again.

Paul sat down beside her and vigorously rubbed her back and arms. After a while the spasms lessened and he eased her into a more upright position. She offered no resistance when he put an arm round her and began to stroke her hair. 'I'm sorry about the unpleasantness in the bathroom, *dushka*, but I wanted to be sure that you really hadn't swallowed an overdose.'

She murmured something into his shoulder and he rubbed his head against hers. Without thinking, she put her arm round his neck…then went rigid, pushing herself back to the end of the sofa and sat starting at him, scarlet-faced. 'Oh, I'm terribly sorry, I…I didn't mean…to…to…be…' She buried her head in her hands.

He looked at her in amusement. 'To be a forward hussy?'

She nodded.

He pulled her hands away gently, amusement turning to concern. 'Not at all, just the opposite. You strike me as being someone who's in urgent need of help.' He started to run a finger over her cheek. 'When did you last see a doctor?'

'My final check-up after my hysterectomy, probably mid-summer.' His stroking had a hypnotic effect on her: her jaw slackened and her eyelids fluttered and drooped. He pulled her to him again and went on stroking. After a while, she said sleepily, 'Would you mind very much if I put my arms round you for a few minutes?'

'Go ahead.'

She settled herself against him with a sigh and went on, half to herself, 'It wouldn't have been so bad if I'd had a daughter, or the boys were a bit younger…then we could have had a little cuddle together…but you can't do that with them now, they'd be embarrassed… That was the worst thing after my operation, knowing I'd never have a daughter… It was unlikely before, but there was always a little hope and now, it's gone for good… You've no idea what it's like not having anyone to cuddle…'

'On the contrary, I know all about loneliness and insomnia, my wife died of ovarian cancer after we'd been married barely three years.'

She looked up at him and he gave her a sad smile, which nevertheless revealed a dimple in each cheek. She shyly touched one of them, then said, 'Poor you,' and put her head back on his chest. A little later she enquired, 'How did you get over the insomnia? Did you take pills?'

'There are certain services,' he said dryly, 'which are more easily bought by a man than a woman.'

There followed a few seconds silence, then a shocked 'Oh!' as Jill sat up and edged away from Paul, embarrassed by the effect she was having on a man she hardly knew.

He drew her towards him again, tilted her head, kissed her gently on the mouth. 'Relax. I'm going to give you what Sonja used to call one of my special sleeping pills.'

'What's that?'

In reply, he gave her a much longer kiss, caressed her breasts and slid his hand down to her thighs. Jill began to respond to him, slowly at first…then hungrily…but she suddenly pushed him away and catapulted back to the end of the sofa, where she buried her head in the corner. 'Oh my God! What am I thinking?' Her shoulders started to heave again.

A thoroughly frustrated Paul hauled her upright and gave her a shake. 'You need to learn a few facts of life, ma'am.'

'Wha-hat d'you mean?' She tried to pull away from him. Her visitor didn't seem so nice now.

'Soviet labour camps aren't single sex. There isn't supposed to be fraternisation between male and female prisoners, but inevitably it occurs and the circumstances are such that friendships blossom and ripen very quickly.'

When she took in the implications of what he was saying, Jill went rigid with shock and outrage. 'You mean…? He's probably having it off with some Russian woman?'

Paul gave her another shake. 'For heaven's sake, woman, be realistic! If you, who are living in familiar surroundings with family and friends on call and plenty to eat, are suffering from insomnia and loneliness, what d'you think it's like for your husband? Surely you aren't such a narrow-minded little prude to begrudge him a bit of companionship and comfort?'

'Oh Christ! Why does life have to be so utterly hateful? I wish I were dead!'

He let her cry for a few moments before he went back to being "Mr Nice Guy".

She suddenly disengaged herself again, but this time she tugged his arm and pointed upstairs. 'It'll be warmer up there, there's a heater on. You can get undressed in the bathroom.'

Before removing her nightie, Jill picked up a photo of Steven from the dressing table and placed it face down.

What was sauce for the gander was going to be sauce for the goose.

*

The first time they were in too much of a hurry, but after that, it was highly satisfying for both of them.

They eventually fell asleep, but at some stage in the night Jill felt him get out of bed, followed by noises off downstairs and the sound of his car starting up. She sighed and shrugged...it had been great while it lasted... She turned over and was soon asleep again. It was still dark when she awoke the next time, to the novel and exquisite sensation of finding herself already penetrated and aroused.

It was mid-morning before either of them had any inclination to get up. Jill had woken an hour earlier to find Paul smiling down at her. Her eyes widened momentarily in alarm at the sight of a comparative stranger, then she relaxed and smiled at the recollection of the night's events.

'I thought you'd left me.'

'No, I only went out to move the car, local ladies have sharp eyes and long tongues. I also left a message at the college to say I'd be away till Monday morning. Anyhow, did my sleeping pill work?'

'It was magic. I don't know when I last slept so well.' Her face fell at the recollection of what separated her from her last sound night's sleep.

He leant over and kissed her. 'Now then, no morbid thoughts! *Das ist streng verboten!* For the next forty-eight hours, *je suis à votre disposition. Idyomtyeh dushka!'*

She giggled at the linguistic cocktail. 'What does *dushka* mean?'

'It's a Russian endearment: dear; duckie; love.'

'But I thought you were Czech?'

'Only half. Mother was born in Czechoslovakia of Russian parents. *Dyed* – Grandfather – and *Babushka* were White Russians. They were refugees from the Revolution and they helped to bring me up. Father died when I was nine, so Mother had to become the breadwinner. We always spoke Russian at home and in any case, at school it was a compulsory subject.'

She snuggled up to him and began to walk her fingers down his chest. 'Have you any brothers or sisters?'

'A younger sister, Margit – forward hussy!'

'Your sister?'

'No, you, for taking liberties with my person…'

Hunger finally got them out of bed. 'Any chance of a shower and something to eat?' said Paul.

Jill was lying on her back, smiling and waving her arms about.

'What on earth are you doing?'

'Conducting.'

'Conducting what?'

'The symphony at last night's concert.'

'Sibelius' second?'

'That's right.' She stretched languidly and yawned. 'It reminds me of what we've been doing.'

'How d'you mean?'

She gave him a self-satisfied grin. 'It occurred to me just now that the finale is the perfect musical description of multiple orgasm!'

Paul looked at her in amazement and burst out laughing.

She sat up. 'After I've washed, I'll go and make us brunch. Is there anything you fancy?'

'Any possibility of a mixed grill?'

'I can probably oblige.'

Three-quarters of an hour later Paul stabbed his last piece of sausage. 'How nice to sample someone else's cooking for a change.'

'You sound like a housewife on a spree.'

'Well, in a way I am. Either I have to cook for myself in my flat at the castle, or else take what's on the menu in the dining hall.' They were finishing their toast and marmalade when he said, 'You know, you really ought to see a doctor. This insomnia and depression, there must be something wrong.'

'I'm coming round to that idea myself,' Jill admitted. 'Rose, the butcher's assistant, said she'd been very depressed when her Liam was doing time and that she'd got pills which helped. She suggested that I got some, but didn't know the name.'

'Valium? Some of the students have to resort to it during exams.'

'No. I was prescribed it last year during Steve's trial and I didn't altogether care for it. It calmed me, but I think it also made me feel depressed and that's the last thing I want.' She sighed. 'Perhaps I'm a coward, but

I loathe changing doctors – and hairdressers – and I keep putting off registering with anyone here.'

'Dr Grant, the local man, looks after the college and seems to be well thought of. I haven't heard any complaints and he'll turn out in the middle of the night.'

'I wonder if he was the one who stitched up Gregor's leg? Alright then, I'll give him a try next week.' She started to clear the table. 'What d'you want to do now?'

'D'you play golf? I've got my clubs in the car.'

'I used to, but haven't for ages, in fact I sold mine. Steve's are somewhere in the garage, but they'd do as we're practically the same height.' She looked out of the window. 'The weather's not very promising, but there's a better forecast for tomorrow.'

'OK, golf tomorrow. We'll go up to St Andrews and make it a day's outing. And if you're agreeable, we'll go into Edinburgh today, I've never visited Holyrood House.'

The combination of companionship, fresh air and several kinds of exercise wrought a considerable change in Jill over the weekend and by Monday, she was feeling better than she had done for a very long time and said as much when Paul said goodbye early that morning. 'You've been absolutely marvellous, I feel a new person.'

'Good, but promise me that you'll go and see the doctor.'

To her relief, she took to Dr Grant and trusted his judgement when he said he wanted her to see a psychiatrist. Paul phoned her the name of a hairdresser recommended by a colleague's wife and a new, short style was a further boost to Jill's morale. The plumber and his mate were on the doorstep at eight o'clock on Tuesday morning to finish the central heating installation and when the boys arrived back from London that night, it was to a warm house.

The visit had been a success: they had been to the Planetarium and Madame Tussauds. 'Some of it was wet, but the Chamber of Horrors was brilliant,' was Gregor's verdict.

'We also went to the Tower and saw the torture chamber and the block where traitors had their heads chopped off,' added Alan. 'The girls didn't like it, they preferred the Jewel House.'

Later that evening, a pyjama clad Gregor came into the sitting room. 'It's nice being warm again and thanks for the holiday Mum, it was great, I'm glad I went.' He gave her a hug. 'I hope you managed alright without us.'

In Wednesday's post there was a small packet addressed to Jill in unfamiliar writing. It contained a cassette of Sibelius' second symphony and the unsigned note simply said, 'In future, we must try and synchronise the crescendos!'

But it wasn't so easy to arrange "in future".

The psychiatrist prescribed anti-depressants and suggested Jill have another adult to stay with her until she got over the initial side-effects. Her mother would have been the obvious person, but since her father's heart attack three years previously, his wife hated to be separated from him for even one night. When approached, Mickey was delighted to help out, but Jill knew the Lindsay family's housekeeper looked on Steven as the child she'd never had and any suspicion that Jill was even remotely interested in another man would have provoked an almighty row.

She warned Paul about this and when he visited the cottage during Miss Micklethwaite's stay, he was merely a neighbour calling to see if he could help with shopping or give the boys an outing, as Jill was feeling too doped to risk driving or to take any interest in him.

Once Jill had the house to herself during the day, it was possible for them to be alone together, but their meetings were dependent on Paul's duties at the college. Her successful application for a job at the newly-built village library put the final seal on her recovery, but with both of them now working, their tête-à-têtes were less frequent. However, they did manage the occasional weekend together when Jill was able to persuade the boys to stay with friends or relations. The last such interlude had been the previous Easter when Alan and Gregor had joined her sister's family for a winter sports holiday. At Paul's insistence, they'd done a tour of the Highlands as he wanted to see the Loch Ness Monster…

*

'You're looking very solemn.' Steven finished his coffee, picked up the mugs and rinsed them.

Jill gave herself a little shake as she came back to the present. 'I was mulling over the last five years.' She smiled at him. 'But that's past history now.' She stood up. 'D'you want to walk along to the Co-op with me? I was going to prepare vegetables for tonight, but I haven't yet got used to catering for four again.'

CHAPTER 9

Over at Bathgate, Alan had the shakes.

The band members all arrived by midday and having played separately for a while by their cars, came together and walked over to the tuning park at the other side of the football ground where the Highland Games were being held. They staked their claim to a vacant space amidst the dozens of bands already there and made their final preparations for the competition.

At first, Alan felt fine. Duncan set their chanters against his own and gave the drones a preliminary tuning. They had played through a couple of march selections when he announced, 'OK, we'll have a go at the competition set.' They were four bars into the march before Alan realised he was supposed to be playing the march, strathspey and reel and not the medley they'd played at Scotstoun. Willie gave him a dirty look.

When they finished the set, Duncan said, 'Right, same again and we'll now have everyone playing the correct tunes,' which did nothing to boost Alan's confidence. He felt himself going red and mentally kicked himself. He'd been with the band long enough to have learnt they didn't play medleys at a Grade Three Championship...

The next couple of times through the set, all went well, so Duncan lined them up into their marching positions, said that they would practice the introduction and marching into a circle and told them where to stand. As Alan found it easiest to listen to the player on his immediate right, he hoped he'd have one of the more experienced pipers as neighbour, but no such luck. He was placed with a side drummer on his right – not even Sheila – and to his left was Ken Fyfe, a young miner from Brankstone, who had had little more competing experience than himself.

Duncan gave the commands for them to start, but after eight bars, turned round and shooed them back. 'That was bloody awful! If you're going to play like that afore the judges, we might as well go home now. The drones came in all over the place.'

As one of the offenders, Alan's confidence dropped another notch. However, at the second attempt, it was the drummers who incurred Duncan's displeasure. 'Pipers, that was much better. Drummers, could we please have the introductory rolls sounding more like tearing a sheet of taffeta and a bit less like emptying a sack o' tatties down a flight o' stairs.' The drummers shuffled their feet and muttered under their breath.

As they lined up yet again, Ken whispered to Alan, 'Someone's got out o' bed the wrong side this morning.'

‘Perhaps he’s planted a customer in the wrong hole again.’

‘Quiet there at the back!’ yelled Duncan. ‘This is no’ an old wives’ tea party!’

At the third attempt, the band made a satisfactory start and marched into the circle, but halfway through the strathspey, Alan’s stomach began to churn when he was hit by the realisation of what they were about to do. He could hear the tone of his drones wavering as his blowing became increasingly unsteady and a few bars into the reel, his mind went blank. By the time Duncan started to go round to give the drones their final tuning, he couldn’t stop shaking. He also wanted to relieve himself, but the nearest Portaloo was some distance away. There were some bushes between the tuning park and the pitch, but he would have been too embarrassed to lift his kilt against them with so many people around, even if other bandsmen didn’t suffer from such inhibitions.

Alan gazed around, stamped his feet to try and dispel the shivery feeling and caught Sheila’s eye. She rubbed her stomach. He grimaced at her and got a sickly grin back. He looked at his companions, considering the different styles of playing: chipmunk, where the cheeks were puffed out; bullfrog, where the neck swelled; or rabbit, where the upper lip somehow lengthened and compressed. Their drones were held at an angle anything from the vertical, down to nearly forty-five degrees and there were folk who rested the bass drone against the side of their head, which looked most uncomfortable.

During the last run-through, he was aware that his pipes weren't the only ones making the wrong noises and realised Duncan was having trouble with Bob's bass drone. Eventually the pipe major said, 'Sorry lad, it's double toning and I haven't time to sort it, you'll have to stand down,' and gave Bob a sympathetic slap on the shoulder.

As Duncan came behind him to tune his drones, Alan half-hoped he too would be told to stand down. But after his father's remarks about competing in a British Championship, he didn't want to disappoint him.

His drones were tuned without comment and just as Duncan finished, the secretary's rotund figure came trotting towards them. 'Come on, lads' puffed Ian, waving his programme. 'Time you were off. The lot in front of us is getting ready to march over to the starting point.'

The bandsmen moved off in a bunch, with Duncan giving his drones a final tuning on the hoof. They formed up at the bottom of the slope at the end of the tuning park and proceeded round to the starting point, playing the march The Brankstone Boys, written by a late resident of that ilk.

Alan found he no longer had the shakes and was feeling perfectly calm. I wish to heavens Duncan would stop blethering to one of the judges, he thought, so we can get on with it… And why are judges at piping competitions always craggy, elderly chaps in hairy tweed jackets and faded kilts? Perhaps he and Duncan would be chatting like that one day: pipe major and judge.

Suddenly, Duncan was giving the commands.

'Band–' Pay attention.

'Get ready.' Pipes up and a bit of air into the bag.

'Ready.' Drumsticks poised.

'By the right–' Right hand snaps smartly off the bag to your side.

'Quick march!' Left foot forward and we're off. A couple of good puffs and a gentle pat on the bag, but no squeals from the drones. Left foot down for the third time and drones in. Right foot. Left foot again: chanters play the introductory E – I think we all came in together – and start the march. Know your place in the circle and make it a neat, tight one. Keep marking time until the end of the first measure of the march. After that, only the pipe major beats time.

Alan remembered one practice when a foot had suddenly pressed down on his own and he had turned round to find Ian grinning at him, yet when he'd first taken up piping, he'd found it impossible to play and beat time simultaneously. No, don't think about that… concentrate on the job in hand. Watch the pipe major's fingers, listen to the others, listen to the bass drum and don't rush the music. Take that bit at the end of the march nice and easily. Oops! Someone boobed there! Was it me? Hope the judges didn't notice. Don't be put off by it. Concentrate…

Into the strathspey now. Think of a little girl hopping, Willie once said, and make the music lift her higher. Coming up to that tricky run of triplets. Relax your fingers. You're not going to muff it… And you didn't! But don't get too confident. Concentrate…

Nice smooth break from the strathspey into the reel. Don't look at that bit of paper blowing across the circle, look at Duncan's fingers. Can't see the judges. Is one standing behind me? Forget him, concentrate... Getting near the end now, don't rush it. Duncan's stepped in a couple of paces to signal to Ron. Boom-boom from the bass drum means finish at the end of this measure. Last two bars coming up. Stop blowing, squeeze bag to expel the air, but keep the drones steady. Drones cut off cleanly and – Finish! Right hand down smartly. Watch Duncan for cue to put pipes down. March off in time to Jimmy on the side drum. Keep in ranks till dismissed. Band: fall out.

And it was all over: everyone breathing sighs of relief; flexing their fingers; shaking their arms; stamping their feet – anything to dispel the recent tension.

'That wasnae too bad.'

'How d'ye think we did?'

'Thae new reeds wuz much better.'

'D'ye think we're in wi' a chance?'

'Whaur's the beer tent?'

As Alan was putting away his pipes in the car boot, Duncan came up to him. 'How're ye feeling, lad?'

'Great, now that it's all over, but I was awful nervous beforehand, couldn't stop shaking.'

'Well, it doesnae really improve as ye get older, but ye did no' bad at all.'

'I thought I made a mistake at the end of the march.'

'Naw, that was Joan. She was too busy looking at Ron when she should have been watching my fingers. I'm away for some lunch now.'

'What time d'you want us to assemble for the march-past and where?'

Duncan got out his programme. 'The last bands in grades one and two are due to play at about four-fifteen, so we'll say about then, at the tuning park. Same spot as before.'

He had gone a few steps when Alan called after him. 'Duncan, Mum got me the new bag. Can you tie it on some time?'

'Aye, bring it and your pipes along on Monday and we'll sort it then.'

'Thanks a lot, see you later.'

*

Steven reluctantly agreed to accompany Jill to the jumble sale that afternoon. He acknowledged the necessity of buying something to wear while his physique was recovering from years of privation and also of not spending too much on it. The day had turned out to be very warm and Jill put on a cotton dress for the first time that year. Steven was wearing one of Alan's tee-shirts and a pair of Gregor's jeans which were too long and by his way of thinking, far too tight, though he was assured that they weren't a bad fit.

On arriving at the school, Jill plunged into the scrum round the second-hand clothes stall. A few minutes later she backed out, slightly dishevelled, with several garments. 'I forgot to measure you before we left, so try these shirts on.'

'What! Here?'

'Yes, just put them on over your tee-shirt to see if they fit round the collar.'

One fitted very well and was discarded as not having enough room for expansion, but another was pronounced to be satisfactory. A plain blue one had a collar which Steven remembered as being the "in" thing five years ago, but was evidently now considered to be well out of fashion. A checked shirt which he didn't like was not allowed to be returned to the stall: it would do for gardening.

'If you're going to be so choosy,' said Jill, 'You'd better come and have a look for yourself,' and she pulled him into the fray.

He was debating between two more shirts when a voice said, 'Why don't you take them both, Dr Lindsay, they're only twenty pence each.' The speaker was one of the helpers at the stall, a woman in her mid forties who had gone prematurely and prettily grey. She wore thick-lensed glasses and had a face which seemed to smile, even when in repose. He had never seen her before.

'I'm Kathy Grant.' She took some money from a customer and went on, 'You must be awfully glad to be home again.'

Jill elbowed her way to Steven's side. 'I was about to introduce you, but Kathy's done it for me.' She made a sudden grab at a garment and held it up against Steven. 'How about that?'

"That" was a green pullover.

He shook his head, 'Green suited me before I went grey, but I think blue would be more flattering now.'

Kathy rummaged in the pile in front of her. 'What chest size are you?'

'I used to be forty-two, but I think I'm about thirty-eight at the moment.'

As they searched for something suitable, Jill said, 'It was Kathy who really launched me into village society and she even baby-sat for me, knowing that I wouldn't be able to reciprocate.'

Kathy took some more money, then handed Steven a pullover. 'That any good?' She went on, 'Not reciprocate? Who used to answer the phone for me when I wanted to go out for a couple of hours when Angus was on call? You'll have it? Thanks.' She turned to another customer and Jill and Steven backed out of the crowd.

'They're such a nice couple.' Jill steered Steven in the direction of a clothes rail filled with jackets, trousers and suits. 'We must have them along for a meal sometime.' She picked up a plastic bag from a pile under the rail. 'Put that lot in here. Oh, hello, I wouldn't have thought jumble sales would be your scene.' This last remark was directed at Paul, who had just come in. 'And how come you're not at Bathgate with the band?'

'I had some tutoring to do this morning in view of looming A-levels and as for sales, I have a weakness for second-hand book stalls.'

'Books are in room two,' said a passer-by who had overheard his remark.

Jill wandered down the rail, inspecting the garments. 'We're trying to get Steve temporarily kitted out until he grows into his own clothes again.'

Steven gave Paul a wry grin. 'What she means is that I was dragged along so she would have an excuse for a good rummage.'

Jill pointed. 'Look, your suit's still here. Are you sure you don't want it back?' She explained to Paul how the suit came to be in the sale, then took a jacket off the rail. 'Try this. The size is right and the colour's inoffensive.' A few moments later she came back with a couple of pairs of trousers. 'That looks OK. How about these?'

'I'm not taking them without trying them on.'

'Well go into the boys' loo, it's opposite the main door. I'll wait here with the jacket.'

'I'm off to the books,' said Paul. 'Perhaps I'll see you later.'

While Steven was trying on the trousers, Jill looked at the other goods on offer. She bought a fruit tart from "home baking", bypassed "unwanted treasures" and started to fight her way round again to Kathy's stall. As she glanced across the hall to see if Steven was back, she suddenly had a clear view of the clothes rail. Paul hadn't gone into the other room, he was looking at a jacket very carefully, going through the pockets and it looked uncommonly like Steven's cast-off. How odd! Her attention was suddenly caught by a garment in her favourite shade of blue, but it turned out to be a child's dress.

Steven tapped her on the shoulder a few minutes later. 'These'll do. Can't we go now? I've had enough.'

'Then go and wait at the entrance, I haven't finished.' She turned back to the stall.

Steven paid for his clothes: two pounds for the jacket and trousers. Perhaps it was worth the scrum after all. He fought his way out of the hall and subsided onto a bench near the main door in exhaustion. Crowds were a trial after being cut off from the world for so long. A few minutes later Paul flopped down beside him. 'Phew! I'd sooner take on the Red Army than a battalion of British housewives in search of a bargain.'

'Did you get any books?'

'A few.'

Steven turned his head sideways to read the titles and gave a hoot of laughter. 'That's a child's book.' He pulled a copy of *Wee McGreegor* out of Paul's hand. 'Why d'you buy that?'

Paul reclaimed it with a sheepish expression. 'Curiosity. You see, it's my nickname at school. I bought a kilt recently and as my patronymic is Grigorovich, I reckoned that I was entitled to wear the McGregor tartan, after all, the names mean the same thing.'

'And I suppose you're "wee" because of your size?'

Paul nodded.

The crowd in the hall suddenly ejected Jill, who joined them on the bench. 'Ouf! My skin's leaking, as the boys would say. If you've finished, let's get out of here.'

As he got up to go, Paul gave a groan. 'Oh Gawd! Here comes Brunhilda!'

Steven turned round and saw advancing towards them a handsome blonde in her mid forties. She was generously proportioned, had neat ankles and was carrying a book of raffle tickets and a plastic box.

‘Oh Jill, deah, there you are. Now do tell me, is it really true about your hubby?’

Jill indicated Steven: ‘This is my husband,’ placing a strong emphasis on the last word. ‘Steve, this is Judith Waterfield, an invaluable member of the PTA committee.’

‘And of every other committee in the neighbourhood,’ muttered Paul, not sufficiently *sotto voce* for the remark to escape the newcomer.

‘Paul deah, wouldn’t you like to buy some tickets. There’s evah such nice prizes.’

Paul rolled his eyes and put his hand into his pocket. In a stage aside he said to Steven, ‘Judith doesn’t approve of me, she reckons I lead Eric astray at the nineteenth hole. What are your nice prizes, deah?’

Judith gave him a smile which did not extend to her eyes. ‘Rennies have donated a bottle of whisky, there’s a dinner for two at The Stag’s Head and Peggy Findlay’s given a voucher for five gallons of petrol. And there’s others as well.’

‘I’ll settle for any of those.’ He put a coin in the box. ‘I’ll take a quid’s worth.’

Steven felt obliged to contribute.

‘That’s very generous of you both.’

As Judith was writing their names on the tickets, Jill nudged Steven. ‘Look there goes your suit, someone’s got a bargain.’ She explained to Judith about the suit, ‘And if I’d known that he was going to discard it, I wouldn’t have bothered to take it to the cleaners while he was in hospital.’

The three of them started to move off, but Judith said, 'Oh Jill deah, just before you go...'

Paul jerked his head at Steven. 'Let's wait outside, too much hot air in here.' Once through the doors, he went on, 'When Judith gets going, you can write off the next ten minutes.'

They strolled over to the wall bordering the playground and sat down. Steven looked slowly round him, shaking his head. 'I still can't get over the feeling that I'm dreaming. A week ago I was labouring *In the Steppes of Central Asia*, so to speak, and now I'm at a jumble sale in a Scottish village. It's surreal.'

Paul got out his pipe and started to fill it from a pouch. 'How are you settling down? It took me a while to adjust to being free again after even only a few months and I went through a period of having nightmares.'

Steven nodded. 'The psychiatrist at the hospital warned me about that. He called it the "concentration camp syndrome" or some such fancy name, but so far, so good. I'm revelling in my freedom and with no side-effects.'

'Freedom's like good health. When you have it, you take it for granted and when it's taken away from you, you realise just how precious it is.' He tamped down the tobacco. 'Why were you released?'

'Haven't a clue. I was hauled out of the camp in Kazakhstan with no warning, flown to Moscow on a military plane, tidied up, given back my clothes and passport, plus some cash, then put on the next flight home. Someone must have decided that I was a hot property, thank heavens.'

Paul struck a match and held it to his pipe. 'No strings attached?' he said, between sucks. 'You weren't to act as a courier? Nobody asked you to carry something out of the country?'

Steven stared at him in amazement. 'Good heavens, no! Well, you saw me unpack and nobody touched my luggage at any of the airports, at least not to my knowledge. It wasn't locked though, so I suppose it could have been tampered with.'

'Sorry, I didn't mean to be impertinent, but the Soviets don't usually do things for no apparent reason. Time will probably tell.' He tilted his head back, half shut his eyes and extinguished the match with a long exhalation.

The gesture struck a remote chord with Steven. Somewhere, he had seen somebody blow out a match like that. 'There's no need to apologise, the two chaps who quizzed me on my experiences asked the same thing, but I assured them that I hadn't any secret messages to hand over to glamorous spies and I hadn't been brain-washed into working for the other side. I was simply treated as a common criminal.' He looked towards the school entrance. 'That woman certainly knows how to blether. What was her name?'

'Judith Waterfield.'

Steven thought for a bit and then remarked, 'Boggy meadow.'

There was a few seconds puzzled silence, then a bellow of laughter. 'Oh man, I like that! Brunhilda Boggy

Meadow! That's bloody marvellous!' Paul gave Steven a slap on the shoulder which nearly unseated him. He was still chortling when they were joined by Jill.

'Sorry I took so long. What's the joke?' When told, she laughed even more than Paul did. 'Poor Judith,' she said when she calmed down, 'we shouldn't make fun of her. If there weren't people like that in a community, nothing would ever get done.'

'I did her an injustice,' Paul said as he stood up. 'She isn't on the pipe band committee, thank heavens.'

They set off down Castle Lane together and Jill linked arms with both men, but after a few steps, Paul disengaged himself. Neither gesture escaped Steven and his dislike of the other flared up again.

The three of them paused to look at the small cascade on the hillside below the castle. Jill went across the road and watched the Tullum Water as it emerged to flow down Burnside. Such a lot of water had passed under the bridge since she and Steven had last stood in this spot together. She turned round and leant against the parapet, the sun warm on her back. She looked dispassionately at the two men opposite: the one, big and blond; the other, emaciated and grey. Comparisons are odious, she told herself. She turned back to stare at the water, humming under her breath. When she identified the tune, she stopped, appalled at herself. It was MacHeath's couplet from *The Beggar's Opera*: "How happy could I be with either, Were t'other dear charmer away." She hoped the sound of running water had prevented the others from hearing anything.

Steven crossed the road to stand beside her. 'You're looking very serious.'

'I was thinking about what a lot of water had literally flowed under this bridge since we last stood on it together.' In an effort to lighten her mood, she went on, 'D'you see the wee footbridge opposite the pub? It was awash at the end of one winter when we'd had a lot of snow. The inhabitants of that row of cottages didn't take kindly to a longer hike for their pint.'

'Would you like a drink?'

'I wouldn't mind some well-chilled lager, but the pub'll be shut by now.'

'Can you get it anywhere else?'

'Sure, the Co-op's got a licence.'

Steven felt in his pocket and brought out some coins. 'Will that be enough? I'm so out of touch with prices.'

'No.'

'Blast Mrs Boggy Meadow and her raffle tickets!'

Jill laughed. 'It's alright, I didn't quite empty my purse at the sale, we've enough between us.'

He took their carrier bags on one arm and put the other round her waist, '*Idyomtyeh, dushka*,' he said as they set off down Burnside.

She'd heard the phrase before. 'What's that mean? Is it Russian?'

'Yes, I suppose you could translate it as "Let's go, love", or something like that.'

*

Paul, forgotten, watched them saunter off like a pair of teenagers. His outward appearance would have earned him a contract from any advertising agency with a tobacco manufacturer on its books, but inwardly he was anything but serene and contented. Before setting off up the road to the castle, he identified his uppermost emotions as made up of fairly equal parts of jealousy and a sense of loss.

*

Jill put down the Sunday colour supplement with a sigh. 'I do so resent having to reach for my glasses after having read only half a page. Anybody seen them?'

'Top of your desk,' said Alan through a mouthful of toast, while reaching for a bit of the paper to read.

'Thanks.' When she came back into the kitchen she said, 'Oh, I forgot to ask, how did you get on yesterday?'

'No' bad. We were fourth on a piping preference.'

'What does that mean?' said Steven.

'Our overall marks for piping and drumming were the same as another band, but our pipers did better than theirs. Why, I don't know, Joan made an obvious blooper, the judges must have been deaf.'

'And I'll bet the pipers crowed over the drummers,' remarked Gregor. 'Dad, would you like me to hold the paper a bit farther away for you?'

'Your mother may complain about having to wear glasses, but at least she does have some.'

'Try them, if you want,' offered Jill.

'I've already done so, thanks and they make matters worse.'

He got up, cleared the table and was half way through washing the dishes when Alan gave an exclamation.

'Here, get a load of this! I think Uncle Tony may have had something to do with Dad's release. Look!'

The family crowded round him as he pointed to an article on the front page of the business section. The caption to the accompanying photo said, "Anthony Roper, managing director of Celtic Biotechnics (Scotland) Ltd., clinches a multi-million pound deal with Moscow." Steven started to read it and cursed when the print went out of focus. 'Hell! I can't see what it says. One of you read it out, please.'

The gist of the article was that his brother-in-law's company was providing the know-how and machinery to set up a plant for the conversion of farmyard slurry into vegetable protein suitable for animal consumption, which was urgently needed in view of the succession of disastrous harvests in the Soviet Union.

Steven looked at the others in bewilderment. 'I don't get this, I thought Tony worked in a lab? And what's biotechnics?'

They all started to talk at once, but Jill gestured for the boys to be quiet. 'Biotechnology is one of the up-and-coming sciences. It's to do with getting bacteria – bugs and the like – to work industrial processes. I believe quite a lot of sugar is now made that way. It's Tony's speciality and his team produced this bug. I don't know if it's a mutation or if it was genetically engineered, but somehow it gobbles up what comes out of the back end of a cow and makes part of it fit to go in at the front end again. The product isn't yet suitable for human consumption, but they're working on that.'

'But what's this about Tony being managing director?'

'Once they developed the bug, the parent company in Wales opened up a new plant in Ayrshire to get the process going. It was some government-sponsored thing in a disused steelworks and Tony was put in charge of it. He seems to have developed as much flair for admin as he has for lab work, though he does rather less of the latter nowadays.'

Gregor leant forward, eyes wide. 'I wonder if Uncle Tony refused to deal with the Russians while they had Dad in prison?'

'Phone him and find out,' suggested Alan.

'Shall I?' said Gregor.

'No, if anyone phones, I'd better,' said Jill.

'Well, go on then, Mum,' they said in unison.

She looked at Steven, who gave a non-committal shrug. 'Perhaps it might be as well to enquire.'

She came back a few minutes later. 'We guessed right. Tony'd known that there was a possibility of using the negotiations to free you, but didn't dare say a word about it until it was a *fait accompli*. Even Helen was in the dark until you'd returned safely. He meant to phone earlier.' She pulled a face. 'But the media got in the way.'

Steven didn't know what to think. It was marvellous to be home, but he felt that for the rest of his life he would be beholden to his brother-in-law…and even more so after his financial assistance to the family.

Some of this must have shown on his face as Jill gave him a hug. 'Cheer up. I know this puts us in Tony's debt for evermore, but personally, I'm only too thankful to have you back, you might not have survived the full stretch.' In order to distract him, she went on, 'Is Russian agriculture in as much of a mess as we're led to believe?'

'Well, I only saw a very small part of it in, but that was pretty inefficient and corrupt. There was a frightful stushie a couple of years ago because one of the overseers was nicking part of our bread ration and selling it to the locals for cattle feed.'

'I should bloody well think so!' said Gregor. 'Your need was a damn sight greater than any old cow's.'

Steven gave a wry laugh. 'They weren't worried about us. The row was because the price of bread is subsidised by the government and cattle feed isn't. The chap got a three year prison sentence, and of course, people like Fyodor Alexandr'ich didn't help the system either.'

'Who was he?'

'A fellow jail-bird. He was in for large scale fraud. A lot of grain went in the wrong direction for a very long time before they caught up with him. He reckoned that he was lucky to get hard labour instead of the firing squad, though in retrospect, he probably wished it'd been the latter.'

'What happened to him?'

'He was eventually sent to work on the Siberian gas pipe line and their labourers rarely last more than eighteen months.'

'How awful,' said Jill. 'Was he a friend of yours?'

Steven thought for a few moments. 'It's difficult to say. I suppose that on the surface we were pals, but I never really liked the man.'

He remembered the big, blond, hearty Ukrainian who had befriended him when he arrived at the Butyrka jail in Moscow, in transit from Leningrad… It was a cross between a new boy being taken up by the captain of the first Rugby fifteen and living with a potentially dangerous animal, but he learnt to read the storm warnings. Fyodor soon found out that Scots object to being called English. Get called *Schatlandyets* and it was plain sailing, but *Anglichanin* meant take shelter… At times he resented being regarded as an exotic pet, but it did have its advantages. Wherever Fyodor went, he was cock o' the walk, even in jail and any perks usually went in his direction, but he did give his pals a share in the goodies… If his benefactor hadn't wangled those felt boots on arrival in Siberia, he'd certainly have lost some toes to frost-bite. And the padded jacked was another life-saver…

Steven shivered as he thankfully came back to the present. 'No, I'm not going to complain about Tony bailing me out of that lot. I just wish all the other poor devils could be released as well. Paul was right. You don't know how precious freedom is until it's taken away from you.'

CHAPTER 10

In a room overlooking Dzerzhinsky Square, two men were talking. The younger was standing in front of the other's desk, a man in his late thirties, of medium build and who wouldn't have looked out of place in many European capitals. The older man indicated a paper. 'I have just received a report from Nesterenko and he says that if "Augustin" did manage to plant a message on Lindsay at the airport, then to the best of his knowledge, it has since been lost or destroyed and I believe him. After all, he has no means of knowing the traitor is dead and that his reaction to the information was intended to show us where his loyalties really lie.' He shrugged. 'The tethered goat can stay in place a bit longer, we can always find another use for it. So, Oleg Sergeyevich, it would appear that your "Operation Birdkill" has only been partially successful.'

Oleg Sergeyevich Koshachin took a deep breath and wished his boss wasn't addicted to cheap cigarettes. 'I put it in place myself, comrade.' He swallowed hard. 'I take full responsibility–'

The other held up his hand and smiled. 'There is no need to start blaming yourself. That part of the operation was set up at extremely short notice and with very little chance of working. The other part, however, has been most successful. I believe that it was you yourself who brought to our attention the connection between Dr Lindsay and Celtic Biotechnics when he booked that cruise to Leningrad?'

'Yes, comrade.'

'The President has asked me to tell you that he is delighted that "Operation, er, Cowdung" has been concluded so satisfactorily.'

Koshachin smiled to himself. The operation had been named rather more earthily, but the boss was a bit of a prude.

'Regarding the other matter.' The speaker paused and smiled again at the man in front of him. 'I have decided that it needs further consideration. Our Ambassador to the Court of Saint James's – such a decadent expression – will shortly be acquiring a new chauffeur so remember to drive on the correct side of the road. You must never attract the attention of the British authorities.'

CHAPTER 11

Jill straightened up and rubbed her back. Weeding was a chore and she could never make up her mind if it was easier to hoe and then bend down and pick up the rubbish, or to crawl along the rows of vegetables with a hand fork. Either method left her aching and the new bed didn't help matters, though Steven was happy with it. She must remember to phone Duncan about making a headboard with integral bedside tables, like they'd had in Glasgow. She looked at her watch. Time for another row before she got ready for the late shift at the library.

A few minutes later there was a call of, 'Hello, anyone at home?'

She bobbed up like a startled rabbit from between the broad beans to see Paul standing on the terrace. She hadn't encountered him since the day of the sale and suspected he'd deliberately been avoiding the household.

'Oh, there you are. I was beginning to think you were all out. I came to see if anyone wanted a round of golf on Friday evening.'

‘I’m working then, but Steve might. He should be home soon. D’you want to wait and ask him?’ Jill suddenly felt awkward at the prospect of being alone with Paul and regretted her invitation.

He sat down on Gregor’s seat. ‘OK then.’ He looked round the garden. ‘Everything seems to be flourishing. Does McGinty still help you?’

‘He hasn’t been along recently, but I haven’t given him the heave-ho. Steve just about had a hairy fit when I told him that I’d been employing an alcoholic, ex-jail-bird as a part-time gardener! I haven’t yet convinced him that when the man’s sober, he’s a good worker.’

Paul laughed. ‘Well, you took a bit of convincing too.’

‘D’you blame me? After all, the first time I saw him was when he was weaving an unsteady course down Burnside on a Saturday morning, but everyone I asked about getting someone to knock the garden into shape said, “Oh, get McGinty, he’s a wee bitty erratic and it’s best you give Rose the money, but he’ll do a good job”.’ She got up stiffly. ‘The hedge’ll soon need to be cut, I must ask Rose when I next see her. The doctors said that Steve wasn’t to do any heavy work because of his back, and in any case, he’s started on his book now. Not that he was ever much of a gardening enthusiast.’ She dumped the weeds on the compost heap and went into the garage with her tools. As she came back round the side of the house she called out, ‘Sorry I can’t stop to blether, but I’ve got to go and get ready for work.’ She looked at her watch. ‘Perhaps Steve’s missed the bus,’ and with that, she went inside, hoping their visitor would go away.

Paul stayed where he was and idly began to make a daisy chain. He was jerked out of a daydream about his childhood by a mocking voice. 'I'd have thought you were a bit old for that.' He did a double take at the speaker before realising it was Steven, who sat down beside him and bared his teeth. 'D'ye no' recognise me wi' ma wallies, glasses and a bit more hair?'

Paul looked blank.

'That's obviously one bit of Glaswegian you haven't come across. "Wally" is slang for china, hence "wallies" for false teeth and "wally dugs" – those awful china dogs which used to adorn Victorian mantelpieces.'

Paul looked slightly less blank. 'I've heard people talking about being "peely-wally". Is that the same word?'

'Yes, if you're peely-wally, you're the colour of china with the glaze peeling off, in other words, off colour.'

'Oh, I see.' Paul swung the daisy chain around his finger and gave Steven a slightly shamefaced look. 'This reminds me of my sister. I used to make them for her. She always said that the daisy was her flower as her name's Margit.'

'D'you ever see anything of her?'

Paul shook his head. 'I get the very occasional letter, but I haven't seen her since I was arrested.'

'Ever thought of getting her to join you?'

'Often. There's nothing that would make me happier, but it's hopeless. She'd never be allowed a permit and in any case she's now got a husband and two children. I've got three relatives whom I've never seen and am never likely to.' He suddenly crushed the daisy chain and threw it in the direction of the compost heap. It landed short. He got up and kicked it across to join the other rubbish. After staring at it for a few seconds, he said, 'I came to ask if you'd like a round of golf on Friday evening. I know you'll be out of practice, but my handicap's the proverbial bag of clubs.'

Jill came out in time to hear the last bit. 'Do go Steve, you know how much you used to enjoy it and I'm working that evening. I swapped with Kathy as Angus has the weekend off.'

'OK then. Is it going to be just the two of us, or will there be more?'

'It depends. Sometimes I meet up with some chaps from Rosyth, including Eric Waterfield, but Judith's brow-beaten him into doing something else on Friday.'

Jill chuckled. 'Perhaps now Steve's home, Eric'll feel a bit less uncomfortable in my presence.' She explained about the abortive interview at the dockyard. 'I can laugh about it now, but it was no joke at the time. Eric's in charge of civilian personnel there and I'm sure he regarded me as a latter day Mata Hari, all set to worm out naval secrets in exchange for my husband's freedom. But I came to say there's a pot of tea brewed if you want some.'

The three of them adjourned to the kitchen where Gregor was devouring a jam sandwich. Paul ruffled his hair. 'How's school these days?'

'Putrid as ever, but we finish soon.'

As he sat down, Paul glanced at Steven and was jolted to see a flash of intense dislike cross his face. The next time he looked, the polite host was back in place. The camps quickly taught you to conceal your emotions, but there was no disguising Steven's resentment at another man's intimacy with his family.

Oblivious to the undercurrents, Jill poured their tea, gestured at Steven and said to Paul, 'Don't you think he's looking heaps better already?'

'I do indeed. I hardly recognised him when he came into the garden, probably due to his glasses. He's still too thin, but he's lost that awful, emaciated look.'

'It's bliss being able to see and chew properly,' said Steven, 'and eat a normal helping. 'I thoroughly enjoyed our raffle prize dinner at The Coo's Heid.'

'Me too,' said Jill, 'but he's still getting cravings for things, particularly chocolate.'

'Is that why I saw you walking up Burnside when I went past on the school bus?' said Gregor. 'You might have got some for us.'

'Bad for spots,' was the reply.

'And you took your time in getting home,' continued his son.

'I got in tow with some twittery old bird at the post office. I did my good deed for the day and carried her bag for part of the way. A nice little old lady she was, most interested in me and knew all about the family – why are you all looking at me like that?'

Jill narrowed her eyes. 'Any idea what she was called?'

'One of the ladies at the post office, the one who's well-corseted and cantilevered and whose jet-black hair doesn't quite match her complexion, called her Aunt Chrissie.'

This was greeted with groans and hoots of derision.

Paul clutched his head in mock dismay. 'Your "nice little old lady", your "twittery old bird" has a facility for gathering information that makes the CIA and the KGB look like a lot of fourth division amateurs.

'Huh!' grunted Gregor. 'That's you labelled, pigeon-holed and cross-referenced.'

'You have just met our neighbourhood busybody,' added Jill. 'Namely Mrs Oliphant, alias Old Elephant Ears.'

'Well, how was I to know?' retorted Steven. 'She looked harmless enough with her pink cheeks, blue eyes and rows of neat white curls. Everyone's ideal Grandma.'

There were further derisive comments.

'I'm almost certain she bullied her nephew, Johnny the postie, into having a nosy round when we moved in,' continued Jill. 'Before we arrived, the odd letter was simply pushed through the flap, but a couple of days after we got here, I found him on the upstairs landing. His explanation was that the place was in such a mess that he felt it was safer to hand over the letters personally, so that they wouldn't get lost.' She snorted. 'A likely story! Aunt Chrissie put him up to it to satisfy her curiosity.'

'The old girl's about as shy as a docklands tart,' commented Paul. He indicated his pullover. 'The first time I appeared in this round the village, she toddled up to me and asked what it was, was it my car registration number?'

Steven had been wondering what the letters and numbers knitted into the pullover signified. 'And is it?'

‘No, it’s my radio ham call sign. One of my girl friends made it for me.’

‘Was that the one in Portsmouth or the one in Dunoon?’ asked Jill.

He shrugged. ‘Can’t remember. Easy come, easy go. Safety in numbers.’ As soon as the words were out of his mouth, Paul regretted them.

Jill got up abruptly. ‘Time I was off to work. Don’t guzzle all the biscuits.’

Paul cursed himself when the front door slammed behind her: that was two black marks against him from people he’d no wish to hurt.

Gregor was saying to Steven, ‘Paul’s got the most super transceiver, Alan’s pal Andy loves to have a go on it. He’s a ham as well, though not a full one, he’s still to pass the Post Office Morse test and isn’t allowed to transmit abroad, but you can get anywhere in the world on Paul’s machine.’

‘Talking of Handy Andy,’ said Paul, ‘reminds me that my razor’s gone temperamental. Tell him if he mends it, he can come and play with my toy for the evening.’ He grinned at Gregor. ‘That ought to get me prompt attention once he’s back.’

As he poured them a second cup, Steven said to Paul, ‘You seem to have a liking for seaside places, or at least waterside ones.’

Paul pondered. ‘I suppose so. I find the sea fascinating and all the more so as I never saw it until I was in my twenties.’

Gregor looked at him as though he had suddenly sprouted two heads and six legs. 'You what? But that's crazy…never to have seen the sea until–'

'Until I had one foot in the grave? Young man, you forget I come from a landlocked country whose inhabitants are given no incentive to travel. There are millions of people in the world who pass their whole lifespan without ever seeing the sea.'

The two men looked at Gregor in amusement as he sat there, shaking his head.

'I remember trying to describe the sea to someone at Tabaga and got nowhere fast,' Steven said. 'He was a native-born Siberian and it wasn't just my halting Russian which was the stumbling block.'

Paul looked at him. 'Tabaga?' He pulled down the corners of his mouth. 'You're lucky to be home.'

'And how!' Steven grimaced and shivered. 'Snow, barbed wire and vicious guard dogs… At one point I got pneumonia and reckoned I'd had it.' Open-mouthed, Gregor stared at his father, who patted his arm and flicked a sharp glance at Paul as he did so. 'But they gave me what was red carpet treatment for a prisoner – hospital and antibiotics – and moved me to Kazakhstan, north of the Caspian Sea, for the rest of my stretch… And of course, now I know why they wanted to keep me alive. It was like a rest camp after what had gone before, though in retrospect it was still slave labour… But it's already beginning to feel like a bad dream, thank heavens.'

Paul got up. 'I know what you mean and I only had a few months of it. Anyhow, I'll see you on Friday evening. Will five-thirty be too early?'

'Which course are we playing?'

'Dunfermline.'

'In that case, could you pick me up from the Carnegie Library? I've taken to doing my writing there. I've no study here and it also makes me feel as though I were going out to a job, which is no bad thing psychologically. But I seem to be spending a fortune on bus fares.' He gave a wry smile. 'I can thank the Russians for one thing. When I get writer's cramp, I can swap hands.'

'Your working arrangements sound to be a good idea. I'll see you in Dunfermline then. Shall I collect your clubs on the way past? You won't want to take them to the library.'

'Would you? That'd be a help.'

'Nae sweat, as the locals say and thanks for the tea. Don't get up, I'll see myself out. 'Bye.'

Driving back to the castle, Paul savagely over-revved the car engine as he negotiated the steep, twisting drive. He now realised that he missed being a part of the Lindsay family more than he had thought possible. No longer was he able to drop in casually and suggest an outing, give the boys a hand with their homework, or try and help Jill to bridge the generation gap. He had been a fool to get involved, but that was no excuse for being deliberately unkind to her, she hadn't started it all. He thought bitterly: this is what it must be like for a divorcee who sees another man move in and take over his family – except he was the interloper and Steven Lindsay had come back to reclaim his own.

*

At dinner that night, the talk was mainly of holidays. The previous weekend Steven said he very much wanted to have a family holiday before the boys went their separate ways. So long as she didn't have to do cooking or housework, Jill had no particular preferences. The boys were vociferous in their dislike of boring museums and old buildings.

'I fancy somewhere where there's some sports.' said Gregor as he shovelled in the shepherd's pie Jill had left for them. 'Swimming; sailing or suchlike. And I'd love to try surfing, it looks great.'

'I want somewhere with a bit of nightlife, with birds and discos,' added Alan. 'How about Majorca? I've several pals who went with their parents and enjoyed it.'

His brother was unenthusiastic. 'You can't surf in the Med, not enough waves in summer.'

'Yes, but you can sail and swim there.'

Steven put an end to the argument. 'We are staying very firmly put on British soil, I've had more than enough of abroad and I want to enjoy my own country.'

The boys looked at each other and pulled faces.

'There's no need to be bolshie. From what I've heard since I got back, it sounds as though Aviemore might keep everyone happy. I know you won't be able to surf, but there's lots of other sports and there should be plenty of night life. How about it?'

His sons brightened up. 'Sheila once went there for a weekend with the Guides and said that it was great.' Alan ran his fork round his plate and licked it appreciatively.

'OK then? Subject to Mum's approval and provided we can get a booking at this late date, Aviemore it shall be. Now, what's for pudding?'

'It's in the oven,' said Gregor.

'Well go and get it,' said his brother. 'It's your turn.'

'No it isn't.'

'Yes it is!'

'Will the pair of you shut up and stop arguing!' bellowed Steven. 'You keep complaining I still consider you children. If you want to be treated like adults, try and behave like them. Alan, put the plates in the sink. Gregor, get the pudding out of the oven – and don't scrape back your chairs like that!'

An oval Pyrex dish was shortly plonked down in front of him.

'You'd never make a living as a waiter. Where are the plates?'

Gregor looked in the top oven. 'Someone forgot to put them to warm.' He glared at his brother.

'You mean, you did.'

'For God's sake stop bickering and get some out of the dresser and don't forget a serving spoon.'

Steven peered at the dark sponge pudding, floating in some sort of sauce. He sniffed at it. 'What's this? I haven't seen it before…it smells good.'

'Chocolate walnut pudding,' said Gregor. 'Mum saw it demonstrated on the box. It's jolly good, you'll like it.'

Steven prodded it with the spoon and the sponge bobbed up and down in the sauce. He grinned at the boys. 'Gludge-sludge!' and they all burst out laughing.

CHAPTER 12

Jill glanced at the library clock. Another five minutes and she could finish. She picked up a dog-eared book which would have to be replaced and took it into the office. The outer door banged and someone walked over to the desk. Blast! Borrowers who came in just before closing time and then took ten minutes dithering over their choice were a pest. She sighed and went out to deal with the latecomer and was even less pleased to see Paul. She gave him an unfriendly look and said nothing.

'I…er…I forgot to ask you to tell Alan there'll be a few seats available in the mini-bus on Saturday.'

'Where for?'

'The Scottish Championships in Edinburgh. I'm taking some students along now that exams are over and I've room for band members or the drums.'

'In that case, why don't you phone Duncan, or Ian, or Jimmy? It's nothing to do with me and if you don't want any books, I'm about to shut up shop.' She snapped shut the lid of the ink pad and put it and the date stamp at one side of the counter.

Paul made no move to depart.

She looked at him in irritation. 'What else d'you want?' She picked up the long wooden box of tickets from the evening's withdrawals, but he grabbed hold of the other end to stop her from moving away.

'Please! I…I came to say I'm sorry about earlier on. I didn't mean to hurt you. It…it was unforgivable of me and quite untrue.' The words came out in a rush. 'I shouldn't have started it all and…and it certainly isn't "easy go", at least, not for me.' Paul's accent became more noticeable. 'You don't know how much I miss not coming to see you and the boys. It's like being cut off from my family all over again.'

If the counter hadn't been between them, Jill would have flung herself into his arms. Instead, she put down the box and gave him a little smile and a shrug. 'Thank you for saying so,' she said after a couple of seconds. 'I did feel hurt, but I also admit that there have been times in the last few weeks that I've missed you too. After all, you were part of my life for what…? Nearly four years…very much a part of my life. And I think you've already realised,' she went on, 'things have changed. I – I mean…' She looked down in embarrassment.

He took her hand. 'There's no need to go on, I understand.' He stood up straight, clicked his heels together and bowed formally. Jill felt him move to let go, but she held on to him.

Pressing his hand to her cheek for a few seconds, she turned it over, kissed the palm and folded his fingers over it. She said huskily, 'You have my very grateful thanks for all your kindness and help and for all the fun we had together. I don't regret any of it, but it would make things easier if you could continue to keep out of the way for the next few weeks, as you have obviously been trying to do.'

He nodded. 'That's probably best for all concerned. Anyway, I'm off to Austria in a fortnight.'

She was relieved that he had moved to the safer topics of holidays. 'To stay with your friends and gaze longingly over the frontier?'

'I gave up doing that years ago. Even if I could go back, I don't think I'd want to unless I could bring Margit and her family out with me.'

'Poor you. I wish you could, then there'd be a happy ending for both of us.'

He gave her a smile which revealed his dimples and walked over to the door.

He was nearly outside when she called to him. 'I nearly forgot! Thank you for the dinner at The Coo's Heid. I recognised the writing on the envelope, but I wish you'd kept your raffle prize for yourself.'

Paul acknowledged her thanks with a wave and as an afterthought, he put his head back round the door. 'What did you tell Steven?'

'I simply said that one of the raffle prizes had come our way – which was quite true – and the reaction was "Bully for Mrs Boggy Meadow"!'

When Jill arrived home, Steven was stretched out on the sofa, watching a ballet on the television and she recognised the music for *Swan Lake*. Ming was lying on his lap with one paw hanging down. She briefly opened an eye and yawned.

'Are the boys favouring us with their presence tonight?'

'No, they're both out. Alan's at band practice. Someone appeared on the doorstep at the end of dinner and Gregor went off with him, didn't even help with the dishes. However, we all enjoyed the Gludge-Sludge, you can add it to the repertory as far as I'm concerned.' He laughed at her expression. 'The chocolate pudding.'

'Thank heavens you haven't lost your wacky sense of humour. What ballet company's this?'

'Don't know, I missed the start.'

'Where's the paper? Here we are…the Kirov.' She looked critically at a group of huntsmen and their maidens. 'Scottish Ballet's almost as good as that.'

'Did you say the Kirov?' Steven jerked upright, to Ming's indignation. 'That was Kaiya's company. When was it filmed?'

'It doesn't say, but as Plisetskaya's dancing Odette-Odile, it can't be all that recent, I think she's retired now.' She sat down by Steven and snuggled up to him. 'Let's have a good snog in the back row of the stalls now we've got the place to ourselves.' He put an arm round her, but his attention was wholly on the ballet and she could feel he was very tense. She looked at him. 'What's the matter? Are you expecting to see your friend in the back row of the chorus?'

He shrugged, but a few minutes later edged the sofa nearer the screen. However, he relaxed and pulled her to him while Odette and the prince danced a pas de deux, but as soon as the swans reappeared he was on the alert again.

She pulled his arm round her more closely. 'Russian ballerinas seem to be quite a different shape from western ones, much sturdier. Some girls there have quite respectable frontages, instead of being all skin and bone – and the Prince certainly has a sexy bottom.'

Jill's attempt at humour was greeted by a grunt, which was followed by a choking noise as they were given a brief close-up of the four cygnets before they started their dance. Steven threw himself across the room and landed on his knees in front of the television. Ming gave an angry yowl at such cavalier treatment and slunk off round the back of the sofa. 'Oh Christ! That's her…second from the left…'

The camera panned over a row of bosoms bobbing up and down in unison and then cut to the footwork.

'Damn you!' said Steven in a strangled voice with his nose practically touching the screen. 'Let's see their faces again.'

The camera obliged.

'It's her, alright.' He stayed where he was until the dance ended, occasionally wiping his eyes. The second cygnet from the left looked an ordinary girl, with a round face, high cheekbones, slightly oriental eyes and a snub nose, but she'd obviously been someone very out of the ordinary as far as Steven was concerned.

Jill suddenly felt like hurling something hard and heavy at the screen, but the fit of jealous rage subsided abruptly when she remembered her own feelings earlier on, when Paul apologised to her. Everyone seemed to be crying for the moon this evening. She knelt behind Steven, put her arms round him and rocked him gently in time to the music while Odette danced ecstatically. By the end of the act he was in control of himself, but nodded when she asked if he wanted a cup of tea.

When she came back with it, she said, 'I've put in an extra spoonful of sugar, you look as though you need treatment for shock. D'you want the electric radiator on?'

He nodded again as he warmed his hands on the mug.

Steven stayed sitting on the floor, with his back to the radiator, for the rest of the ballet and simply pointed wordlessly when the same girl appeared as one of the Spanish dancers in the court divertissement and again, when the name "Kaiya Kassapian" appeared in the credit titles.

As soon as it disappeared off the top of the screen he went up to bed, leaving Jill with very mixed feelings. She wanted to try and comfort him, but didn't relish the possibility of being repulsed. On the other hand, if he did turn to her, would they each be imagining that they were holding someone else? Damn the Russians! Why did they have to mess up so many innocent lives?

*

When the pipers arrived in the village hall, Duncan said they needed to spend time on the competition medley. 'I know it'll be the march, strathspey and reel on Saturday, but it's no' bad and we can polish it up on Thursday. There were two very obvious mistakes last weekend and they were reflected in the marks. Get the music out. I want to be sure that everyone's playing what's written down and no' your own personalised version.'

There was a general scraping and shuffling as tables and chairs were taken from the stacks at one end of the hall and the pipers settled themselves with practice chanters and music. Some of them kept the duplicated sheets in ring binders, others used loose folders and one or two produced a fistful of crumpled bits of paper from the bottom of their pipe cases. Sandy Henderson favoured the latter method of filing.

Willie looked at him over the top of his glasses. 'Is that the dog's dinner ye've got there?'

'Looks more like its bed,' said Ken, to chuckles.

Neil picked up a piece of paper at random. 'It's no' that, it's Jeanie's shopping list.' He read out: 'Tea bags, nescaff; cornflakes – man, does she no' gie ye porridge? – bread; sugar; baked beans–'

'Beanz meanz jet-propulsion,' commented Alan.

'–sausages; tatties; almond oil.'

'I use almond oil on my pipes, but I didnae ken ye could fry chips in it,' remarked Duncan, straight-faced.

'It wuz for ma pipes,' growled Sandy as he snatched back the bit of paper, but his expression changed from a scowl to puzzlement as he looked at both sides. 'Tha's no' mine. I dinnae play pibroch,' and he pushed it away.

Willie picked up the music and peered at it. 'Well, I suppose it is that. The range is correct, low G to high

A, but it's a funny way o' writing it, wi' no clef sign.' He tried it tentatively on his chanter, then with more confidence. 'Aye, that's it. It's the ground for *Red Rory's Desire*.' He pushed the paper in the direction of Alan and Bob, 'One of you lads might as well take it, ye'll be learning it shortly.'

The two of them looked at each other, shrugged and left it where it lay.

'Red Rory, wasn't he one of the McTullums?' asked Alan.

'Aye, he was brother to one of the earls back in the seventeen hundreds,' said Willie. 'A well-known piper, he composed several good pibrochs, that among them. His ghost's said to haunt the castle.'

'What happened to him?'

'His "desire" was someone else's wife and the jealous husband strangled him with his own drone cords.'

Duncan cut in. 'And that's what I'll be doing if you lot don't improve your fingering. Some pipes sounded as though they were being played by bunches of sausages last Saturday.'

Joan nudged Fiona and whispered, 'What does he expect in weather like that? Flamin' June and ma fingers was frozen.'

'Thank you ladies, that's enough,' said Duncan firmly. 'We'll start with the march.' An hour later he looked at his watch. 'Go and get your pipes warmed up, we've time for a wee blow.'

Alan picked up his practice chanter and folder. Sandy's rejected piece of paper was still lying unclaimed, so he put it with the rest of his music, got out his pipes and went into the lobby. He started with a couple of marches, continued with a selection of hornpipes and after tuning his drones, went through the competition medley. That would have to do. As he lowered his pipes, he became aware of a banging noise. At first he thought it was the drummers, then realised that it was coming from the ladies' cloakroom. He went over to the door and listened. Yes, it was definitely coming from in there. He had a quick look round, but there was nobody else in sight. He opened the door a crack and was met by a strong smell of fresh paint. He called out, 'Is anything wrong?'

'The door's stu-huck. I can't ge-het out!' a voice sobbed.

'Just a minute then.' Alan laid down his pipes carefully next to the wall, had another look round and furtively slipped into the cloakroom, feeling thoroughly embarrassed. One of the two cubicles was shut, so he knocked on the door.

'Get me out of here!' He recognised Sheila's voice.

He gave the door a push and saw that it was stuck at the top of the frame. 'Stand clear,' he instructed.

'I can't, there's no room.'

'Well, climb up on the loo seat then. OK? Here goes.' He thumped the top of the door with his fist. It flew open and Sheila literally fell into his arms.

'Oh thank God! I thought I was going to be in there for the night. I've been banging and shouting for what seems like ages, but it was impossible to make myself heard over you lot.'

‘Och, you poor thing.’ As she made no effort to move away, he kept hold of her. ‘It was my fault, I was standing by the door and must have drowned you out completely.’

Sheila nodded against his chest and said between sniffs, ‘When you started on the medley, that really finished me off. I knew that I’d no chance of being heard until you’d completed it and I couldn’t even climb out of the window, it’s stuck as well.’ Something inside him started to do somersaults when she looked up and said shyly, ‘I’m awful glad it was you who came to my rescue.’

‘Are you really?’ He gave his reflection in the mirror above the basins a gleeful grin and rubbed his face against her head.

She wriggled an arm free and put it round his neck. ‘Uh-huh. I really am.’

He bent his face towards her upturned one – and the door was thrown open and Joan bounced in.

‘Oy-oy! Whit’s goin’ on here?’

They hastily moved away from each other. Alan stood staring at Joan in frustration and embarrassment, wishing that the floor would open and swallow him.

Sheila recovered her composure first. ‘The loo door was stuck with the new paint and I couldn’t open it. The inner knob’s still off and there’s only the slip-bolt to pull on and there isn’t even room to hook a foot underneath. He heard me banging and came to let me out.’

Joan leered at them. ‘Oh aye? It’s a good story, but I’m no’ buying it.’ She jerked her head at Alan. ‘Oot laddie, I want tae use the place for its intended purpose.’

As soon as he was gone, Sheila said angrily, 'Joan Bruce, just 'cos you're a filthy-minded little flirt, it doesn't mean that everyone else is. It's true what I told you.'

Joan shrugged and went into the toilet.

As Sheila washed her hands, she too grinned at her reflection: Joan was enthroned in the trap from which she'd just been liberated.

Alan was waiting outside as she hoped he would be and before he could say anything, she said, 'Joan's about to find out I was telling the truth. Get your pipes up.'

His playing for the next few minutes wouldn't have won any prizes as he was trying not to laugh at Sheila's gestures and expressions as she lounged against the cloakroom door, ignoring Joan's shouts for help.

Before they went back into the hall, he said, 'You'd better tip Ron the wink that Joan's waiting to be rescued.'

'Ron? You're out of date. He's behaving himself these days.'

'That's a change. What happened? They were very good friends indeed at Bathgate.'

'I know, and they didn't get home till about ten that night. My friend's boyfriend's dad's car broke down the far side of Stirling and the AA Recovery van brought them back to the garage just in time to hear Peggy welcoming him home. She told him if he ever went near that slut again, she'd kick him out. Mind you, she must have known what she was taking on–'

This interesting recital was interrupted by Ken who opened the hall door and made a shooing gesture.

'C'mon you two, we're ready to start.'

Alan retuned his drones while Sheila collected her drum and sticks.

Duncan looked round the band. 'We're still one short,' he said, frowning. 'Where's Joan?' In the following silence, faint bangs and yells could be heard coming from the ladies' cloakroom.

When the practice was over, Alan waited outside the hall until Sheila emerged. 'Can I carry your drumsticks?'

She swung the drawstring bag round a finger. 'Och, they're no' heavy.'

They walked down the street side by side in silence and had passed Rennie's Mini Market when Alan grabbed hold of her hand. She didn't try to pull away and a few steps farther on he said, 'You were telling me something about Ron when we were called into the hall. Something about Peggy knowing what she'd taken on.'

Sheila giggled. 'He's always been one for the girls. I can remember Dad and Mum talking about him, they must have thought I was too young to understand. He got several girls into trouble, including Peggy.'

'Was it a shotgun wedding?'

'More likely old man Jamieson's largest spanner, unless Ron decided that it was no bad thing to marry the only daughter of his boss.'

'But how d'you know he got Peggy into trouble?'

'You know I baby-sit for them occasionally? Well, one of the first times I did it was last summer, at the end of term and I remember distinctly that it was their tenth wedding anniversary, she told me before they went out. I also sat for them just before Christmas and the mantelpiece was full of the older girl's birthday cards.'

'So what?'

'It was her tenth birthday and the end of June to mid-December doesn't add up to nine months.'

Alan digested this tit-bit in silence for a few steps. 'I don't know that I like the idea of you baby-sitting for Ron.'

She let go of his hand. 'Who d'you think you are to dictate where I baby-sit?'

Alan looked down at her. 'Well…I mean…I – I wouldn't like him to get you into trouble…'

They walked on a bit in silence. Sheila slipped her hand back into his. 'Don't be daft! He's not my type at all. I suppose you could say that he's quite good-looking in a flashy sort of way, but his skull's beginning to grow through his hair and bald men turn me off.'

Had not both his hands been occupied, Alan would have furtively patted the back of his head. He took a deep breath. 'And what sort turns you on?'

She gave him a sidelong look. 'Redheads are no' bad.'

Alan covered the rest of the distance to the Grants' house feeling as if he were floating several inches above the ground. As Sheila released his hand and turned to go up the path, he pulled her back. 'There's a disco on in Brankstone on Friday night. Would you like to go? I think I'll be able to get the car.'

Sheila looked him up and down and he felt as though she was seeing him for the first time. After what seemed like an age she said, ‘OK then. Seven-thirty. See you,’ and walked off, twirling her bag rapidly. She was nearly at the door when she turned round and grinned at him. ‘Thanks for coming to my rescue. ’Bye.’

He stood staring after her until the door shut and then walked home in a state of rapture. He found his mother curled up on the sofa, reading a book. ‘Hi there, can I have the car on Friday night?’

‘I suppose so, if you were to say “please”,’ she said without lifting her head. ‘I’m working and Dad’s golfing with Paul, who’s giving him a lift.’

‘Please.’

His tone made Jill look up. ‘What’s happened? You look as though you’ve just come into a fortune.’

He tried to sound casual. ‘I’m taking Sheila to the disco.’ When he met his mother’s eye, he grinned from ear to ear.

‘Aha! So she’s suddenly woken up to the fact that you’re a fine fellow. OK then, but soft drinks only and no snogging on the back seat.’

Alan found himself going scarlet as that was precisely what he was hoping to do. Why did mothers have to be mind-readers?

CHAPTER 13

'Bluidy cheek!'

The sentiment resounded over hill and glen, strath and ben as throughout Scotland, readers unfolded their papers to learn that, as a gesture of friendship, the Russians were sending a team of athletes to compete in the open heavyweight events at the principal Highland Games. Or strictly speaking, two teams: one for the professional categories and the other for amateurs, which the public took with a large pinch of salt.

'My dear, whoever heard of a true Russian amateur sportsman?'

'Och, they're a' state subsidized. They're no' like our lads who have tae hold doon a job as well.'

'It were bad enough wi' yon Englishman Capes muscling in on the game, but fuckin' Russians, what do they know aboot it a'?'

'Ah'm no' sae sure. Yon Russkies is no' bad at the shot.'

'Aye, but they'll drop the caber on their tootsies.'

'I don't believe it, it's all a hoax.'

But it was no hoax. A well-known firm of kilt makers confirmed that the Russian embassy had supplied them with a list of measurements so that their athletes would be correctly dressed for the competitions. Several dowagers promptly closed their accounts, declaring that they were not prepared to do business with an establishment that would be entitled to display the words “By appointment” under the hammer and sickle.

CHAPTER 14

No matter how hard he tried, Steven couldn't make any impression on the tree trunk. He worked the saw until his arms ached, but it refused to cut. The guard shouted his bread ration would be reduced because he wasn't fulfilling his work norm and then swung his rifle at him…the rifle changed into a chain saw, but he was too tired to duck away from it…it was coming down onto his shoulder, buzzing loudly…the buzzing turned into the door bell and he woke up, sweating and shaking, with his heart pounding.

It took him several seconds to realise that it had all been a nightmare and he was lying in bed at home, in Scotland. The bell rang again. He looked at the alarm clock: half past seven. Who on earth could it be at this hour? He got out of bed, shoved his feet into his slippers, pulled on his dressing gown and went downstairs.

The caller was Johnny the postie. ''Mornin' Dr Lindsay, sorry to get yer aht o' bed so early on a Sa'erday morning, but I'm orf wiv the band terday. Gotta do me rahnd quick.'

‘Don’t apologise. I was delighted to be woken from a nightmare.’

Johnny commented sympathetically, ‘Dreaming abaht the camp, wos yew? That’s wot ’appened to me Uncle Solly. ’E wos in one o’ them Nazi ones. Stayed wiv us after the war and ’ad nightmares fer years. Nah then, there’s this ’ere Recorded Delivery letter ter sign for.’ He started to pat his pockets and mutter under his breath in German, finally locating a pen. ‘Got a job yet?’

Steven handed over the receipt with a shake of his head.

‘Ah well, never say die. ’Bye.’

“Never say die” indeed! The letter contained a contract from his publisher, plus a cheque.

Jill’s initial reaction to it was less than enthusiastic. She gave a protesting groan and grabbed the bedding when he rejoined her, and an even louder one when she saw what time it was. ‘What on earth are you doing up at such an unholy hour on a Saturday morning?’

‘Signing for a letter.’

‘Anything interesting?’

He shoved the cheque under her nose.

She pushed it farther away and squinted at it. ‘Blimey! Am I seeing correctly? What’s it for?’

‘Advance on my book.’

‘That’s terrific!’ She flung her arms round him. ‘It’ll boost our resources rather more than somewhat.’

Half an hour later Steven retrieved a crumpled cheque from under Jill’s thigh. He smoothed it out and put it on the bedside table, thinking how good it was to be contributing to the household exchequer again. He said suddenly, 'How come the village has a postie who is bilingual in broad Cockney and educated German?'

'You mean Johnny Morgan? I gather he started life in Leipzig as Johannes Morgenstein, but came to this country as a baby when his parents fled the Nazis. He went into the navy and met Elspeth when he was stationed at Rosyth. They'd been married for several years when he was invalided out with hepatitis and as her uncle and aunt wanted to retire, the Morgans took over the post office.'

Steven mulled this over. 'I suppose that they must have spoken German at home and it explains why he had an uncle who'd been in a concentration camp.'

'I knew about the German, I've heard him and Paul talking together, but the uncle's news to me. How did you find out?'

'We got onto the subject of nightmares.'

Jill sat up and gave him a worried look. 'Was it very bad last night?'

He shrugged. 'I've had worse, but I think they're getting a bit less frequent.'

'Are you sure there's nothing that can be done about them?'

'The psychiatrist did say at my last visit that he could try drug therapy using hallucinogens, but I don't fancy that.' He gave her a reassuring smile, 'But what I do fancy is some breakfast. I've been cutting trees all night and I'm famished!'

Alan was already in the kitchen. Gregor was the last to appear and he gave his father a disapproving look as he started his porridge. 'You must have had a good session at the nineteenth hole last night. Even Alan was back before you.'

Jill looked at husband and elder son. 'I gather you both enjoyed yourselves last night?'

They both nodded.

'Well, we know Alan spent the evening snogging Sheila,' remarked Gregor, 'But what were you doing, Dad?'

'Playing billiards with Paul, mostly. I used to be quite good at it. Oh, by the way, I've arranged with him to pick up Alan here at ten as for once, I want the use of the car. And we're all invited to the college's end-of-term ceilidh next Friday evening. He hopes you'll play a few tunes for them, Alan.'

Gregor pulled a face at this announcement.

'Yes, all of us. Time you learnt to be a bit more sociable. For once, you can emerge from your work-shop, put on a shirt and tie, brush your hair and look respectable.'

This prospect held no attraction whatsoever for Gregor.

'Alan, you're out today,' said Jill. 'Gregor, what are you doing? Dad and I are going into Edinburgh. D'you want to come too? No? Then you can get your own lunch. We'll have our main meal in the evening. Alan, will you be back by six-thirty?'

'Should be. I expect Paul's lot will have had enough by the end of the march-past and prize-giving. I'd better go and get ready.'

‘Not until you’ve helped with the dishes. You and Gregor are getting rather good at sneaking off and leaving Dad and me to do it all.’

Alan came downstairs just before ten and was inspected by his father. ‘That’s a different outfit from usual.’

‘Full dress. Duncan said there were likely to be quite a lot of tourists about and we might as well tart ourselves up for them.’

‘Why are you wearing a different tartan? No pun intended.’

‘We got this stuff second-hand from a band run by some firm in Glasgow that went into liquidation. I think this is McLaren, but we usually wear Mackenzie.’

‘But why don’t you wear the Mackenzie kilts with that lot?’

‘’Cos we’d look daft in green kilts and red plaids.’ A horn hooted outside. ‘That’s Paul, I’m off.’

‘Good luck.’

*

When Jill and Steven returned home in the late afternoon, it was to find an elderly Mini and several bicycles parked outside the house and a kitchen full of teenagers who were gathered round the table, chatting and drinking coffee.

Steven had met them all before, with one exception. ‘Who’s the skinny fair-haired lad with glasses?’ he whispered to Jill while she was unpacking the shopping.

'Andy Cameron. He must be home from university.'

'Is he the one who mends things?'

'Yes. Oh gosh! Thanks for the reminder.' She called out, 'Andy, have you time to look at my hairdryer? It keeps sort of hiccupping.'

Andy put down his mug. 'Sure, though I can't guarantee to mend it on the spot, it depends what's wrong.'

Ten minutes later she was presented with a smoothly-running hairdryer and as Andy pocketed his Swiss Army knife, he explained, 'Loose connection inside, that's all.'

'Thanks very much indeed and while I remember, Paul would be grateful if you could look at his razor. Says you can play with his radio afterwards, but you'd better be quick, he's off on holiday shortly.'

Andy's face lit up and for the next few minutes he rhapsodised about Paul's transceiver, but finished his recital of its virtues and finer points with a puzzled shake of his head. 'It's funny, y'know. Paul isn't like the other hams I've met. He doesn't go to any of the Radio Society meetings or get any of the magazines, isn't even interested in borrowing them. It's almost as if he was a ham because he had to rather than because he wanted to.' He looked at his watch. 'I'd better be off, otherwise Mum'll be nagging. Thanks for the coffee, Gregor. Oh, thank you very much, Mrs Lindsay. Tell Alan I'll be seeing him.'

This prompted a general exodus and Jill and Steven were left on their own in the kitchen. 'Nice lad,' said Steven. 'Pity about the limp. What happened?'

‘Motor bike accident. Two years ago he spent part of the summer holidays in hospital with a compound fracture of his shin and he used to be in the school football team. That’s when Alan began to understand why I refused point blank to let him buy a motor bike. Andy’s accident was a gypsy’s warning to quite a lot of local lads.’

‘I seem to remember you saying something about Alan and a bike in your letters. Said you’d persuaded him not to get one.’

‘I think that was one of the episodes I glossed over. I had an awful time with him for a few weeks, with rows and sulks when I told him I refused to accommodate one on the premises… He even went behind my back and asked Duncan if he could keep it at the workshop, but Duncan warned me what was up. I was just about demented when he threatened to leave home because he was sixteen. Paul talked him out of that one, thank heavens, he can be very persuasive, but Andy’s accident put a different perspective on it all.’

*

Alan arrived home when the rest of the family were in the middle of their evening meal, looking as though he had spent the day at the local coal face instead of a piping competition. They all burst out laughing when they saw him and he stared back in indignation. ‘What’s up with you lot?’

‘You’ve got black streaks all over your face,’ chuckled Gregor.

'Go and look at yourself in a mirror,' Jill advised.

Alan rubbed his face and inspected his fingers. 'Must be the dye out of my feather bonnet. There was a cloudburst during the march-past and prize-giving. The water had to be emptied out of the cups before they could be presented.'

'If you've got a lot of wet gear,' Jill said, 'go and hang it up in the utility room, don't leave it in a pile on the bedroom floor. And if you want a shower, I'll put your food back in the oven.'

The others had finished eating by the time he came back. Gregor said, 'How did you get on?'

'We came fourth.'

'Jolly good.'

Alan stuffed in a few mouthfuls and waved his fork at his brother. 'Joan's got a new boyfriend and you'll never guess who!'

'Who, then?'

'Paul. She kept fluttering her eyelashes at him all day and I heard him invite her out for a meal this evening as we were getting into the bus to come home.'

At the sink, Jill suppressed the urge to smash a glass down on top of the pile of crockery. Paul, going out with that little tart? Oh be reasonable, she told herself, it's none of your business now, he's nothing to you any more. But for the next few minutes she had to fight for self-control.

While Alan was finishing his meal, Steven went out into the hall and came back with a carrier bag, tipped a pile of car brochures onto the table and started to study them. ‘Pipe-dreaming, Dad?’ said Alan as he picked one up and flicked through it.

‘No, trying to decide which I prefer.’

Gregor paused from drying dishes. ‘Is there something wrong with the Metro?’

His brother shook his head. ‘Not that I’m aware of. Ron serviced it recently.’

The conversation gradually penetrated Jill’s thoughts. ‘What’s this about cars?’

‘How d’you fancy the latest Rover?’ Steven waved the brochure at her.

‘It’d be very nice, if we could afford it.’

‘Of course I can, with this morning’s cheque.’

‘I dare say, but the Metro’s barely three years old and there’s lots more important things to spend your money on–’ she put down the dish cloth and went and stood over him, hands on hips, ‘–like updating your National Insurance payments for a start.’ At the boys’ enquiring looks, she went on, ‘Your father seems to have forgotten that he needs to make good nearly five years’ backlog.’

‘Bloody hell!’ exclaimed Alan. ‘You never told us that.’

‘It’s none of your business,’ snapped his father.

‘With that amount owing, you need a new car like a hole in the head,’ added Gregor.

‘There you are,’ said Jill. ‘Out of the mouths of babes and sucklings, though they wouldn’t put it quite so crudely.’

Steven glared at them in tight-lipped anger. He stood up abruptly, nearly knocking over his chair, threw the brochure down onto the table and stormed out of the room. The house shook as two doors were slammed shut.

His wife and sons looked at each other, rolled their eyes and exhaled gustily.

When Jill went through to the sitting room a few minutes later with their coffee, he was sitting hunched on the sofa. 'I don't understand my family.' He scowled as he took his mug from her. 'I'd have thought everyone would be delighted with the idea of a new car and all I get is reproaches.'

'Oh, try and be realistic, love – and be thankful your sons have some financial nous.'

'Implying I haven't?'

She sighed as she sat down beside him and after a couple of sips, went on. 'Not a bit. In the light of what you've been through, your reaction to all that lovely money is perfectly rational.'

'The boys didn't seem to think so,' he grumbled.

'I think that some of the trouble is that they're jealous and not a little resentful.'

'Of who?'

'You.'

'Me? Why on earth should my sons be jealous and resentful of me?'

Jill gave another sigh. 'It may be my fault. Perhaps I expected too much of them too soon, but you see, when you were away, we tended to act as a team. I always discussed any important matters, purchases, any major decisions and so on, with them. When we were initially on our own, they were very protective of me, particularly after my operation. I remember one of the first things Alan said to me after your trial was, "Try not to worry, Mum, you've still got me and Gregor to look after you." And I do know that thereafter he thought of himself as head of the family.' She patted Steven on the arm. 'Can't you try and see it from their point of view? Now you're back, they feel they're being relegated to children again. They think they're being kept out of things the three of us on our own used to cope with together.'

He gave her a bleak look and shrugged.

She took his hand and squeezed it. 'Teenagers are hell to live with at the best of times and you've suddenly been landed with two of them, when for years you've been thinking of them as nice, polite, biddable little boys. That's bound to cause rows.' She put her arm round his shoulders and gave him a little shake. 'Try treating them as sub-adults, rather than overgrown children. It does work – occasionally…'

A little later Steven went back into the kitchen. The boys were sitting at the table chatting while Alan was doing something to his pipes. Steven rinsed the mugs, wandered over and by way of making amends for his earlier behaviour, said, 'I'd no idea there were so many bits and pieces in a set of pipes. What are they all for?' Alan had dismantled the instrument and was carefully wiping the parts with a soft cloth. Steven picked up a tube and blew down it. Something flapped at the other end.

‘That’s the blowpipe you’ve got hold of. The loose bit’s the valve. It’s made of leather and when you squeeze the bag, it stops the air from going back up again.’

‘I see. What’s this?’ He picked up a long, thin, conical tube with holes in it, a disc at the wider end and a reed inserted at the other.

‘That’s the chanter, the fingerboard. If you ever pick up a set of pipes, make damn sure you’ve got a good grip on it. If you drop it and it doesn’t bounce, that’s a good forty quid up the spout.’

Steven put it down very carefully and looked at the reed. ‘Is that like an oboe reed?’

‘Well, it’s a double reed and it’s made of cane, but it’s much shorter and fatter.’

‘And a different noise.’

Alan wiped the chanter, picked it up and played the nine-note scale. The volume left his father’s ears ringing.

‘Can’t you play it a bit quieter?’

Alan grinned and shook his head. ‘You can’t modulate it, that’s why you need the gracenotes–’

‘The chirrupy and bubbly bits?’

‘Yes, you need them to emphasise notes and to separate two or more the same as you’ve got a continuous flow of air passing over the reed. It’s not like the orchestral woodwind instruments.’ He chuckled. ‘There are no rest signs in pipe music!’

Gregor stretched and got up. ‘If you’re going to lecture Dad on piping, I’m off.’

Alan gave his father an anxious look. 'Sorry, was I boring you? I do tend to get carried away at times.'

'On the contrary, it's most interesting.' Steven sat down in Gregor's place and picked up the practice chanter from the box. 'What's this?'

'Beginners start with it and you also learn new tunes on it. It's a smaller version of the pipe chanter, but with a straight bore, plus a mouthpiece. The reed's different too, much quieter and easier to blow.'

'Can you swap the reeds round?'

'No, put a chanter reed in that and it's like a cock with laryngitis and vice versa, you sound like an Indian snake charmer.' He demonstrated and Steven pulled a face.

The latter pointed to another part. 'Is that a drone?'

'Yes. That's one of the two tenor ones and you tune it by sliding the upper bit over the lower, which holds the reed.' He pulled the drone out of the stock which was tied into the bag and showed his father a piece of bamboo about three inches long, with a tongue cut into it and one end blocked by a blob of sealing wax. 'The open end goes into the drone and the air passing over the tongue causes it to vibrate. It's tuned to A and the bass drone is an octave lower.' He demonstrated again.

'Sounds like a cow in labour. What sort of wood is that?'

'The very best. African blackwood and the mounts are ivory, though nowadays they're made with a variety of tropical hardwoods, plus plastic mounts.'

'So they aren't new?

'No. Duncan got them for me. They belonged to a former band member who died recently and was related to a well-known pipe-maker. I'm bloody lucky to have such a super set.'

By now the pipes were completely dismantled and dried. Steven picked up the bag with its dark green velvet cover. 'What's this made of?'

'The traditional material's sheepskin, but that one's hide. I'm a wet blower and cow hide doesn't rot so quickly. You can even get them made of kangaroo leather!'

'What was the gunge you heated up and poured in last week?'

'Seasoning to rub into the bag to keep it airtight. If the leather gets dry, it becomes porous. In the olden days they used treacle, but now we use a proprietary brand.'

Alan had been reassembling the pipes while he talked and when he had finished, took them out to the utility room and played a couple of tunes. Back in the kitchen, he found his father looking at the folder of music. 'I take it that the notes which look as though they've been sprinkled over the music with a pepper pot are the gracenotes?'

'S'right, and they've all got to be learned by heart.'

'On the practice chanter?'

'Yes. Pipe bands don't have the music stuck up on the instruments like brass bands.'

'D'you have one of those chaps at the front twiddling a baton?'

'You mean a drum major? We used to, but he was football daft and took himself off to a grade one band.'

'So what?'

'Grade one bands take it in turn to play at all the big football matches.'

Steven pulled out a sheet of music. 'This doesn't look the same as the rest.'

Alan came and looked over his shoulder. 'That's pibroch, the classical music of the pipes. What you usually hear played is the low- and middle-brow stuff. Pibroch is for solo players and very much an acquired taste.'

'What's so special about it?'

Alan though for a few moments. 'It's quite different. Mum once said that it's like trying to assimilate Bach toccatas and fugues when you're used to Strauss waltzes – difficult to play and listen to, but if you do get to like it, it can be very addictive.'

'And have you acquired this taste?'

'I – I think so. I didn't at first, but it grows on you. If you get really good at it, it becomes a sort of self-hypnosis. Very basically it's in the form of a theme, the ground, and variations on it which get more and more complicated till suddenly, you're back where you started. Someone once told me to think of it as a musical version of a Celtic knot pattern, which is quite a good description. Let's go into the sitting room and I'll put something on the record player to show you what I'm talking about.'

Steven followed Alan and while the latter was locating the record, he gave Jill a quick wink and a thumbs-up. 'I gather we're going to be treated to some pibroch.'

Jill's face fell. She raised her eyes heavenwards and mouthed, 'Oh Gawd!' then said in feigned interest to Alan, 'What are you putting on?'

'*The Desperate Battle of the Birds.*'

'That's not so bad then, so long as we're not going to be subjected to twenty minutes non-stop of some ghastly dirge.'

Alan looked down his nose at her. 'Some people don't appreciate fine music when they hear it.'

'Chacun à son gout, son, if you can dredge up a bit of O-grade French. And my gouts–' she pronounced it like the illness '–incline more to Mendelssohn than Macrimmon.' She turned to Steven, 'Actually, this one isn't too bad, it really does sound like birds.'

'It's supposed to depict the display of Blackcock,' said Alan, 'But it always makes me think of eagles soaring over some Highland landscape.' As Steven settled down to listen, he was handed the record sleeve. 'It tells you about it here.'

He read the notes, then looked at the photo of the piper on the front. 'I thought pipers were great big hairy he-men? This chap looks more like a schoolmaster.'

'Let me see – well, you're not so far out, he's a university lecturer.'

Steven looked at the photo again. 'Now that you mention it, he does look vaguely familiar. I probably saw him in days gone by.'

‘From what I’ve seen of pipers,’ Jill said, ‘they strike me as being stocky, middle-aged men whose waistlines are indicated by the position of the belt on the bulge. I hope you aren’t going to look like that in twenty-five years time, Alan.’

‘Not unless I develop a taste for whisky with beer chasers.’

Steven suddenly held up his hand for silence. ‘Listen, I thought you said there were no rest signs in pipe music?’

Alan explained: ‘In that variation the theme notes are separated by a high A, which is being lost against the harmonics of the drones. You have to have them tuned spot-on to get that effect and keep your blowing rock-steady. Actually, when you blow, you’re only topping up your reservoir, you control the flow of air over four reeds with your left elbow and forearm.’ He went out of the room and came back with a book of music. ‘Look, you can follow it in here.’ He put it down on his father’s knee, open at the appropriate page.

For a few bars, Steven tried to follow the music, but soon got lost. He leafed through the book, looking at the titles. ‘*Massacre of Glencoe; Lament for–* some unpronounceable Gaelic name. They were a cheerful lot in those days. *My dearest on earth, give me your kiss*, that’s a bit more like it.’ He turned a few more pages and then gave a mirthless laugh. ‘Here’s one that’s very apt: *The unjust incarceration*, that’s me alright. Hmm, *The wee spree* – perhaps they did have a bit of fun at times.’

‘Oh aye,’ said Alan. ‘There’s even a march called *Behind the bush in the garden*!’

That produced chuckles from his parents, then Steven gave a hoot of laughter. ‘Here’s one written by someone with an almighty hangover: *Too long in this condition*.’

‘Oh no it wasn’t,’ said his wife. ‘It was written by a lady piper nine months after the previous tune.’

*

‘Don’t forget we’re going out tonight,’ Jill reminded the family at breakfast the following Friday.

‘I haven’t,’ said Alan, through a mouthful of toast. ‘I practiced my “Top of the Pops” selections when I was warming up yesterday.’

‘Do I have to come?’ Gregor sounded like a small child as he banged his bowl down onto the table.

‘Yes,’ said his father in a tone which brooked no arguments. ‘You were included in the invitation and Paul would think it rude if you didn’t turn up.’

Gregor consoled himself with extra sugar on his porridge.

*

The ceilidh started at eight, but Alan asked that they be there by seven-thirty to give him time to warm up. Paul handed him over to a lad of his own age with instructions to take him along to one of the classrooms and asked the other Lindsays if they wanted to have a walk round the grounds as it was a fine evening. ‘Can we go up to the top of the old keep?’ Gregor said, ‘I’ve often wondered what it was like up there.’

‘Certainly, if you don’t mind climbing over a hundred steps up a spiral staircase. Just a minute, I’ll get the key from the office.’

As they puffed their way up, they paused at each landing and had a quick look at the single room per floor, used by the students for common rooms and recreational purposes. When Paul unlocked the door at the top of the building, they agreed that it was worth the effort as there was a marvellous view over the river, with the two Forth Bridges to the left. After they’d discussed various landmarks, Gregor asked, ‘Did I see a telescope in the last room we looked at? Could we bring it up for a few minutes?’

‘Sure.’ Paul went down to get it.

The telescope was a great success and they took it in turns to use it. ‘You get a good view of the dockyard,’ said Jill. ‘You can even make out the numbers of the ships there.’ She read out, ‘D88.’

‘That’s a destroyer,’ said Paul, as he came back out onto the roof after lighting his pipe. ‘*HMS Glasgow*, I think. Wasn’t she damaged in the Falklands campaign? And last month they had a light cruiser in.’

‘You seem to know a lot about ships,’ said Steven. ‘Particularly for someone who comes from a land-locked country.’

‘That’s probably why. After all, they’re a common-place sight for you, but I find them fascinating.’ He waved his pipe at the wooded slopes around the castle. ‘Actually, one of my favourite views is of this place later in the year when the leaves are turning colour. It's like sailing through a sea of gold.'

A sea of gold… The expression took Steven back to his first autumn in Siberia, to the moment when he had discovered that there was some beauty to be found in the purgatory into which he had been pitchforked one night in Leningrad.

It was a crisp autumn day and he was working in a small clearing of silver birches. He straightened up to rest his aching limbs and stared at the sky above, trying to shut out of his mind the thought that his family and friends might be staring at it too. A little breeze got up and he was suddenly surrounded by a swirling shower of golden leaves as they were swept off the branches. He stood there, entranced by it all: the golden leaves dancing over the silver trunks against a background of vivid blue… Even the guard was moved by it. He let Steven stand for longer than usual and instead of shouting at him to get back to work, gave a quick smile which made him seem quite human and merely jerked his head in the direction of the other prisoners.

By this time, Steven had decided the only way in which he could come to terms with the catastrophe that had overtaken him was to tell himself he'd died that night and been reincarnated into his present existence…everything that had gone before was just a pleasant dream…he was doing penance for some terrible misdeed committed in a previous incarnation – and the sooner he died again, the better. When his Russian improved to the extent of being able to hold philosophical discussions with his fellow sufferers, he discovered several of them thought along similar lines. He also discovered that the political prisoners who were diehard Communists often found it the hardest to come to terms with their fate, being convinced the whole thing was some ghastly mistake.

There were several attempted suicides, but nobody was allowed to quit the Soviet way of life of their own volition.

After the incident in the birch wood, Steven decided he would survive so long as he could find one thing to be thankful about or to look forward to in each day…a few grams extra in the daily bread ration…a kind word or gesture from a fellow human, be they prisoner or jailer…a poem or piece of prose recited from memory as they lay on their bunks at night…

'A penny for your thoughts?' Paul's voice brought him back to the present.

'I was thinking about trees.'

'Siberian ones, if your expression was anything to go by.'

Steven gazed out over the wood and nodded slowly. 'How we hated those bloody trees, but paradoxically there were times when we were all too thankful for them. One of our lot was a botanist and he showed us how to make pine needle and birch bud teas to counteract vitamin deficiencies. He also taught those of us who had the energy how to forage for edible plants and berries. He was one of the lucky ones.'

'What happened to him?'

'He was one of the very few prisoners I came across who was fully rehabilitated. He ended up with us because he didn't toe some party line. He disagreed with the theories of a famous geneticist who then fell from favour, or his ideas did, and the botanist found himself *persona grata* again, lucky devil.'

'Genetics? That was Sonja's subject. She graduated in Botany and was doing research on plant mutations when…' Paul went on, half to himself. 'I can't help wondering if her work killed her… She worked a lot with irradiated material… But the specialist assured us…' He pulled himself together and looked at his watch. 'If you've all finished with the telescope, we ought to go downstairs again.'

The ceilidh was voted a success, even by Gregor. Groups of students provided some comic sketches; some of them sang and accompanied themselves on guitars; Alan piped a couple of selections and provided the music for a *Gay Gordons*. In this, Gregor was hauled onto the floor by an American girl and seemed quite taken by her. Paul sang some Czech and Russian songs, accompanied by one of his colleagues on the piano and Elspeth Morgan had brought along members of her Scottish Country Dancing class to give a demonstration.

Just before this started, Paul turned to the group at his table, which included Steven and Jill, Angus and Kathy Grant. 'D'you want to go up into the gallery to watch the dances?' he said. 'You'll get a better view of the formations up there.'

'Oh yes please,' said Kathy. 'Elspeth said to try and watch from upstairs.' When they arrived in the gallery, she went on, 'The first one's *Mairi's Wedding*, it's pretty to watch, one of the figures looks like the petals of a daisy.'

'That'll remind Paul of his sister,' remarked Steven and went on to tell them about Paul making daisy chains, to the latter's embarrassment.

Sensing this, Jill said, 'What else are they going to do?'

'A jig called *Bonny Anne* and then a fearfully complicated thing called *Schiehallion*. It starts off in strathspey time and ends up with bodies flying in all directions.'

When the final applause died down, Elspeth invited the audience to take the floor for *Mairi's Wedding* and said she would walk them through the figures before they performed it. Joan was in the demonstration team and gestured at Paul to come and join her.

Steven asked Kathy to dance as they headed for the stairs and Angus waved at a friend. Jill turned to follow them, but Paul took hold of her arm and pulled her to the back of the gallery. 'Please, *dushka*, just a few moments. It's important. You see, I might n–'

She freed herself, saying, 'I think Joan wants to dance with you,' and ran off downstairs. There, she was claimed as a partner by one of the staff who was a regular at the library.

As Paul came onto the floor, several young females headed towards him, Joan included, but he ignored them and bowed to the wife of a colleague. However, in the last waltz, Jill noticed Paul and Joan were dancing at very close quarters and she couldn't suppress a stab of jealousy.

It was a long time before Jill settled down that night. That was the worst of going out for the evening – come bedtime, you'd got your second wind and your mind was in overdrive, replaying the events, the music, the conversations. An owl hooted outside and she found herself reciting the final lines of *Love's Labour's Lost.*

Tu-whit, tu-who, a merry note,
While greasy Joan doth keel the pot.

…And was greasy Joan labouring with her new love? Was Paul thinking of his lost loves when he was with her? Oh, shut up! If he wants to fornicate with greasy Joan, let him, it's none of your business and to be brutally honest, you're older than him. You can't blame him for going with someone younger. Greasy Joan… that's not a bad description of the girl, with her oily complexion… Now then, you're being prejudiced, she's quite pretty and you have to admit, she does cut hair well…and with any luck her fancy will move on while Paul is on holiday. I wonder what he was going to say when I choked him off? Jill heaved an irritated sigh and turned over.

Steven grunted and touched her shoulder. 'Can't you get to sleep?'

'No, I'm too busy jigging and reeling.'

'Me too.'

'Mind you, I'm not complaining. It was wonderful to go to a social event feeling a whole person again.'

'How d'you mean?'

'In your absence I always felt a sort of half-person... neither wife, nor widow, nor divorcee.' And, she thought, I was never able to go anywhere as Paul's partner. 'Folk were generally sympathetic as the wives didn't see me as a threat, but I was still in a sort of social limbo.'

'I hadn't realised that that was one of your many problems, but then, single men are always more socially acceptable than single women.'

She snuggled up to him. 'S'not fair, as the boys are so fond of saying, but at least it's less of an issue at ceilidhs. Scottish country dancing is very accommodating to "loose women", you get used to doing sudden sex changes on the dance floor!' She laughed. 'Elspeth certainly put you through your paces in the *Eightsome Reel*.'

'And how! She doesn't half generate a centrifugal force when you twirl her, but I prefer to put my arms round uncorseted flesh…'

Some time later Jill murmured, 'What did you think of Gregor's girlfriend?'

There was a non-committal grunt. 'I suppose it proves his glands are working properly after all.'

She giggled. 'About time too. So far, he's never displayed any interest in the opposite sex, though I think she was making most of the running.'

'Well, he didn't appear to be objecting to the way she was draped round him in the final dance, almost as bad as that girl Paul was with, no inhibitions there.'

'You were a bit mean to him up in the gallery, telling tales about daisy chains. After all, the man was our host.' She felt him shrug and after a moment's silence, she ventured, 'You don't like him, do you?'

This time it was more of a wriggle than a shrug. 'I don't really know… It's kind of love-hate…'

'Like with your Ukrainian "Mr Big"? Theodore something?'

'Fyodor Alexandr'ich? Possibly… They're quite similar in looks, perhaps that's why I keep getting the feeling I've seen Paul before. No, I don't like him, he's not my type, yet there are times when I find myself craving his company. He's the only person I can really talk to about the last five years.' Steven put his hand out to soothe Jill's movement of protest. 'I don't mean that unkindly, you're very patient and sympathetic with my nightmares and bad temper.'

He continued on a pleading note. 'You see, Paul's the only person here who really understands what I've been through. He's been there himself. No matter how much I tell you, you'll never truly know what it's like – and pray God you never do.' He pulled her closer. 'Some people just don't want to know about my Russian experiences, I can see their eyes glazing over if I mention it, but with him, I can get it off my chest… I find myself coming out with far more than I intend to, he's so easy to talk to.'

'You mean, you use him as a sort of father-confessor?'

'I suppose so. That's why I was late back last Friday. We did play billiards, but after the others went, the two of us sat and talked hard, or at least, I did most of the talking. It was far more beneficial than any session with my shrink. But dammit! I don't even like the man.'

'Well, forget about it all,' she said. 'And think of the fun we're going to have together up at Aviemore in three weeks' time.

Steven was soon snoring gently, but Jill was unable to follow her own good advice and continued to lie there, wide awake, trying to obliterate images of Paul doing with Joan all the things they'd done together in the past. She eventually fell asleep with the consoling thought that the girl was unlikely to appreciate Sibelius.

CHAPTER 15

'Well folks, I hope you enjoyed your holiday,' said Steven as they approached Auchentullum from Dunfermline.

'Yes, thanks,' said Jill. 'It was bliss not to have to do any cooking or housework, even if it was only for a week.'

'Are you going back to work on Monday or are you taking a further week off?'

'Going back to work. I've already had time off this year and I want to keep some days in reserve for the autumn. So far, I've taken them at the October mid term, but we'll see about that later.'

As they passed the sign for the village, Steven said, 'Can anyone tell me what Auchentullum means, if anything?'

'I can,' said Gregor. 'It's derived from the Scots words meaning the "field by the hill", which refer to the flat bit of ground around Burnside. Brankstone is something to do with a Celtic chieftain and the standing stone in the field at the far side of the village.'

‘I never knew that,’ said Jill. ‘How did you find out?’

‘English teacher.’

‘Old Ratty?’ asked Alan.

‘’S’right. You learn more about Scottish dialects in his classes than you do about English – Aw shit! Our exam results are due out today.’

‘Gregor! Language!’ said Jill sharply as the car drew up in front of the cottage.

‘Home, sweet home, with Ming waiting to greet us,’ announced Steven. The cat was sitting on the wall and as they got out, she jumped down and wrapped herself round their legs, purring loudly.

Jill picked her up and stroked her. ‘Anne’s obviously been looking after her well in our absence.’ She handed the cat over to Gregor, unlocked the doors and went into the kitchen.

The boys came in with the luggage, which they dumped in the hall. ‘Where’s the post, Mum?’ asked Alan.

‘Anne’s put it all on the table.’ She picked out a couple of large brown envelopes and handed one to each son. ‘Here you are. Here’s your fates.’

After a few moments silence, Alan beamed at his parents. ‘That’s me home and dry. Dentistry, here I come.’

‘Let’s see,’ said Steven, holding out his hand for the results. ‘A grades in all your sciences and you’ve passed Higher English. Jolly good, son. Congratulations!’ and slapped him on the back.

Meanwhile, Jill was looking anxiously at Gregor, who was staring at the paper with an expression that she couldn't interpret. 'Well?'

'I've got A for woodwork and Technical Drawing, B for Art and C for Arithmetic.'

'What about English?' Wordlessly, he handed her his results. 'Oh dear!'

Gregor had got an E grading. He tried to make light of it by saying, 'Well, E is for English.'

'You got an E in your English exam?' said a horrified Steven. 'That's appalling! You'll certainly be going back to school for another year.'

'Steve, you're being less than fair to him. He's done well in his other subjects, particularly in Woodwork.' Jill went and hugged her younger son. 'Congratulations, I'm sure Duncan'll be pleased to hear that.'

Gregor shrugged her off and jerked his chin at his father. 'I dare say, but he isn't.' He glared at his parents. 'S'not my fault if you gave Alan all the brains. And it's not my fault either about English. It's that silly old bugger of a teacher. He's absolutely hopeless.' He strode out of the cottage, slamming all the doors behind him, leaving the others staring after him in dismay.

Alan was the first to recover from Gregor's outburst. 'He's right, Dad, it's not really his fault. Mr Rattray's a lousy teacher, everyone's marks go down when they get into his class and he's always had his knife into Gregor, he's never liked him.' He held out his hand. 'Give me the car keys, I'll put it away if everyone's finished unloading.'

After he went out, Steven snorted, 'If the man's such a rotten teacher, why do they employ him?'

'If the school tried to sack him, there'd probably be trouble with the teachers' unions. I did try to get Gregor out of his class at the start of third year, I even had an interview with the head of the department, but it was a waste of time.' Jill spread her arms in appeal. 'Steve, do try and be a bit more tolerant, it's not entirely his fault. Try and praise him for what he's achieved, rather than bite off his head for his failure.'

Duncan said much the same thing to Steven a few days later when he came to install the headboard in the bedroom. In the interim, the family had seen very little of Gregor, who spent most of his time in his workshop with only Ming for company, or else was out of the house and when asked where he had been, merely shrugged and gave an evasive answer. However, when he emerged onto the landing one morning to find Duncan manoeuvring lengths of timber into the other bedroom, he asked if there was anything he could do to help.

The joiner gave the pyjama-clad figure a disapproving look and said that he hadn't brought along a mate as he had expected to find one ready and waiting for him on site.

Gregor dressed and breakfasted in record time.

The two of them were tidying up when Steven arrived home. After inspecting the job and expressing his satisfaction, he asked Duncan if he'd like some tea. Before going downstairs, he asked how the mahogany veneer was going to be finished off.

'Wax, not varnish,' said Gregor, which was met with a nod of approval from Duncan.

Gregor downed his tea and then departed upstairs with a tin of his own turpentine and beeswax polish, some cloths, an old bristle nail brush and his electric drill with a sheepskin pad fitted in the chuck. 'Not what Chippendale used, but it'll do,' chuckled Duncan after he left.

'Can't wait to get on with the job,' said Steven.

'Oh aye, the lad's keen as mustard, it would be a pity to put him off.'

'D'you think so?'

'Definitely.'

Steven swallowed his pride and looked Duncan in the eye. 'You probably know my son better than I do now. What d'you think would be best for him?'

'Let him become a cabinet maker, like he wants. The ability's there, alright.' Steven digested this in silence and as he picked up his mug, Duncan went on, 'Try not to be sore at the lad over his exam results. He did his best.'

Steven stared into his drink and nodded. 'I realise I was a bit sharp with him, but come what may, he'll have to have another go at English, preferably with a different teacher.'

'You're right there, Dr Lindsay. Me and my brother, we were never good at exams. I never worried about it, I'm happy where I am, but Robbie, he was made redundant a year or two back and wished he'd got his wee bit of paper.' He finished his tea and put down the mug with a decisive thump. 'Tell ye what, one o' my men is due to retire next summer. If that lad o' your goes back to school and gets his English and a couple o' Highers in whatever subject he likes, I'll take him on as an apprentice. Once he's got a trade under his belt to stand him in good stead, then mebbe he can go and study cabinet-making with that chap Makepeace down in England. How about that?'

Steven considered Duncan's offer and held out his hand. 'OK then. If Gregor likes the idea, I'll give him my support. We'd better see what he thinks.'

Gregor was none too pleased to be interrupted – until he learnt why and then he was too overcome with joy to do anything other than stand looking from one to the other, grinning from ear to ear.

On the way out, Duncan punched him lightly on the shoulder. 'Now mind, lad, I'm no' taking ye on unless ye pass your exams. And that won't be the end o' your studies either. Ye'll be off to a 'tec one day a week until ye're qualified.' At the door, he turned round and gave Steven a conspiratorial wink from behind the boy's back.

Gregor sat down with a slightly dazed expression.

'Well?' said Steven. 'D'you feel a bit happier now?'

'Oh gosh! Yes. Thanks.' His grin faded. 'But another year of manky old school…'

'Try and look on it as a means to an end. I know it seems a helluva long time at your age, but now you've got a goal to aim for.' He smiled in encouragement. 'Try and see that it's to your advantage in the long run to get all the qualifications you can, even if it's only to wield a hammer and saw.'

His son gave him an indignant look. 'There's more to cabinet-making than that.'

*

Now that Gregor's future was settled, the tension which had never been far from the surface of the Lindsay family since Steven's return eased considerably and doors were slammed much less often. Jill had never worried about Alan's abilities, but her younger son had given her sleepless nights and more recently Steven's attitude to anything non-academic was no help.

Steven himself became more relaxed. He gained weight, the nightmares and bouts of bad temper lessened and his book progressed satisfactorily. Jill wondered how writing it would affect him as after the first two chapters she refused to read any further, saying in apology he'd have to find someone else to type out the manuscript, it was far too harrowing.

> *The Old Masters had got it wrong with their depictions of* The Last Judgement: *hell wasn't hot, it was endless, unrelenting cold. A place where Hades' henchmen included Hunger, who sunk his long, sharp teeth into your stomach. And Frostbite, who gleefully grabbed fingers and toes with his pincers. But worst of all was Delilah-like Despair, enticing exhausted men into her snowy embrace, from which they never got up.*

When she asked how he could bear to write about it at all, he said it was as if he was writing about another person and the whole exercise was a form of catharsis.

With Paul on holiday and Steven becoming more like his old self, Jill found herself thinking much less about her ex lover.

If anyone in the family had something on his mind, it was Alan, August being the month when the most prestigious pipe band competitions take place. Strathtullum had been first in grade three and sixth in grade two at the Dunfermline Highland Games at the beginning of the month, which was excellent for their morale, though it was not a major competition. They knew they were unlikely to do as well in the World Championships in the middle of the month, or at the Cowal Games at Dunoon on the last Saturday as bands from as far away as Canada and Australia came to compete in these events, but they were determined to put on a good show.

Even allowing for this, the other three Lindsays and their neighbours became fed up with Alan's constant practising and eventually he was banished to a local field in fine weather. This was a case of "out of evil cometh good" as the licencee of The Stag's Head heard him while out walking his dog and on learning why Alan was there, invited him to play outside the pub whenever he liked, as a tourist attraction, on condition that he wore a kilt. The takings went up on these occasions and the piper benefitted.

‘How much longer does this competition lark go on for?’ asked Steven one evening when Alan came in. ‘I’m making coffee. D’you want some?’

‘Please.’ Alan put his pipes on the table and went into the hall to get his folder of music out of his case. ‘I’ve got a list here, somewhere.’ After a bit of hunting around, he read out, ‘The World Championships are this weekend, Cowal a fortnight later, the European Championships at Shotts a fortnight after that and finally Dunblane in mid-September. That’s the final one of the season.’

‘And not before time,’ muttered Steven under his breath as he added milk to their mugs. ‘Take this along to your mother, please.’

A little later Alan returned to the kitchen with their empty mugs and realised he had still to put away his pipes – and there was a passage in the strathspey he wanted to check. By the time he had found the sheet of music, there was paper all over the table, so he decided he might as well tidy his folder.

He was doing this when a chocolate and cream paw came out from under the table and started to pat one of the tassels on the drone cords which were hanging down. He watched the cat playing for a minute or two, but when she started to attack it with tooth and claw, he hauled the tassel up to safety with an indignant, ‘Oy! Pawzaff! That’s band property.’

Ming sat up and squinted at him, tail twitching.

‘OK then, I’ll make you another toy.’

He looked round for inspiration and his eye lit on the piece of paper which Jeanie Henderson had used as a shopping list. That would do nicely. Willie had recently given him the proper setting for *Red Rory's Desire*, so a bit of the pibroch was of no further use. He crumpled the paper into a loose ball, got out the reel of yellow hemp thread which he used for binding the drone slides and other joints, broke off a length and wrapped it round the ball several times. He dangled the new toy in front of Ming, but she merely sniffed at it, jumped down and stalked off into the utility room. The tassel had been much more fun. Alan shrugged, tied the free end of the string into a loop and hung it round one of the drawer knobs on the dresser and went back to sorting out his music.

Jill noticed Ming's new toy and left it there, where it remained for about ten days.

*

She was on her own one evening, finishing a large pile of ironing, when the bell rang. On opening the front door, it took her several seconds to recognise the visitor. 'Paul!' His hair was cut very short and he had grown a moustache.

Jill stood staring at him until he said, 'May I come in?'

'Oh, sorry. I was a bit fazed by your appearance, you look so different. Of course, do come in. D'you mind being received in the kitchen? I've got the iron on.'

He followed her, started to pull out one of the chairs and Ming leapt off. She snarled at him and retreated under the dresser until only the knobbly tip of her tail was visible, lashing angrily from side to side.

He sat down with a rueful grin. 'That's another black mark against me.'

'She's never liked you, but I can't think why.'

'It's my own fault. I once laughed at her when she missed her footing on a leap. I think she was still groggy after her speying operation, but I've never been forgiven.' He went on, 'You're looking well. Did you have a good holiday?'

'Aviemore was great fun, thanks, but horribly expensive. From that point of view, it was just as well we were only there for a week. How did you get on?'

'I had an excellent holiday, thank you.'

She looked up from ironing a shirt and grinned. 'You obviously haven't been speaking much English, your accent is more pronounced than usual.'

'I've been staying with some exiled Czechoslovakian friends. We went on a camping holiday in Austria. That's when I grew my moustache… I grew a beard as well, it saved having to shave in cold water.'

She eyed him. 'Hmm, I suppose you do have a faint reverse five o'clock shadow which isn't tanned as much as the rest of your face. But why the crew cut and moustache now?'

He shrugged. 'I felt like a change of image.'

Jill was glad of the change: it made him seem different from the man who'd been her lover. She started to gather up the pile of garments which had been accumulating on the table. 'If you can wait till I've put this lot in the airing cupboard, I'll go and get Steve and Gregor from the workshop and we'll have something to drink.'

‘How did the boys do in their exams? That’s what I really came to find out.’

‘Alan did well and’ll be off to do dentistry. Gregor failed English with ignominy and went back to school last week to resit it and do Higher Technical Drawing and Woodwork.’

‘How did he react to that?’

‘Badly at first, but with Steve’s blessing, Duncan’s going to sign him on as an apprentice next year, so he’s not so bolshie now, thank heavens, particularly as he’s got a different English teacher.’

After Jill went upstairs, Paul sat back in his chair and stared out of the window. He was soon aware of a movement at the edge of his vision. He turned round and saw a paw come out from under the dresser and bat the ball of paper which was still suspended from the drawer knob. He got up and went over, detached the loop and started to jerk the string to encourage the cat to come out of her hiding place.

Ming allowed herself to be enticed into the centre of the floor then suddenly subjected the ball to a concerted attack, lying on her back and boxing it with all four feet, but just as quickly tired of the game. She gave Paul a disdainful look, turned her back on him, stuck a hind leg into the air and proceeded to wash.

The ball had been freed from the hemp which Alan had wound round it. Idly, Paul picked it up and unfolded it. He sat down again and read: “Tea bags; nescaff; cornflakes; bread; sugar; baked beans; sausages; tatties; almond oil” and raised a puzzled eyebrow at the last item. He glanced at the other side. Some pipe music, to judge by the range of the notes. He tried to hum to tune, but it wasn't anything he recognised.

His train of thought was interrupted by a yowl from Ming, who was sitting by the door to the utility room.

Paul smoothed out the paper, all the better to read the music and his finger tips registered a small irregularity. He passed a finger over the surface again. One of the dotted notes–

At the top of her Siamese voice Ming broadcast to the world exactly what she thought of him for ignoring an aristocratic lady who had an urgent duty to perform.

He jumped up with an irritated exclamation and headed towards the back door, unaware that his sleeve had caught the edge of the paper and rotated it through one hundred and eighty degrees. He was halfway across the kitchen when he heard Jill come downstairs and he hovered in indecision between paper and cat.

To his relief, she called to him, 'Be an angel and let Ming out. I'm just going round to the garage. Shan't be long.'

Paul let the cat out and returned to his study of the piece of paper. Yes, one of the dotted notes was definitely standing proud of the surface. He looked at the notes again and they gradually began to arrange themselves into the old German folk tune *O du lieber Augustin.*

Augustin?

O du lieber Gott!

Augustin!

Paul stared at the paper, heart thumping, his stomach tying itself into a tight knot. He took out his wallet and with a shaking hand folded the paper, music innermost, and placed it carefully inside. He went quickly over to the cupboard under the sink and from the waste bucket, scavenged a white paper bag. He tore a bit off and crumpled into an approximation of the other ball and rearranged the hemp round it. He had just hung it up when he heard the others come in.

Steven gave him a friendly greeting. His eyes took in Paul's changed appearance, but he made no comment.

Gregor was less inhibited. 'Jeez-oh! You look like a cross between a blond Che Guevara and a skin-head! What prompted that?'

Jill and Steven tut-tutted at their son's lack of tact, but Paul didn't seem to mind and retaliated in kind. 'I got fed up with the me that I saw in the mirror and decided on a change.' He peered at Gregor and went on innocently, 'I do believe you're trying to grow a moustache as well, or won't Alan let you borrow his razor?'

Gregor reddened: for some weeks his parents had been telling him it was time he started to shave.

Jill suppressed a smile. 'What d'you all want to drink? Tea? Coffee? Hot chocolate?'

Paul got up and said he had to finish working on the new timetable, but eventually gave in to the Lindsays' pressing invitation to stay a bit longer.

'Well, just a small coffee, but I really do have some urgent business to attend to as I'll be away at the end of the week.'

'Aren't you going to Cowal?' asked Jill as she put on the kettle.

'Oh, rather. I wouldn't miss it for anything.' In answer to Steven's surprised look, he went on, 'I'd only just started to work in Dunoon when the annual games took place. I wondered at first what was happening, with the town centre closed to traffic, but found it fascinating, particularly that marvellous bit at the end of the final day when all the competing bands parade down the main street… It must be wonderful to take part in it.'

'Is that when you first got interested in pipe bands?' asked Gregor.

'Yes. I even went to chanter classes for a while, but decided that I'd left it too late in life and was the wrong nationality.'

'Well, I never knew that,' said an incredulous Jill. 'You must have been dead chuffed when the local band asked you to be president of their association.'

'I was indeed – oh, I must remember to phone Ian to tell him I'd like to come back on the coach on Saturday evening.'

'Aren't you going over with them as well?'

'No, I'm going to Glasgow by train on Friday to meet some friends from Dunoon at the theatre and I'm travelling back with them, so I want to be sure of my return transport.'

Paul left almost as soon as he had drunk his coffee, turning down the suggestion that he should wait to see Alan, who would soon be home from band practice. 'No, really, it's time I left, I've got a lot to do. I'll catch up with his news on Saturday. Are you going?'

Jill glanced expectantly at Steven and Gregor, who gave unenthusiastic shrugs. 'It doesn't look like it, does it?'

*

As soon as he got back to the school, Paul went into the deserted office and collected the keys for the biology laboratory. There, he unlocked the cupboard where the microscopes were stored and carried one to his flat. He removed the instrument from its box, put it on his desk and switched on the reading lamp. From his wallet he took the piece of paper which had had such a chequered career and placed it on the viewing platform. He rotated the objectives until the low power one was in line with the eyepiece and adjusted lens distance and the light. His shaking hands slowed up the delicate manoeuvres. He finally located the suspicious dot and when it swam into focus, he let out a long sigh. As he had suspected, instead of being a granular dark grey, the image resolved itself into rows of writing in Cyrillic characters.

Paul increased the magnification and stared until his eyes started to ache. He lit his pipe and sat gazing into space, the final pieces of the puzzle of Steven Lindsay's imprisonment dropping into place. When his pipe was finished, he went back to the microscope and gave the dot another long look. Just to be sure, he subjected the other dotted notes to the same scrutiny, but they were innocent of any hidden message. He took the paper into the kitchen, burnt it in the sink and rinsed the ashes down the plughole. After making a long-distance phone call to an ex-directory number, Paul replaced the equipment and went to bed.

CHAPTER 16

About thirty-six hours later, a news flash was handed to a man in room overlooking Dzerzhinsky Square. After his initial surprise, he smiled to himself – an unpleasant smile – and wrote out a message in a code known only to the chauffeur of their British ambassador. He rang for his secretary and handed the paper to her. 'This is to go out immediately, top priority.'

CHAPTER 17

The following morning, Jill staggered downstairs as usual at seven-thirty, opened the outer front door, picked up the rack of milk bottles and nearly dropped it when a photographic flash went off in her face. Once she had stopped seeing "suns", she recognised one of the reporters who had pestered the family after Steven's return.

'Good morning, Mrs Lindsay,' said the woman. 'My paper would be interested to know if you consider the spy scandal at your brother-in-law's firm has any bearing on your husband's imprisonment?'

Jill gaped at her. 'What on earth are you talking about?'

'But surely you heard it on the news last night?'

'Heard what?'

A newspaper was thrust into her hands and she had taken in the headline of "Another Philby mole unearthed." and something about Tony's firm, when the flash went off again.

Jill grabbed the milk and slammed the door in the reporter's face. She picked up the family's copy of the *Glasgow Herald* from the letterbox and went into the sitting room in search of her glasses. The two papers told much the same story: one of the senior research biochemists in Celtic Biotechnics had been a Communist sympathiser since university days and had confessed to passing on information to Moscow, though it was not yet clear how his activities had been uncovered. The opposition was calling on the government to conduct a full investigation… She read through each article twice before going upstairs to shake Steven awake.

Breakfast was a much livelier meal than usual. Jill and Gregor had been eating together since school started and the other two came down later, considerably later in Alan's case if he was on an evening shift at the Co-op. However, when the noises departed from their usual pattern, he guessed that something unusual had happened and appeared shortly after Steven, still in his pyjamas.

Once they'd all read the papers and watched the news, Jill said to Steven, 'There's something I don't quite understand. If this chap has been passing secrets to the Russians, they'd have known all about Tony's bugs and wouldn't have needed to buy the process with you as a bargaining counter.'

They all looked at each other. 'Suppose,' Alan said slowly, 'suppose this chap only knew about a bit of Uncle Tony's research, knew roughly what was going on, but not the details, or couldn't get hold of a sample of the bugs. Suppose he tipped off the Russians that something important was in the pipeline and they snatched Dad as a pawn when they had the opportunity and kept him on ice till he could be of use to them. That would make sense.'

Steven asked Jill, 'When did Tony start on this line of research?'

'I've no idea, but it's certainly been on the go for some time.'

'Phone him and find out.'

'Remind me to do it this evening when the cheap rates come in.'

'Damn the cheap rates! Do it now. I want to know.'

She came back a few minutes later. 'The line's engaged.'

'Well, keep trying, then.'

'Keep trying yourself! It's time I was off to work.'

It was mid-morning before Steven got through to his harassed sister-in-law. 'Who? Oh, Steven. That makes a change from the press… You too? It's been simply awful since the news broke… Yes, we know him. I can't believe it. Tony's absolutely shattered, they were great buddies when we lived in Wales… I know it's not exactly state secrets he's been passing, but it leaves a nasty taste… I don't know if he's been arrested… There's no need to shout… How long's the cow-pat research been going on? Let me see, I think it started about the time of Victoria's eighth birthday and she's now fourteen… Oh yes, before you were imprisoned… Oh Steve! You don't think… But how perfectly frightful! Perhaps traitor's not too strong a description after all… You want a word with Tony? I'll get him to phone you this evening… I hope you're right about it being a nine-day wonder… Well, an assassinated president or divorced Royal would certainly take the heat off us lesser mortals. Bye.'

Jill had a trying morning at the library, the borrowers having but one topic of conversation: 'Is that firm wi' the spy no' something to do with your family, Mrs Lindsay?', and there was no respite when she got home.

Steven was beside himself with fury. 'It's all the fault of that filthy traitor that we both went through five years of hell. He robbed us of our family home and made me a stranger to my sons… I'd like to use his guts for garters! No, that's too good for him. Something long and lingering involving boiling oil – or better still, boiling cow shit! That'd teach him to pass information to the Russians.'

She eventually gave up trying to calm him and told him to go and work off his feelings on the hedge, it was time it was trimmed. Which job he did with more force than finesse: for all that McGinty steered an erratic course on occasions, at least he did leave the top of the hedge level.

Even more did Jill regret her suggestion about the hedge when Gregor came storming into the kitchen, brandishing a saw, while she was dishing up the evening meal. 'Who the hell's been mucking about with my tools?'

'What's the matter now?'

‘Some idiot’s ruined this saw! It’s as blunt as butter and the teeth are all out of alignment.’

She sighed. ‘You’d better blame it on me. I asked Dad to cut the hedge and perhaps he needed a saw for–’

‘Surely to God he knows to use secateurs or a pruning saw for the thicker bits and not a tenon saw?’

‘Obviously not. But please don’t say anything about it. He’s been frothing at the mouth all day about this biotechnical mole.’

Gregor managed a chuckle at the expression.

‘Is it so special? Can’t it be mended?’

‘It’s the one Grandpa gave me a couple of years ago.’ He scrutinised the tool. ‘It’ll probably be OK if I can get Duncan to sharpen and reset the teeth.’

‘Well if it can’t be restored to its former glory, let me know and I’ll buy you a new one. Now go and tell the others that dinner’s ready – and don’t forget to wash your hands.’

*

Alan was up very early on Saturday morning, which meant the rest of the household was also thoroughly wakened then, with little chance of getting back to sleep after his usual noisy departure to catch the band’s coach, which was due to leave the village hall at seven-thirty.

The journey over to Dunoon, via Stirling, Loch Lomond and Rest and be Thankful took nearly four hours and the band liked to have at least two hours in hand before arriving and competing, which this year was to be around one forty-five.

On arriving in Dunoon, the coach would drop them off at the sea front in the centre of town and after a preliminary tune-up in a small park, they would march up through the main shopping street to the sports stadium where the games were held, a march which was uphill a lot of the way. When Alan had heard the others talking about "going up the hill" at Cowal, he had gone there for the first time expecting to have to scale a mountainside while blowing his pipes, but was relieved to find a much less fearsome gradient. He was greatly looking forward to the outing, which for many pipers, was reckoned to be *the* band competition above all others, even out-ranking the world championships.

*

Jill bent over Steven and kissed his nose. 'As I'm unlikely to get back to sleep now, I might as well get up.'

He pulled her down on top of him. 'What's the hurry? You're not working today.'

'No, but I've got lots to catch up with and in any case, I'm hungry.'

'Then a bit more exercise, my love, will sharpen your appetite…'

Steven and Gregor eventually arrived downstairs at the same time. 'Your porridge is on the table,' said Jill. 'I'll be with you when I've made the toast. I can't wait for Andy to get back from holiday and mend the toaster, the grill isn't nearly so–'

'Eeeyah! D'ye no' put any salt in this?' said a disgusted Gregor. 'Yuk!'

‘Sorry. Sprinkle some on and stir it round. Steve! Whatever’s the matter? You look as though you’ve seen a whole regiment of ghosts.’

Steven was staring wide-eyed at nothing and the colour had drained from his face. He got up slowly and went out of the room like a sleep walker. There was a few seconds silence, followed by him pounding upstairs, swearing furiously.

Jill and Gregor stared at each other in utter bewilderment and after a few moments, she switched off the grill and followed her husband to find out what was wrong.

*

Gregor’s exclamation of disgust had registered in Steven’s brain as *yad*, the Russian word for poison.

‘Poison! That man’s absolute poison!’ spat a fellow prisoner as they were lined up in the yard at the Butyrka transit prison in Moscow.

Steven and Fyodor looked over at the big, blond man who had come to one of the doorways to talk to a guard. ‘Doesn’t look too bad a chap,’ said Fyodor. ‘Reminds me of one of my cousins.’

The other prisoner spat again. ‘That’s why he’s so dangerous. They give you a dose of the bully boys and then turn you over to him. Sits and smiles at you, puffing his pipe and before you know where you are, you’ve sobbed out your life history on his shoulder.’

‘What’s he called?’

‘Rodyon Nesterenko. He’s KGB and like I said, pure poison. If you ever come up against him, button your trap.’

Steven could barely follow this conversation, but the name, coupled with "KGB" and the prisoner's expression, registered with him, as did the odd gesture when the man took a pipe out of his pocket, lit it and blew out the match with a long, slow exhalation. His gaze panned over the prisoners like a camera taking a school photo and Steven edged behind Fyodor's bulk. Having looked his fill, the KGB officer flicked the spent match at the men ranged in front of him and left them to contemplate a future which offered not even the comfort of an occasional smoke.

*

When Steven was able to review dispassionately the events of that extraordinary day, he had no recollection of covering the ground between kitchen and bedroom. One minute he was peacefully eating his breakfast and the next, he was upstairs, angrier than he'd ever been in his life, searching for the sponge bag which he had used in hospital.

'Whatever's the matter? What are you looking for?' said Jill from the doorway.

'Where's my sponge bag?' he shouted at her. 'Where the hell have you hidden the damn thing?'

She walked over to the wardrobe, felt around at the bottom, then took out the bag and handed it to him. 'Here you are, but what's all the fuss about. What's the matter with you?'

He snatched it from her. 'I'll get him for this, the filthy traitor! He'll swing for this! They still hang 'em for treason, don't they?'

‘What on earth are you talking about? Telling tales about cow pats is hardly a hanging matter.’

‘I’m not talking about that stupid Welshman.’ In his rage Steven started to stutter. ‘I m-mean Mr. P-Paul b-bloody Holland, alias Rodyon Nesterenko, m-member of the KGB.’

‘You’re raving!’

Steven grabbed hold of his wife and dug his fingers into her shoulders. ‘No I’m not! You know I’ve said he looked vaguely familiar? Well I’ve just remembered where I saw him. It was in the Butyrka and he was pointed out to me as a member of the KGB and a thoroughly nasty bit of work. And the goddam bastard hasn’t even bothered to change his initials.’

Jill freed herself from his painful grasp and flopped down onto the unmade bed, utterly aghast. ‘But RN isn’t the same as PH.’

‘It is, in the Cyrillic alphabet.’ Steven rummaged in the pockets of the sponge bag and found the card which the MI6 agent had given him. He waved it at her. ‘I’m sure they’ll be most interested to know about dear Mr Holland.’ He took a couple of steps to the door, turned round and said bitterly, ‘I spend five years in Soviet labour camps and come home to find the local, friendly KGB agent has been bringing up my sons and bedding my wife.’

Jill opened her mouth, but any denial she was about to make was negated by the flush which swept over her face and neck.

'He was, wasn't he? And don't try and deny it, I've overheard village gossip and seen the way he looks at you.' He sneered. 'You must have been devastated when I turned up out of the blue, but no doubt you managed to go on meeting whenever I was in Dunfermline.'

She forced herself to meet his furious gaze. 'Alright then, we were lovers. But it finished the moment you came home and I'll swear to that on anything you like.' On the principle that attack was the best method of defence, she got up and advanced on Steven. 'You can say what you like about Paul, but if it hadn't been for him, you wouldn't have had a family home to come back to, large or small. I'd have slit my throat long ago. He propped me up when I had my nervous breakdown – he even made me be sick when he thought I'd taken an overdose of sleeping pills.'

'I'll bet he enjoyed doing that,' jeered Steven. 'Just the sort of job the KGB would relish.'

Jill raised her hand to slap his face, but he grabbed her arm before the blow landed. By this time, her fury was on a par with her husband's. 'Since we're on the subject of marital fidelity, what about your precious little ballerina?' she yelled at him. 'I'll bet you didn't spend your time together discussing the finer points of *Swan Lake*!'

Steven gave her a shove which sent her sprawling back onto the bed. Again, he headed for the door, but what stopped him this time was the urge to hurt – anything, anyone – to make them pay for what he'd been through. He paused and said casually over his shoulder, 'As it appears to be confession time, you might as well know that Kaiya died of a haemorrhage while miscarrying a daughter…our daughter,' and he marched off downstairs to use the phone.

Jill felt as though she'd been kicked in the guts. She curled up into a tight ball, hugging her hysterectomy scar and burst into tears. Once she calmed down, she lay staring at the ceiling, shivering occasionally, until there was a quiet knock on the door.

Gregor said in a subdued voice, 'Are you alright? D'you want any breakfast?'

She pulled herself together. 'I'll be down shortly. Make me a pot of tea, please.'

When she arrived back in the kitchen, having washed her face, Steven was hidden behind the paper and Gregor was doing the dishes. He looked at his mother. 'I – I couldn't help overhearing part of Dad's phone call…something about Paul being a spy…' His voice tailed off.

Jill slumped into a chair, poured her tea and sugared it liberally. After a couple of mouthfuls said, 'I think he's right.'

Steven emerged from his paper. 'Of course I'm right.'

'But why, Mum?'

'Straws in the wind, but they all seem to add up to something pretty damning. First of all, there are the obvious things. He's always lived near a naval base since he came to this country and he seems to know a lot about ships. He's also got a powerful radio transmitter–'

‘Yes, but that doesn’t make him a spy. Lots of radio hams must live near naval bases.’

‘Let me continue. He was always most insistent that Dad would come home sooner or later and when he did arrive, Paul was the first person outside this household to know about it.’

‘Optimism and the village grapevine,’ defended Gregor.

‘Maybe. But how do you explain away this next bit of evidence? I’ve never told anyone before, but at the jumble sale the weekend after Dad got back, I briefly saw him going through the pockets of the suit that Dad had donated.’

‘Yes,’ said Steven. ‘And both he and the MI6 men asked if I’d been given anything to do or to bring home as a condition of my release. He must have been looking for something… I wonder if I unwittingly brought it back with me? And don’t you remember, he was present when I unpacked my case and he asked for it when I was about to throw it out.’

Still clinging to hope, Gregor said, ‘But there could be another reason for that.’

Jill shook her head at him. ‘It’s no use love, Dad saw him when he was in prison in Moscow and Paul was pointed out as a member of the KGB.’

‘I don’t believe it. I just can’t believe it. He’s such a nice chap.’

‘Huh!’ Steven snorted. ‘That’s what your uncle said about his colleague.’

Gregor looked at his father. ‘What’ll happen to Paul?’

'I hope he'll be arrested very shortly.'

'Is that what you were told on the phone?'

'Not exactly. I couldn't speak to either of the men who questioned me, but I was told that the matter would be dealt with promptly.'

Gregor screwed up the dish cloth into a tight ball and slammed it into the sink, showering water in all directions. He elbowed aside Steven's paper, scooped up an unprotesting Ming from one of the chairs and strode out of the room with her cradled in his arms.

Jill stood staring after him, wishing she had someone or something to turn to for a bit of comfort. Instead, she went over to the grill, extracted a piece of cold toast, scraped off the burnt bits and spread it with butter and marmalade, hoping some food would make her feel better, which it did not. After another cup of tea she got up and said politely to Steven, 'Would you like anything else, or have you finished?' She interpreted the grunt to mean that he had, so she cleared the table, mopped up Gregor's mess and finished doing the dishes.

After folding the cloth neatly and placing it on the draining board, she went over to the table. Steven did not look up. The silence lengthened. Jill took a deep breath and let it out slowly. She said flatly, 'We've both done and said things to hurt each other and although two wrongs don't make a right, life's got to go on. Please will you dry and put away the dishes as I've got jobs to do round the house... And will you also go and see if your son's alright, he too has had a very nasty shock this morning.'

Which was putting it mildly.

As Jill did her chores, she kept telling herself that it wasn't true, that it was all a ghastly mistake, that there would be a rational explanation for it all, but in her heart of hearts she acknowledged that it really was true. Paul had indeed been working for the Russians and they had all been thoroughly fooled. After she cleaned the bathroom she went into the garden and found Steven tidying up the hedge cuttings. 'Where's Gregor?'

'In the workshop.'

'How is he?'

'Not saying very much.'

Gregor was sitting on an upturned bucket, axe in hand, demolishing the old chaise longue with a vicious expression on his face.

'I shan't be lighting the fire for a few weeks yet.'

'I feel like chopping sticks.'

'Oh. Whose head are you chopping off?' That produced a faint smile. She patted him on the shoulder. 'Come and give me a hand with making some sandwiches. I could do with a bit of company.'

'OK then.' He got up, scooped the sticks into the bucket and put away his axe. 'And if they're for my lunches, can I have some raspberry jam ones?'

They had just finished making the sandwiches and were enjoying the crusts, thickly spread with the newly-made jam, when a car drew up outside. A few seconds later the doorbell rang and when Jill answered it, she recognised one of the men who had interviewed

Steven. She invited him in with a heavy heart and called her husband.

Their visitor introduced himself as John Brooks. 'I'm sorry to bother you, but can you tell me where I can find Paul Holland. I need to get hold of him urgently. I've been up to the college and couldn't understand half of what the janitor said, something about a cowl, which didn't make sense. I know he's friendly with you and I wonder if you could help?'

Jill's heart sank further. 'How did you get here so quickly? Did you–'

'I'll tell you where that filthy traitor is,' growled Steven as he came in. 'He's at the Cowal Games, over at Dunoon. I'll be delighted to help you to arrest him and I hope they hang him.'

To their amazement, Brooks burst out laughing. 'That's the last thing I want to happen to Paul.' He sobered down. 'But it's the least the Soviets will do if I don't get to him quickly.'

The three Lindsays gaped at him and started to speak at the same time.

'Then he's not a–'

'You did get my phone message?'

'Why are the Russians–?'

'I don't understand.'

Brooks pulled out a chair and gestured to Jill. 'Sit down a minute and I'll try and explain briefly. It's quite true that Pavel Holandov, who you know as Paul Holland, was recruited by the KGB as Rodyon Nesterenko shortly after his wife's death and eventually sent over here. However, he didn't do it willingly, they blackmailed him – threats against his family – and we were on to him almost as soon as he arrived. He needed no persuasion to work as a double agent and he's been very useful. We arranged for him to get jobs in suitable places, not that it was difficult as his teaching qualifications are excellent and we've been using him to feed back misinformation.'

Steven looked stunned, but Jill and Gregor exchanged looks of joy and relief. 'Why d'you need to get hold of him so urgently?' said Gregor.

'On two counts. Firstly, we got word last night that his sister and her family have arrived safely in Austria. He's been trying to get them out for years and in fact went back into Czechoslovakia last month to set up their escape route.'

'So that's why he changed his appearance,' commented Jill.

'But, much more important than that, his cover's just been blown. The Soviets now know that he's working for us and we have to get him away before they catch up with him. We were going to do this anyhow because of his sister, but it's suddenly become much more urgent.'

'How did they find out?' asked Gregor.

'The information which exposed your uncle's colleague came from Paul.'

Steven suddenly found his voice. 'From Paul? Good God!' He sat shaking his head in disbelief.

'From Paul. Somehow, he got hold of a message sent out by one of our agents in Moscow.' Brooks looked at Steven. 'I suspect that it may have been planted on you without your realising it, though I don't understand the time lapse.'

'My accident at the airport,' said Steven. 'I tripped over a suitcase. The owner was most apologetic and helped me up again. He could have put something in my pocket.'

Brooks nodded. 'It sounds a possibility.'

'So that's why Paul was going through your suit.' Jill told Brooks what she'd seen at the jumble sale.

'Whatever its route to him, Paul passed on the information about the mole on Monday evening and as you know, it was acted on immediately. But what has really put the cat among the pigeons is that last night we learnt that our agent had been arrested back in the spring, which means Paul's information must have come from the KGB. They evidently had had their suspicions about him and decided to use Dr Lindsay as a means of testing his loyalties.'

'In other words, I was used to kill two birds with one stone,' said Steven bitterly. 'I've been pushed around like a pawn in someone else's game.'

'But the whole thing seems very hit-or-miss,' commented Gregor. 'The KGB obviously knew that Paul lived near us, but there was no guarantee he'd find the message.'

'I agree,' said Brooks. 'I suspect the "sting" was thrown together on the spur of the moment when the KGB learnt about the order for your father's release, which would have come from a different government department. They took a gamble that they might just succeed – and they have. They knew that if the Welshman was exposed, the information could only have come from Paul. "Taffy" had served their purpose and they were prepared to sacrifice him to–'

'Oh my God!' Jill clapped her hands to her mouth and stared at the others in wide-eyed horror. 'They may have got Paul already!'

Brooks gave her a worried look. 'Why should that be?'

'There'll be Russians at Cowal. Don't you remember? They've got a team of athletes competing in the heavyweight events. They're sure to know about his connection with the band and'll be watching out for him there.'

Brooks frowned. 'And what exactly is this Cowal thing?'

She explained.

'And how far away is it?'

'The other side of Scotland, across the Firth of Clyde and for a lot of the way it's not a road you can hurry on.'

'Can you get there more quickly by ferry?'

'Yes, but they'll all be booked solid this weekend.'

He beat a tattoo on the table with his fingers. 'From what you've told me, it's unlikely anything'll happen to Paul until the end of the afternoon, or at least until your band has competed. The opposition won't want to make any unnecessary fuss. They'll try and persuade him to go quietly before they use force. After all, he doesn't know they've rumbled him, or about his sister.'

‘Yes, but the band’s due on at about one forty-five,’ said Gregor.

Brooks looked at his watch and pondered for a few seconds. ‘There may be just enough time if I do some string-pulling. May I use your phone?’

As soon as he’d gone into the sitting room with it, shutting both doors behind him, Gregor punched the air elatedly. ‘There! What did I say? Paul’s one of the goodies after all!’

Jill looked from happy son to a husband who had just had his cup of triumph dashed from his lips. She touched his arm briefly. ‘I don’t know how you feel, but I’m all at sixes and sevens. I could do with a stiff whisky, even though the sun isn’t anything like over the proverbial yardarm.’

He gave a brief nod.

‘Don’t I deserve one too?’ said Gregor, after Jill poured the drinks.

Steven passed over his glass.

Gregor sampled the contents. ‘Not bad at all.’

Jill removed the drink from his hand and returned it to Steven. ‘The odd glass of watered wine’s OK, but you’re still too young for that.’

When Brooks returned, he declined Jill’s offer of whisky. ‘No thanks, I must keep a clear head. If you’ve any ground coffee, as against the instant stuff, I’d appreciate it, along with some of those sandwiches. I’ve already been on the go for hours and it looks like there’s lots more to come.’

‘Didn’t you get my phone message?’ said Steven as Brooks had his snack. He went on to tell him about his recollection that morning of Paul’s brief appearance in the yard at the Butyrka prison.

‘’Fraid not. You probably saw him when he went back with a tourist visa for a briefing prior to starting his present job. Interesting but irrelevant.’

Steven lapsed into sulky silence.

As soon as he’d finished his coffee, Brooks got up. ‘Thanks very much and I must be off now. Rosyth dockyard has a supply helicopter leaving shortly for the base at Holy Loch and they’re holding it for me.’

‘Wow!’ Gregor jumped up. ‘You’re flying over to Dunoon? Can I come too? I’ve never been in a whirlybird.’

Jill started to remonstrate, but Brooks stopped her. ‘Actually, that’s not a bad idea. In fact, if you could all come, it’d be a help. From what you say, even to locate Paul is going to be a problem, let alone get him out of trouble, so it’ll be useful to have some assistants with local knowledge.’

CHAPTER 18

After a drive to Rosyth which barely observed the speed limits, followed by a noisy and uncomfortable flight across Scotland, they landed in a car park at Sandbank on the Holy Loch, where a police car was waiting for them. The pilot and driver explained to an irritated Brooks that this arrangement was the best that could be produced at such short notice.

Brooks was even less pleased when the driver said apologetically that he had been drafted over for the day from Gourock on the other side of the Firth of Clyde and please would they direct him. His three adult passengers looked at each other in consternation, but Gregor said, 'I know a quick way to get to one of the back entrances of the stadium. Go along the shore road to Hunter's Quay on the outskirts of Dunoon and I'll direct you from there.'

'How on earth d'you know that?' asked Jill.

'You remember how I got bored last year and wandered off? I went out of this gate and it wasn't very far down to the sea front where the smaller ferry comes in. After we've passed the terminal look out for a church on the hillside with a white belfry.'

Gregor's instructions soon brought them to their destination at the north-east gate. Brooks paid their entrance fees and they walked across a stretch of grass to a row of caravans, tents and trailers which were parked along the skyline.

As they made their way between them, Brooks stopped in his tracks. 'Christ almighty!' he exclaimed in dismay. 'Jesus wept!'

Dunoon Sports Stadium, host to the Cowal Highland Gathering, lay in a natural amphitheatre and they were standing at the top, looking down the hillside to the arena and grandstand beyond. The whole area was already a seething mass of people listening to and watching the piping and athletic events which were in progress. 'How the hell will we ever find Paul in this lot?'

'Well, we needn't bother to look at anyone in band uniform,' said Gregor. 'C'mon, let's get down to the main gate by the grandstand, then we can get out to the coaches. It'll be easier if we start looking there, some of the lads may have seen him.'

'Yes, but which coach?' said Brooks, looking at the rows parked on the flat ground behind and slightly below the stadium.

'It's not too difficult,' said Jill as they started off down the hillside. 'All the bands are given placards saying who they are, for the morning parade and the final march-past. They usually display them in or in front of the coaches.'

'And just how many bands are there?'

She looked at the programme which she had bought on the way in and did a quick tot-up. 'About a hundred and fifty.'

'Ye gods! And it sounds like it, too.' Above the noise of the crowd and the bands competing in the stadium, there was a background cacophony of numerous pipers tuning up. 'What are your lot wearing?'

'Full dress.' She explained to Brooks what it meant.

'So we're looking for people wearing red tartan and things on their heads which cover half their faces. That describes a lot of them.'

By the time they neared the main gate, Brooks looked thoroughly bemused. They were delayed when two exiting bands met one incoming one and in the ensuing scrum, he narrowly missed being hit on the head by a bass drum which was being held up out of harm's way.

Jill gave him a sympathetic smile. 'You ain't seen nuffink yet! Once the prize-giving's over, it's a case of: "By the right, quick – charge!" and all the bands converge on this exit to be the first off down the road. That was just a Sunday stroll by comparison.' As they reached the exit, she gave an exclamation of annoyance. 'Blast! I've just remembered, you can't use your pass-out after one o'clock.'

Officialdom overheard her, looked at its watch and remarked that she was quite right, dearie.

Brooks got out a card and waved it at the man, who was not impressed and directed him to the secretary's office in a cabin at the far end of the grandstand. Brooks departed, fuming, but his credentials evidently carried more weight with the secretary of the games than with a member of the Corps of Commissionaires as he came back with red and white badges which conferred official status. 'There, now we don't have to pay every time we come into the stadium.'

They hurried out into the park and were debating their next course of action when Steven nudged Jill. 'Look, isn't that the postie's wife over there? She'll be able to tell us where the coach is.'

Jill yoo-hooed at Elspeth who changed course towards them. 'Why hello there. I didnae know ye were coming today.'

'Last minute decision. Can you tell us where the coach is?'

'Oh aye, about half way down that row,' she pointed. 'They'll be on soon.'

'Thanks.'

The four of them set off as briskly as the crowd would permit and soon found the band, formed up in a circle in front of the coach, practicing their competition set. Ian McLellan was standing among a group of wives and fans and Jill beckoned him into the space between the coaches, where it wasn't quite so noisy. Even so, she had to shout at him. 'Have you seen Paul anywhere? This is Mr Brooks who needs to contact him urgently.'

'He was here about half an hour ago. Had a friend in tow. Said that they'd met unexpectedly and that they were going off for a few days together. In fact, he collected the case he'd left in the coach earlier on.'

'Any idea where he is now?'

'He said that his pal had got seats in the grandstand and that they'd be watching from there.' Ian went on in a reproachful tone. 'Last year he cheered on the lads at the ringside with the rest of our supporters and even bought a round of drinks.'

Brooks said thoughtfully, 'I'd like to get a closer look at this friend of his.' He asked Ian, 'Have you any official status with the band?'

'Why yes, I'm the secretary.'

'Then would it look odd if you went into the grandstand and said to Paul that the band would be a bit peeved if he didn't cheer them from the touch-line, so to speak?'

Ian looked slightly taken aback. 'I suppose not.'

'Then I'd be grateful if you could do that – and tell his friend that he'll be very welcome to come along too. I'll explain later what it's all about.'

After Ian had left on his errand, Brooks said to the Lindsays, 'For the time being I want to keep quiet as to why we're really here. Paul may not be in any danger yet, in which case, the less known about him, the better.'

Duncan had just told the band to stand down for a few minutes and a delighted Alan joined his family. 'I thought you said you weren't coming. What made you change your mind?'

'We were offered an unexpected lift,' said Jill. 'Er, it was Dad's idea to make use of it as you may not be with the band after you start your studies and he's never seen you in action with them. We've brought Mr Brooks along as well, he's a friend of Paul's.'

Alan's face fell. 'Aw hell! It'd never occurred to me that I'd have to leave the band when I start dentistry.'

Duncan joined the group in time to hear Alan's remark. 'Cheer up, lad. If you've a long summer holiday and a job locally, then ye can come out wi' us for the fêtes and fundraising events, providing ye do your homework with the tunes.'

Alan brightened up at this. 'Oh thanks – and of course there's the College of Piping in Glasgow, I'll be able to get some tuition there.'

'Aye lad, but it's time I gave the drones their final tuning. Excuse us, folks.'

'What now?' said Jill to Brooks as the pipers departed.

'I need to try and check on Paul's friend, providing the secretary winkles them out.'

'D'you want us with you?'

'Ye-es, I think that might be a help, but I don't want the mystery man to see you in my company, at least not until I've had a look at him… In fact, it'll be better if he doesn't see you three either, I may need your assistance at some stage. We'll go and distribute ourselves among those stalls at the back of the grandstand. They've got to go past there to get round to the arena and we can see without being noticed ourselves.'

As they started to walk back to the stadium, Steven tugged at Jill. 'I've had enough. I'm fed up with this to-ing and fro-ing, fighting my way through crowds. I'll wait in the coach till it's all sorted out.'

'Don't be so bloody selfish.' She glared at him. 'I know you don't like Paul and even less so after this morning, but haven't you the wit to see that whatever happens today, he'll be going out of our lives for ever? If Brooks gets him away, he'll probably be given a new identity in another country. And however much you dislike him, surely you don't want him to go though what you suffered and probably much worse?'

Steven shrugged and stared at his feet.

'Come on, then.' She grabbed his arm and pulled him after her, dodging through the crowd and round practicing bands. They caught up with Brooks and Gregor at the beer tent, which was just inside the main gate.

Brooks beckoned them over. 'Hurry up! I don't want to bump into them.' He pushed his way through the crowd and said anxiously, 'I hope we aren't too late – No! There they are. I can see Paul coming out of that far entrance. Now don't let them see you.'

Gregor joined the queue for an ice cream van; Steven started to leaf through a book of pipe music; Jill examined a tee-shirt emblazoned with the Loch Ness Monster and Brooks tried on a lurid tartan flat cap and looked at his reflection – and those of passers by – in a mirror hanging outside the stall.

After Paul, Ian and the other man had disappeared into the crowd, the Lindsays converged on Brooks. 'Well?'

'That was the Russian ambassador's new chauffeur and I'll stake my pension he's KGB.'

'What now?' asked Steven in resignation.

'We'll have to think of some means of separating them and then getting Paul away.' Brooks rubbed his forehead wearily. 'I wish to God someone would tell those bloody bagpipes to shut up for a few minutes, then perhaps I could think straight.'

'If the "friend" is KGB,' said Steven, 'He probably came here originally to keep an eye on the athletes to see that they don't defect and that means that he won't be leaving till the end of the games. That gives us a bit of breathing space.'

Jill looked at her watch. 'The band'll be on soon. Let's go and listen to them and perhaps we'll think of something.'

'Alright then, but please keep away from Paul's group, I don't want to be seen by the chauffeur.'

As they pushed their way through the crowds, Steven muttered to Jill, 'I don't know what he's fussing about. He's so nondescript, you wouldn't recognise him five minutes after you'd met him.'

The four of them managed to worm themselves into a position by the rails at the end of the arena where the grade three competitions were taking place. They had been there for a few minutes when Brooks moved aside to make room for a scrawny young woman accompanied by two pre-school children.

'Ta, mister.' The younger child started to grizzle. 'This izna ra place furra sma' wean, but ma man wantit tae come, he's awfae keen oan thae heavy events.' She took a dummy out of her bag, wiped it on a grubby handkerchief, stuck it into the child's mouth and picked him up. 'Wheesht noo, pe'.'

Brooks gave her a look of blank incomprehension.

There was a crackle from a nearby loudspeaker. 'Your attention please. Event number seventy-six on page seventy of your programme has been postponed till half past four. Event number seventy-six will now start at half past four. Thank you.'

The young woman asked Brooks, 'Wissat yin, mister?'

'Er… I beg your pardon?'

Jill consulted her programme. 'That's *Tossing the Caber* in the open section. The one where the Russians are competing.'

A few minutes later, the older child whined she wanted the toilet.

Her mother again appealed to Brooks, but Jill opened her programme at the centre pages, which gave a plan of the stadium and indicated the nearest toilet.

'What was all that about?' said Brooks after the family left. 'I used to think that TV comedian was exaggerating with his *Parliamo Glasgow*, but not any longer. It really is a foreign language.'

For the first time since breakfast, Steven laughed. 'It helps if you're bilingual.'

There was another crackle from the loudspeaker. 'The next band to compete in the grade three championship is number thirty-four in your programme: Strathtullum.'

'Now keep all your fingers and toes crossed for them,' said Jill. She explained to Brooks, 'They did well at the World Championships when they were last out, came seventh, but it would be super if they could do a wee bit better and be in among the prizes.'

'Indeed,' was the indifferent reply.

Jill listened to the band intently as they marched into position and started to play. She suddenly remembered Gregor's remark about not looking at anyone in band uniform… If Paul gave his watchdog the slip, would the Russians bother to scrutinise anyone dressed as a piper? She craned her neck to see the musicians. Sandy was approximately Paul's build. Could he and the rest of the band be persuaded to co-operate? And if they did, how to get Paul into the uniform? Some sort of distraction would be needed for a few minutes. She opened her programme at page seventy and studied the list of competitors. Two Russians were going to toss the caber, one was drawn second and his compatriot was six places further down. She turned to the map of the grounds… A plan was beginning to take shape…

As soon as the band had finished, Jill said to her applauding companions, 'Come on, let's get out of here, I've an idea of sorts.' She halted as soon as they were out of the stadium and explained what she had in mind. 'It's pretty hare-brained and will only work if the band helps and even then there are a lot of ifs and buts, but I can't think of anything better. Can you?'

They looked at Brooks. He shook his head. 'With all that row going on, I'm incapable of rational thought.'

'I'm pretty sure they'll co-operate,' Gregor said. 'Paul's popular with them and not just because he buys the occasional round of drinks. And in any case, Big Sandy's rarely in a fit state to take part in the final parade. Here they come now.'

He went over to the emerging bandsmen and came back with Duncan and Alan, who had already taken off their feather bonnets and were unbuttoning their tunics.

'How did that sound?' asked Alan.

'Not bad at all,' said Jill. 'I didn't hear any obvious mistakes. Now don't go away, Mr Brooks wants a word with you.'

'Not too long a word, I hope. My tongue's hanging out and Paul's invited us to the beer tent.'

'Excellent,' said Brooks and went on to tell the other two what was afoot and how Jill suggested they deal with it.

Before he had finished, Duncan interrupted. 'Ye can count on us, sir. We'll do all we can to help Paul. Get him changed and we won't give the Russians a chance to get near him.'

'Where's the best place for him to meet up with you?'

Duncan thought for a moment and pointed to the back right hand side of the stadium. 'Ye see yon clump of bushes up there? Tell him to wait among them. For the march-past, the bands enter at the main gate, walk up the hillside, form up near the bushes then march down through the crowd to the track round the arena. I'll try and bring us in so that after the prize-giving we'll be positioned near the gate for a quick get-away. That do ye OK?'

'Yes indeed,' said Brooks gratefully. 'That sounds fine, and you'll get the big chap's uniform?'

'Aye.' Duncan was struck by a sudden thought. 'But he'll need something to wear instead.'

'Oh Lord! We hadn't thought of that.'

'If you tell me what size he is, I could go down into Dunoon and get him some clothes,' said Jill. 'Or could we give his wife the money for it?'

'Jeanie's no' here. She's off to Edinburgh to the Festival, but we can find out from Sandy himself.'

'OK then. We'll all meet back at the coach in about half an hour and if you haven't been able to pass the message on to Paul, we'll have to think of some other way of getting it to him. This is what I want you to tell him…' Once Alan and Duncan had left them to shed as much as possible of their uniforms before going for a drink, Brooks said to the other three, 'I think we can relax for a little while. Can I offer you something to eat, even if it's only fish and chips?'

*

When Alan joined the rest of the band in the beer tent, Paul was taking orders. 'Will lager be acceptable all round, or would anyone like something different?'

There was a general chorus of assent, though Sheila and another young drummer asked for Cokes.

'Now, if you want to try and get seats, I hope I won't be too long. By the way, this is Yuri, we first met years ago at a student camp in Yugoslavia.'

Alan joined Paul in the queue and lowered his voice as much as the general hubbub would permit, 'I've got news for you, both good and bad, but try and look as though it's all good.'

Paul turned round and nodded at him.

'John Brooks is here. He came over from Rosyth by helicopter and brought Mum, Dad and Gregor with him. He says that your sister and her family have arrived safely in Austria.'

Paul inhaled sharply and briefly shut his eyes. 'Go on. I take it that was the good news?'

'Yes. The bad news is that the message from agent "Augustin" was a KGB plant. They now realise that you're working for the British, but we've got a plan to get you out of here with the band. You must be near the left hand Portaloo on the hillside opposite the grandstand at half past four when the caber tossing starts. Try and time your entry to just before the run-up of the first Russian competitor, who's going second. And once inside, go into one of the cubicles, don't use a urinal. Got that?'

Paul gave a bellow of laughter and clapped him on the shoulder as though he'd just been told a dirty joke, then turned and waved at the waiting group. 'Shan't be long, lads.' He turned back to Alan, grinned at him and said in an undertone, 'I've got it, and praise be to heaven about Margit, that's marvellous.' They were now at the head of the queue and he turned round again and made counting motions.

When they got back to the group Koshachin, alias "Yuri", gave Alan a toothy smile of thanks for his drink, displaying the poor standard of Soviet dentistry.

*

It was nearly two-thirty by the time the band members straggled back to the coach. The Lindsays and Brooks were waiting for them and heaved sighs of relief when Alan said that he had successfully passed on the message to Paul. Brooks asked the musicians to get onto the coach for a few minutes, where he explained briefly that Paul was in danger from the Russians and how he proposed to get him away.

'But why can't he just walk out of the gate?' enquired Joan. 'Why all this pantomime?'

'First of all, the "friend" with him is almost certainly a KGB watchdog,' explained Brooks. 'They've also got men watching the exits because of their athletes, I've recognised some of the embassy staff. They're not supposed to be armed, but I'm not risking any shooting incidents in a crowd like this.'

'Well, tell him to hop over the fence,' suggested Joan.

Jill gave her a withering look. 'It has evidently escaped your notice that the fence round this stadium is constructed to discourage people from hopping over, in either direction.'

'Has anyone got a tool box?' continued Brooks. 'We just want it as a prop, what's in it doesn't matter.'

'You could try Johnny,' said Ron. 'He and Elspeth came by car as we left before he finished his round and he usually has one in the boot.'

'Thanks. Now, if Sandy could tell us his measurements, we'll get his replacement clothing.'

There was silence, followed by consternation.

'Where is he?'

'He was following us.'

'Aye, he did leave the tent wi' the rest of us.'

Elspeth was sitting at the back of the coach, chatting to the other wives. She called to Brooks, 'You can borrow the tool box – and if you're looking for Sandy, I saw him heading into town.'

Neil groaned. 'Ye'd better send out search parties and try all the boozers for miles around, that's where he'll be.'

'Isn't there anyone else who could lend Paul his uniform?' asked Brooks.

They all looked at each other.

'I'm nearly as tall as him,' volunteered Bob, 'but nothing like as broad. My kilt might just fit, but never my tunic.'

'And ma tunic'll go round him, but it'll be too short,' added Willie.

'Right lads,' said Duncan, taking charge. 'Search parties away. Ye ken his favourite pubs?'

There was a chorus of agreement.

'I'd be surprised if ye didn't, but don't stay to drink wi' him. Get him back here as quick as ye can. Ye'd best go in pairs in case he needs some assistance.'

'Just a minute,' interrupted Brooks. 'We've still to get his replacement clothes, presuming he'll be found in time. Anyone able to guess at his measurements?'

‘The largest of everything,’ commented Fiona, to general laughter. ‘Ask Ian. He deals with the uniforms, I had to divulge my vital statistics to him.’

There were cheers and whistles.

As the others set off in search of Sandy, Jill made out her shopping list with Ian’s help. ‘Get the largest size of jeans you can find. I don’t know his inside leg, but he’s about forty-two round the waist. Shirt not needed, they all wear tee-shirts under their tunics.’

‘But Paul isn’t. I noticed he was wearing an ordinary one. Shoes?’

‘Size eleven,’ continued Ian. ‘Doesn’t matter what sort, get the cheapest. And he’ll need socks…and a pullover or light jacket. We don’t know how quickly Paul’ll be able to return the gear. I think that’s all.’

‘Underpants?’

‘Dunno. But you’d better get some.’

‘That the lot?’ asked Jill. ‘Then I’ll be off and I’ll keep an eye open for Sandy.’

‘I’d better give you some money,’ said Brooks, getting out his wallet. ‘And there are some things I’ll need as well. It’d be a help if your husband went too, there may not be time for you to do it all on your own.’

Steven got to his feet with an air of resignation and sighed. ‘What am I to get?’

‘Some chalk, the blackboard variety. Some putty or Plasticine. One of those rubber plungers for unblocking drains and a couple of large bags. It doesn’t matter what sort, so long as we can pack all the uniform into them.' He looked anxiously at his watch. 'Try and be back here not a minute later than four o'clock. I'm off to contact the local police. I noticed from the map in the programme they've an office near the far end of the grandstand and I'm going to need their co-operation again for transport.'

'We'll be back long before four,' said Steven.

'Speaking from previous experience, I wouldn't bank on it,' said Jill. 'It's nearly a mile down to the front and the road'll be solid with people.'

*

It was Alan and Sheila who eventually located Sandy in The Clansman, in a side street near the sea front. He was with a group of fellow musicians and at the stage when the whole world was his friend. He gave them a delighted wave, nearly slopping the contents of his glass over a neighbour. 'Hullawrerr! C'mon 'n' join us.'

'There isn't time,' said Alan. 'You're needed back up at the bus.'

Sandy squinted at his watch. 'Whissa fuss? The parade's no' yet. Plenny o' drinkin' time left. Ah'll buy ye a wee half.' He beckoned to Sheila. 'C'mon ma bonny wee lass, 'n' meet ma pals.'

'Sandy, we haven't time,' she pleaded. 'Please come now, we'll explain on the way.'

He banged his fist on the counter top. 'Ye'll join me in a drink afore we go. Hey, miss!'

Alan looked at his watch and gave a resigned shrug. 'OK then, but a quick one.'

'Tha's ma lad. What'll it be?'

'A Coke, please,' said Sheila.

'And I'll have half of lager,' added Alan.

Sandy gave him a disgusted look. 'Piss 'n' wind! Tha'll no' put hairs on yer chest, lad,' but gave the order.

They both downed their drinks in record time. 'Thanks Sandy,' said Sheila. 'That was great on a hot afternoon. But please, can we get going? Duncan says it's urgent.'

'Better do as the young lady says,' advised one of his companions.

'Huh! Glad she's no' my woman,' muttered another into his drink. 'She'd be aye nagging.'

Sandy emptied his glass. 'Wha's it a' about?'

'C'mon, we'll explain on the way up.' The youngsters took an arm each and steered him out into the street, but their task of getting Sandy back to the coach quickly was anything but straightforward as he seemed to know every other bandsman they met en route.

'Hi there, Sandy! How's yersel'?'

'No' bad, thanks. And these is two o' ma young pals, great wee players they are.'

'It's good to see the youngsters coming on…'

Alan and Sheila stood there, trying to look pleased and interested, but fretting to be on their way.

When they got moving again, it was only to progress another few hundred yards, when it was a case of: 'Hey! Sandy!'

'Davie, good to see ye.' Sandy prodded the other man. 'Ye're no' getting any thinner.'

Davie slapped his paunch. 'Aye, well, Ah'm no' working, but Ah havenae stopped eating.' He prodded Sandy back. 'Ye're no' fadin' awa' yersel'.'

Sandy drew himself up proudly. 'Costs a lot o' money to get a figure like mine,' and they both dissolved into guffaws and back-slapping, wasting more precious time before Alan could get Sandy moving again.

Fortunately, the next encounter was with a group heading in the right direction, which helped them along, but just after they turned off the main street into Argyll Road, leading up to the stadium, they met more friends of Sandy's and everyone stopped for a good blether.

'Tommy! It's a while since Ah seen ye.'

'I'm running my own business now, haven't much time for piping these days. You know Archie here?'

'Oh aye, Ah play some o' his tunes. Did ye hear what happened to–'

Alan looked at his watch and pulled Sheila to one side. 'This is hopeless! For God's sake go and get some of the others to chivvy him along, or we'll never be back in time.'

Sheila needed no encouragement and set off at a trot, dodging through the crowd, while Alan did his best to extricate Sandy from the group. He was brushed aside. 'Dinnae be so impatient, lad.'

It was several minutes before they got moving again and Alan heaved a sigh of relief when he saw Duncan and Neil heading briskly towards them. Like a pair of sheepdogs they cut Sandy out of the throng and waved aside any protests. 'Sorry folks, we've got an urgent appointment. See you later for a drink, mebbe.'

Sandy was highly indignant at this cavalier treatment. 'But Ah hadnae seen Donny since we wuz at Scotstoun–'

'Never mind,' said Duncan firmly. 'Ye can rejoin them as soon as we've got your uniform. Paul would like to borrow it for an hour or so. He wants to dress up so that his pal can take photos of him.'

Sandy's protests stopped abruptly when he was informed that he would be getting a hire fee, which Duncan had briefed Brooks to provide.

By the time they got back to the coach it was five to four and Brooks had been waiting, sweating and literally biting his nails, for half an hour. However, his sighs of relief turned to chuckles as he watched several of the male band members hustle a bewildered Sandy into the space between two coaches and strip him like a swarm of locusts, tossing out sporran; belt; kilt; brogues; *sgian dubh*; stockings and garters. The rest of his uniform had been found in the bus and was already packed, apart from his pipes and feather bonnet which would be taken into the stadium later.

Unlike locusts, the bandsmen revested their prey and by the time Brooks was half way to the main gate with his luggage, Sandy was propped up against the coach, staring down bemusedly at his new clothes, the contents of his sporran miraculously transferred to the pockets. However, his expression cleared when he realised he was holding a half bottle of whisky.

CHAPTER 19

Having bought Sandy's clothes, Jill had no further part to play in her plan and she went back into the stadium to try and concentrate on the scheduled events and take her mind off what was to come. She found Elspeth watching the Highland Dancing, but it finished a few minutes later and she started to wander up past the stalls ranged round the periphery of the grounds. Their contents failed to hold her attention and she began to feel sick with apprehension, not helped by a greasy gust from a fast-food trailer. What if the plan didn't work? What would happen to Paul then? She fingered the sweat shirts on the stall in front of her. They were very reasonably priced and the quality–

'Hello. Fancy seeing you here.'

She jumped at the familiar voice and turned round to face Paul, certain she was going all colours of the rainbow. She forced herself to act casually. 'Hi there. Super day, isn't it? Is this your friend Alan was telling us about?'

'That's right. We haven't seen each other for years, the last person I was expecting to bump into. He's over on business. Turbines for the gas pipeline, isn't it, Yuri? I'm going to show him a bit of Scotland before he goes home.'

Jill said politely to Koshachin, 'That'll be nice. Are you going over to Edinburgh for the Festival?' It was an effort to meet the man's eyes, for all that he seemed so ordinary. The thought of what he represented made her want to claw at his face.

He shrugged. 'I will leave that to my guide.'

Paul looked around and waved a hand in the general direction of the Portaloo. 'Let's move on a bit farther. I think we'll see better from over there when the caber tossing starts.'

Koshachin said in irritation, 'Why did we leave our seats?' He fanned himself with his programme. 'It is hot out here and I can see well with my binoculars.'

'But Paul's quite right, you know,' said Jill quickly. 'If you're viewing from above, it's much easier to assess the way the caber falls after the throw. The nearer it is to twelve o' clock, the better and you can't really judge that from near the front of the grandstand.'

Paul put his arms round their shoulders and urged them forwards. 'There you are, Yuri. The expert opinion of a Scotswoman.' They had made a bit of progress through the crowd when he stopped in front of a stall selling costume jewellery. 'Oops! I nearly forgot. I promised my girlfriend a souvenir of Cowal and I don't want her to be my ex-girlfriend. Come and help me to choose something, we've a few minutes to spare before they start tossing telegraph poles about.' He squeezed Jill's shoulder. 'What d'you think she'd like? I'm not very up in these things.'

She suddenly realised what he was doing and nearly burst into tears. She blinked hard and pointed at random. 'What about that?'

"That" was a cheap gilt chain.

It was the Russian who helped them. He peered at some silver items in a glass display case. 'Those are unusual. I will buy one for my wife.'

The stallholder noticed the customers' interest and unlocked the case. Koshachin picked up a brooch with a Celtic knot pattern and passed it over to be wrapped. Paul's hand hovered over the others and came down on a heart-shaped one set with an amethyst. 'How about that?'

'A Luckenbooth brooch?' said Jill. She swallowed the lump in her throat. 'I'm sure it'll be most suitable.'

He gave it to the stallholder, got out his wallet, paused and said casually to Koshachin, 'Be a good chap and pay for it, would you? That round of drinks nearly cleaned me out, but I've spare cash in my case. I'll settle up with you when we get back to your car.'

His companion looked at him in annoyance, but paid for both brooches.

As they moved away from the stall, Paul said, 'Are you coming to watch with us?'

This is it, thought Jill. This is where we say goodbye for ever – in front of half of the west of Scotland and a member of the KGB. She took a deep breath. 'Thanks, but I promised Alan that I'd go and listen to the grade one bands with him.' She schooled her expression into a smile and held out her hand to Koshachin. 'Nice to have met you. Have a good trip.' His skin felt quite normal, not even sweaty, but she had to resist the urge to wipe her palm down her skirt.

She offered her hand to Paul, unable to say anything.

He pumped it up and down with both of his, transferring the little packet to her. 'Cheerio dear,' he said. 'Glad we met. Give my regards to the family.'

Jill turned away from him and plunged into the crowd, scarcely able to see where she was going.

*

When Brooks reached the Portaloo with his luggage, there was only a short queue and he was relieved to see it was only twenty past four. Pushing his way through the crowds seemed to take for ever. Once inside, he went into one of the cubicles and stacked the bags between the back wall and the lavatory pan, away from the mess on the floor. He opened the door fractionally and put a sausage of putty on the frame. After rattling the cistern handle noisily, he went out, slammed the door behind him and with a toe hooked under it, wrote across it in chalk: "Out of order". He then enquired of the other occupants, 'Anyone know where the stewards' office is? That should be reported.'

'Try the back o' the grandstand,' was the reply.

'Thanks, I'll tell them on the way past.'

In a nearby tent, set up by a purveyor of gentlemen's highland dress, Steven and Gregor were waiting for the go-ahead. Steven wandered round, looking at kilts and jackets. 'It must cost a packet to equip even one bandsman these days.'

'Gregor nudged him. 'Dad,' he whispered.

'Mmm?'

'I'm scared. What if it doesn't work? What'll happen to Paul?'

'It isn't going to go wrong,' said Steven airily. 'It'll be fine, just you see.' He was blithely unconcerned as to Paul's fate, so long as the day's events culminated in the man's permanent removal from the vicinity of the Lindsay family.

'How can you be so confident?'

'It's one of the few compensations of getting older. Things that'd make you curl up in embarrassment at sixteen, once you're forty, you hardly notice them. Remember what Brooks said when he briefed us: "If you've enough brass neck, you can get away with murder".'

'D'you think he has?'

'What?'

'Got away with murder?' Gregor stared at his father, round-eyed. 'D'you think he carries a gun? He's kept his jacket on all the time.'

'If he has, it's none of our business. Now wheesht! Here he comes.' Steven moved to the front of the tent. 'Did you get the stuff into place OK?' he asked Brooks.

'No problems. It's all ready for you two to go and do your plumbers' act and I've just seen Paul and his watchdog heading this way.'

The three of them hovered near the tent entrance and watched as Paul and Koshachin joined the crowd to view the caber tossing, which had just been announced. The queue at the Portaloo vanished. Just before the first competitor made his throw, they saw Paul gesticulate at the cabin, but to their dismay, the Russian accompanied him.

'What if he goes in as well?' said Gregor in an anguished whisper.

'Your brother did tell Paul to go into a cubicle?' said Brooks.

'Yes.'

'In that case, they'll be separated momentarily and you'll just have to evict the other chap.'

To their relief, Koshachin remained at the bottom of the steps leading to the door and as Paul went up, Brooks said, 'Props ready?'

Gregor removed the plastic bag covering the bundle under his arm to reveal Johnny's tool box and a plumber's rubber plunger. Steven took out of his pocket a flat cap which had been found in the coach and pulled it well down over his forehead. As to the rest of their dress, Gregor was in a tee-shirt and jeans and Steven was still wearing his gardening clothes.

'Paul's just going in – now! And good luck.'

Steven and Gregor emerged from the tent, the latter carrying their equipment and marched briskly over to the Portaloo. At that moment, the first of the two Russian competitors took up his stance, and the crowd edged forward, carrying a momentarily distracted

Koshachin with it. With an air of confidence, Gregor pushed past a man heading for the steps, went up them, looked round the door, took in the two closed cubicles, one bearing Brooks' notice and said loudly to his father, 'Yeah, this is it.'

'Sorry chaps,' said Steven to the men inside. 'We've got to clear a blockage. Shan't be long. If ye'd like tae go and watch the Russkies get hernias, we'll get the job done nae bother.'

Within seconds, Steven, Gregor and Paul were in sole possession of the cabin and as a sudden hush fell on the crowd, Gregor chalked "Out of order" on the door and sat down on the top step. Inside, Steven dived into the similarly labelled cubicle, pulled out the bags and handed one to Paul, as he cautiously emerged. 'Right, this lot first. It's Sandy's uniform. Brooks reckons you've got a good chance of getting out of the stadium with the band after the prize-giving. Hurry! We've very little time.'

Outside, a roar and a cheer indicated that the Russian had made his throw.

As Paul reached into the bag, all Steven's dislike of him flared up and he had a strong urge to use the contents of the tool box on the smooth, tanned, well-muscled torso which was revealed when the other man hauled off his shirt and wriggled into the tee-shirt Jill had bought. Instead, he gave a scornful snort of laughter. 'Hah! Your final souvenir of Scotland. I suppose it's my wife's idea of a joke.'

Paul looked down at "Nessie" undulating across his chest. He remembered a "bed and breakfast" on the shores of Loch Ness and smiled to himself.

Steven unpacked the kilt and shook it out. 'This next,' he said curtly. 'Come on, get your trousers off. And if you're going to dress the part properly, take your underpants off as well.'

'Like hell!' muttered Paul as he turned away and unzipped his fly.

Behind him, Steven jeered. 'I didn't think KGB members would be so prudish.'

'Brooks told you?'

'No. You'd always seemed vaguely familiar and at breakfast today I remembered having a certain Rodyon Nesterenko pointed out to me when I was in the Butyrka.'

Paul turned round. 'D'you honestly think I'd willingly work for that lot?' He ignored the kilt and got out Sandy's brogues and stockings.

Steven gave a non-committal grunt.

'They got at me through my family.' He took off his shoes and socks and stood on one of the bags to keep his feet clean. 'If I didn't cooperate, *Dyed* would be extradited and tried for treason. Can you imagine what that would have been like for him and *Babushka*?' He emphasised his point with one of Sandy's stockings and put it on, repressing his distaste for someone else's sweaty footwear. As he adjusted the garter, he continued, 'After they died, Margit was next in line for attention, a pretty seventeen-year-old. They said she'd do very well in a brothel.' He hopped about as he put on the other stocking. 'It was to spare her that that I took part in interrogations – how I cursed my "sympathetic manner" and gift for languages – then for good background cover I was publicly arrested and spent three months in a labour camp before my "escape".' He slid his feet into the brogues, which were a reasonable fit, tied the laces, fastened the spats over them and straightened up. 'Surely you of all people can understand something of what I've gone through?'

As he reached for the kilt, they became aware of angry voices outside and heard Gregor saying, 'Hey! You can't go in there!' in tones an octave higher than usual.

This was followed by a couple of thumps on the door and a voice saying urgently in Russian, 'Nesterenko? Are you there? Nesterenko! Answer me.'

Both men froze momentarily. Paul hurled himself into a cubicle. Steven pushed the kilt at him before the door was slammed in his face and he kicked the bags into the other w.c. He grabbed the plunger, dabbled it in a urinal and armed with this, flung open the door.

Koshachin nearly fell in.

Steven gave the man a dirty look and said to Gregor in a loud, angry voice, 'Can ye no' keep the public off of ma back like I told ye?' He waved the plunger at the notice on the door and addressed Koshachin. 'And can you no' read plain English?'

Gregor goggled at his father and recovered sufficiently to say, 'He sounds foreign.' He tugged at the Russian's sleeve as he tried to advance into the cabin. 'Hey, mister! There's another along there if ye're that desperate.'

Steven recognised the man who had tripped him up at the airport. He applied the still-dripping cup of the plunger to the intruder's chest and propelled him backwards down the steps with it, shouting, 'I gave up ma Saturday afternoon tae do a job an' nae foreign idiot is going tae stop me!' Having found the perfect target for all his recent, pent-up anger, he was thoroughly enjoying himself. The Russians had pushed him around for years and at last he was free to retaliate with impunity.

The altercation had attracted the attention of the crowd and one of a trio of burly bandsmen left his companions and came over. 'Is anything wrong, sir?'

Steven waved the plunger in Koshachin's face and was delighted to see the man recoil in disgust. 'Ah cannae make this furrin eejit understand the loo's no' working. If he's that desperate, there's another alang there.'

The bandsman gestured to the Russian. 'If you'd like to come with me, sir, I'll show you where to go.'

'Thanks,' said Steven. 'Then mebbe I can get on wi' ma job.'

A voice from the crowd called out, 'Dinnae fash yersel', Jimmy. He'll get ye there quick. He's from Strathclyde Polis Band. Can ye no' see the wee blue light flashing on his sporran?'

Koshachin mopped his shirt with a handkerchief and looked from Steven, standing sentinel on the steps, to the beckoning bandsman. As he allowed himself to be led away to the accompaniment of laughter, the Russian glared back over his shoulder at his tormentor.

By the time Steven was back inside, Paul was emerging from his hiding place, wrapping the kilt around himself. 'Phew! That was close! You were terrific–'

Both men froze again as from the level of their knees a slurred voice proclaimed, 'Blurry furriners… Too damn perjink… He should ha' peed agin the wheel like me…'

The two men stared at each other and burst into laughter, which dispelled much of the tension between them. Paul started to fasten the kilt and between chuckles said, 'Sandy must be built like an elephant, this'll go round me twice…and there's no way I can shorten the belt enough.'

Steven felt in the bottom of one of the bags. 'Here, Jill thought you might need these.' He produced a bunch of safety pins. 'Get yourself pinned together and put on the sporran… Forget the belt, nobody'll notice… I'll take it back to the coach.'

As Paul put on the tunic and transferred the contents of his pockets to the sporran, Steven slid the *sgian dubh* into his right stocking. 'Hope you don't need this.'

'Me too. How do these things go on? Is it crossbelt over plaid or vice versa?'

'Oh Lord! I've no idea.' Steven opened the door a crack and whispered urgently to Gregor. 'Does the crossbelt go over or under the plaid?'

'Our lot wear it over the plaid…and under the right epaulette.' There was another roar from the crowd. 'Buck up! Two more to go before the next Russian.'

The two of them wrestled with the folds of the plaid. 'I think that's correct,' said Steven as he finally managed to arrange it diagonally across Paul's chest. 'It falls nicely from your left shoulder. Hold it there while I fasten the brooch.'

'Ouch!'

'Sorry. Now for the crossbelt.' He put it on according to Gregor's instructions, centred the buckle, stepped back and surveyed Paul critically. 'That looks OK to me.'

'Where do I meet the band?'

'The bushes at the top of the hill where they form up for the march-past – and I hope Jill's plan succeeds.'

'Well if it doesn't, it'll be a case of *prashchai svaboda* – farewell freedom.'

Gregor opened the door again, 'Zero hour coming up... They're carrying the caber back for the Russian... It's vertical... He's got his arms round it...'

Paul held out his hand. Steven ignored it. Paul smiled and shrugged. 'Thanks for your help and all the more appreciated in view of the way you obviously feel about me. You've got a super family, take care of them, they need you.' He touched Steven briefly on the shoulder on the way out and ruffled Gregor's hair. While all eyes were on the Russian as he made his run and throw, Paul took a deep breath, squared his shoulders, marched down the steps and was soon lost in the crowd.

Steven gathered up the other man's clothes into one of the bags, rubbed out the chalk notice and picked up the tool box. After checking that nothing was left behind, he joined Gregor, who rubbed out the other notice. 'Go ahead folks,' he said to the queue which was reforming. 'How did the Russkies do?'

'No' bad,' came a reply. 'Yon last throw fell at nearly eleven o'clock.'

The two of them rejoined Brooks in the outfitter's tent and gave him the bag of Paul's clothes. He looked from one to the other and shook his head in admiration. 'You were brilliant. You ought to be on the stage, you'd make a fortune.'

'Well, we did have a bit of unexpected help,' said Gregor.

'Thank God for the policeman,' agreed his father. 'If he hadn't taken charge of the Russian, I don't know what I'd have done.'

'I don't think anyone noticed Paul come out, they were far too busy looking at the arena,' said Brooks. 'Now, let's get back to the coach, or at least to the beer tent and an ice cream stall, you've certainly earned some refreshment. No, not that way, the watchdog's sure to come back for a sniff round and I don't want to bump into him.'

*

After leaving Paul, Jill realised she was wandering around aimlessly, still clutching his present. She found a quiet space behind one of the stalls and unwrapped the packet. She studied the brooch. It would remind her of so much, but after all Steven had suffered, she owed it to him to put the past behind her. This wasn't the time to wear Paul's gift and she zipped it safely into her handbag.

She bought a soft drink at the stall and went to the other Portaloo on the hillside to wash her face. When she came down the steps, she noticed an angry-looking "Yuri" being deposited in the queue at the men's entrance by a large bandsman. She wondered how that had been engineered as once the guide departed, the Russian hurried back the way he had come, heedless of the cheers for his fellow countryman.

Back at the arena, Jill found Alan and several of his friends listening to the grade one bands and in response to his raised eyebrow of enquiry, gave a nod and a smile and received a very relieved look in return. She declined the offer of another drink and returned to the coach, where she flopped into a vacant seat, feeling utterly drained and soon drifted off to sleep.

Steven joined her on the coach about half an hour later. Getting the better of the Russian had lanced and drained the pustule of anger and resentment which had been festering inside him for far too long. As he looked down at his sleeping wife, he could see for the first time how she would look as an old woman and he felt ashamed of his behaviour at breakfast. The last five years had scarred all the Lindsays, but perhaps the family could now have something like a normal life together.

Jill came to as he sat down. She yawned. 'I saw the Russian on his own, looking like thunder, so I gather you were successful?'

'It went off a treat…in fact, I rather enjoyed it.' Steven slid his arm round her.

She rested her head on his shoulder and sighed. 'I don't know about you, but I'm just about done in. It'd be bliss if the helicopter could just waft us home again.' She stiffened. 'Heavens! How are we going to get back?'

Ian McLellan had been dozing in the seat in front of them and turned round. 'Don't worry, Mrs Lindsay, the coach wasn't quite full when we left, so the three of you will be very welcome to return with us.'

'What time will you be leaving?' said Steven.

'It's usually after eight before we get away. The march down the road takes quite a while and the lads like to get some refreshments afterwards.' He got out his programme. 'But if you want to meet up with us after the parade, I'll show you where and when.'

Steven felt Jill droop against him. 'Cheer up. You'll feel better after some food. We'll go and have a decent meal.' He started to pat his pockets and his face fell. 'At least, we will if you've got your wallet or cheque book with you.'

Jill gave him an exasperated look. 'There's one thing about you that hasn't changed over the years.' She kissed him on the cheek. 'That, my love, is what you said the second time you took me out.'

CHAPTER 20

Outside, the bands were beginning to reassemble for the march-past. Brooks found Duncan tuning his pipes behind the coach and tapped his shoulder to get his attention. 'We've got Paul into the other chap's uniform and providing he meets up as planned, the next bit's up to you.'

Duncan nodded. 'We've a couple o' tunes to play, but with over two thousand others in the arena, nobody'll notice he cannae pipe. It's always a bit of a habble, so he'll be OK.'

'The trickiest bit'll be at the exit. The opposition'll be on the lookout there.'

'I'll put him in the middle and tell the band to keep ranks as much as possible. We'll reform as soon as we're out and keep him like that all the way down the park.'

'And I'll have a car waiting to pick him up at the first road junction. You will be able to stop for a few seconds?'

'Oh aye, the lads need an occasional breather.'

'I can't thank you enough. You've all been marvellous and if we do get him away safely, it'll be entirely due to the band.' He gave Duncan a wad of notes. 'Have a celebration on me tonight, or rather on my, er, firm and put the rest towards your funds. I'm off now, I've got Paul's clothes and I'll see that the other chap's are returned. And again, many thanks indeed. 'Bye.'

He got onto the coach to say goodbye to Steven and Jill. 'Are the three of you going to be able to get home alright?'

'It's been taken care of, there's room for us in here,' said Steven. 'We're going to get a meal shortly and we'll rejoin the others when the band gets down to the front.'

Jill would have preferred to wait till they'd seen Paul safely on his way, but wasn't going to argue about it.

After thanking them profusely for their help and waving at a comatose Sandy who was sprawled along the back seats, Brooks departed to make his final arrangements.

*

In the stadium, Paul waited by the bushes as instructed. He thought his friends would never appear. Band after band straggled up the hill, reformed ranks and marched past him down into the arena. Every time one in full dress, red kilts and feather bonnets went by, he peered hopefully at the faces.

When he was beginning to think his band had gone home, he saw them coming up the hill towards him.

Rarely had he been so thankful to see familiar faces as he moved out into their midst. Ian gave him the feather bonnet to put on and Duncan handed over Sandy's pipes. 'For the next bit, all ye have to do is carry them. Left hand round the bass drone, blowpipe and chanter, in that order and let the rest hang down.' He helped Paul. 'Right lads, form up the way I was telling ye. Everyone in place? OK... And for the benefit of our newest recruit, I would remind you that we march off on the left foot and bass drones are to be carried parallel to the ground... I don't want to see anyone's suffering from brewer's droop.'

By the time they had marched down the slope, along past the saluting base and most of the way around the arena, Paul's arm was aching, but when they finally halted, he realised why Duncan had held back until nearly the last of the one hundred and fifty or so bands formed up: they were one of the nearest to the exit.

When Duncan said 'Stand easy,' Paul followed the example of some of the others and carefully put down the pipes on the grass. He gave a sigh of relief, rubbed his arm and looked round. He was well away from the grandstand and hemmed in by musicians on all sides.

Duncan came over to him and picked up the pipes. 'Here, you'd better practice putting them up and down and blowing a bit. I've stopped off everything except the middle tenor drone. Hold them as ye did for coming in and when I say "Band, get ready", ye put them up like this.' He demonstrated.

Paul tried to copy him and got into a thorough mess, but after several minutes of concentrated and patient tuition, he could put up and take down the instrument without feeling as though he was wrestling with an octopus. Even so, when the time came for the massed bands to march into a hollow square to the tune *The Glendaruel Highlanders*, they had played the first measure before he had sorted himself out and similarly with *Highland Laddie*, the traditional salute to the chieftain of the games. He then had a respite during the prize-giving. This was punctuated by cheers and throwing into the air of headgear as the winners were announced.

When the announcer got to grade three, Paul's companions gestured at each other to be quiet. They erupted into whoops and cheers when the loudspeaker crackled, 'Third prize, band number thirty-four.' Duncan marched off to the rostrum, leaving the others to rejoice at their success.

Alan hugged Sheila.

Joan, with fewer inhibitions, turned to Paul, flung her arms round him and kissed him.

Willie gave her a disapproving look. 'This is no' a football match – and he was no' even playing.'

Neil slapped him on the back. 'Dinnae mind him, lass,' he said to Joan. 'He's just jealous, that's all.'

Paul let go of Joan and she advanced on Willie. He flapped a hand at her and backed away.

'Shame on you Willie, to refuse a lady!'

‘Make the most of your opportunities, man!’

‘Go on, lass!’

‘He’s feart o’ what his missis’ll say!

In her enthusiasm, Joan had dislodged Paul’s feather bonnet and once she’d turned her attention elsewhere, he tugged it forward to shield his face again, hoping no Russian binoculars were trained on the band.

On Duncan’s return, they crowded round him to admire their silver trophy. Ian took charge of it to carry in front of the band during the march through town. He also took charge of an envelope containing their prize money.

As soon as the announcements for grade one were over, Duncan called the band to attention. ‘Now then lads – and lassies – this is it. Ye all know what we’ve got to do and for God’s sake, try and keep Mr Holland surrounded on all sides. Reform ranks as soon as we’re out of the gate and go straight down the park to yon lock-up garages. We’ll come out onto the road there, rather than at the top end. OK? Form up… By the right, quick march!’

The band headed for the exit and Paul was swept along with it. A seething scrum of spectators and musicians had already amassed ahead of them, all pushing their way out into the park. Paul tried to look round for Russian watchdogs, but it was impossible: his feather bonnet was knocked down over his fore-head and all he could do was clutch Sandy’s pipes to his chest, woodwork vertical and let the flood of bodies carry him forwards. When he sensed an easing of pressure, he pushed back his headgear, looked around and breathed a large sigh of relief. He was out!

The band reformed ranks round him and set off past the parked coaches, Jimmy beating a brisk pace on his side drum. They were headed by Ian holding their trophy and one of the girls from chanter class carrying their name placard. Paul wondered at what stage he would be leaving them all.

Paul heard Duncan call to Ian as they marched along. 'When we approach the nearer row of garages, go on ahead and see if the road's clear. I'll start up the band, we'll do a left hand wheel and we'll follow through with a right hand wheel, once we're clear of the garages.' He swung his pipes onto his shoulder. 'Then we've to stop at the first junction to let Mr Holland leave…that'll be at Argyll Road.'

'And if we can't get out immediately?'

'We'll keep on playing and mark time till the coast's clear.'

Ian went on ahead and Duncan passed back his instructions. 'We'll start off with the retreats: *Green Hills of Tyrol* and *When the battle's over* – appropriate under the circumstances. Band, get ready…'

Paul realised something had gone wrong when he caught a glimpse of a police car parked in a cul-de-sac opposite the garages and Brooks standing beside it, waving in open-mouthed dismay. Duncan must have misunderstood the instructions about the pick-up point. For the first time that afternoon, Paul came close to panicking. He looked wildly round him, but he was boxed in on all sides, being marched away from safety. He was trapped on a treadmill.

He pulled himself together. He might be hemmed in by the band, but in such a position, he was likely to be safe for the time being, even if the opposition spotted him. He had better try and look as though he was playing the pipes. He hitched the drones further up his shoulder and tried to remember the fingering for one of the simple tunes he had learnt on the practice chanter. Bits of a conversation he'd had with Alan a couple of years ago floated through his head.

'Learning to play the pipes is a case of one step back for every two steps forward–'

Paul looked down at Alan's feet in front of him to check that he was keeping in step with the others.

'You learn perhaps six or eight simple tunes by heart on the practice chanter and when you think you really know them, someone sticks this contraption under your arm and every note of music goes out of your head.'

Too damn true. He couldn't even remember the fingering for the *Skye Boat Song*.

'Even with the drones corked, after two minutes you're seeing black spots.'

Lots of black spots, which keep threatening to coalesce, and your lungs are red raw, too.

'Once you get rid of a couple of corks and you think you're doing no' bad, someone bawls at you "By the right, quick march!" and again, every note of music goes out of your head and either you're rooted to the spot or else you set off on the wrong foot.'

And if you don't keep up with the others, Ron's going to bump into you with the bass drum. Paul lengthened his stride.

'Once mobile, you have to maintain a steady flow of air over four reeds with the pressure of your left elbow and at the same time, watch where you're putting your feet. Then when you get all three drones going and you think you're doing fine, you're told that you're no' blowing a steady tone.'

"Haw-hee" went the drone in Paul's left ear. Nobody else's drones seemed to be making that noise. He was suddenly aware of a "boom-boom" behind him and knew enough about band procedure to recognise the signal for "stop playing at the end of this measure". He stopped blowing immediately. They were at the end of the housing estate and about to wheel left into the main street. He looked up to his right, but there was no sign of Brooks or a car.

The policeman on traffic duty halted them and came over to speak to Duncan. Paul caught the gist of his words: a car would be waiting for him near the ferry terminal. He waved to show he had heard the message and rolled his shoulders while Duncan had a brief conversation with Willie and Neil. There were smiles and nods and Duncan beckoned to someone who had been following the band. Johnny and Elspeth Morgan joined the group. Duncan said a few words, gave them what looked like a roll of banknotes and the couple stood aside on the pavement when the policeman signalled for the band to continue.

By the time they passed the gas works, Paul was ready to give up. The feather bonnet was tickling him, his lips couldn't grip the blowpipe and his left elbow was pierced by a red-hot needle. "Haw-hee" mocked the drone as he stumbled on, putting one foot in front of the other, with the brogues chafing the backs of his heels, unable even to work out if he was in step with the others. Puff, squeeze, left foot, right foot. It would have been easier if he could have coordinated blowing and marching, but it didn't seem to work like that. Paul told himself, if children can master this hellish instrument and keep going, then I bloody well can! He screwed up his eyes to dispel the black spots in his vision and plodded on.

Above the sound of the pipes and drums, he gradually became aware of another noise, which threatened to obliterate everything else. He had kept his eyes firmly fixed on Alan's back, concentrating on trying to keep in step, but he risked a quick look round to see what was happening.

He faltered out of sheer amazement.

They had got as far as the Town Hall in the main shopping street of Dunoon and were marching between packed ranks of spectators: spectators who were five and six deep on the pavements; who were overflowing onto the road; who were waving and shouting, clapping and cheering.

Paul briefly caught the eye of a grey-haired matron whose rosy cheeks clashed with the orange cardigan strained across her bosom. She blew him a kiss. He winked at her, pulled back his shoulders and hitched up the drones. God bless the British public. Their support and enthusiasm acted like a high-powered stimulant and he strode on down the street in a state of elation, all his fears and discomforts forgotten. This was on a par with being driven down the Mall in a state landau.

It seemed no time at all before they wheeled off the road into a little park, marched on a bit farther and came to a halt at the top of a short flight of steps leading down to the road bordering the sea. Paul managed to put down his pipes at the same time as the rest of the band. Duncan thanked them for everything they had done that day and told them to fall out.

Paul stood there with his ears ringing. He gasped for breath as the drummers shed their instruments and got scant sympathy from Ron. 'What d'ye think it's like wi' this thing in front of me?' He unclipped the bass drum from its supporting harness, narrowly missing a kilted spectator who was sitting on a stone wall bordering a flower bed, watching the parade from behind mirrored sunglasses.

The spectator merely smiled toothily at them and placidly resettled himself, hands clasped over his sporran.

Duncan took the pipes and feather bonnet from Paul. 'Look, they're waiting for ye. Off ye go now, and the best o' luck.'

Paul saw Jill, Steven and Brooks standing beside a car on the Esplanade, talking to two policemen on traffic duty. He waved at them and turned back to Duncan and the band, a lump in his throat. 'Words fail me. I can't thank you all enough.' He clasped Duncan's hand. 'That was one of the most mind-blowing experiences of my life. If I were to drop down dead right now, it would be as a very happy man.'

'I shall be glad to oblige you,' a voice said in Russian,

Paul whirled round and stared in horror at the man in the mirrored sunglasses.

Koshachin!

The world shuddered to a halt and after several eons, lurched forward in slow motion. Several things happened as Paul watched, mesmerised: Koshachin's hand came up towards him like a striking snake; a squid-like object floated through the air and lovingly embraced the Russian's face and something tugged at Paul's left leg.

Koshachin disappeared under a flurry of tartan as Ron hurled himself forwards, padded drumsticks whirling. Spectators shouted and screamed. Time had resumed its normal pace.

Paul saw Alan pick up his instrument, the chanter reduced to a jagged stump.

'Alan!' he gasped, when he recovered his powers of speech. 'Your pipes! I'm–'

'Oh bugger the chanter! What's that against your life? Now get moving before Duncan has to measure you up.'

Paul took a step towards the car, but Sheila yelled at him to keep still. Reversing her drumsticks, she bent down and used them cautiously to ease away something hanging from one of his spats. She held up a little metal dart with a discoloured tip.

Brooks came running up the steps with one of the policemen, who took charge of the dazed Russian and his weapon, which Sheila had wrapped carefully in a paper handkerchief. Brooks beckoned to Paul. 'Come on man! Don't hang around. There may be more of them nearby.' He said over his shoulder to Alan, 'Thanks, lad. That was quick thinking. I'll see you're compensated.'

On the pavement, Paul paused in front of a white-faced Jill. '*Prashchai, dushka*' and he touched her gently on the cheek before Brooks pushed him towards the open car door.

CHAPTER 21

Jill stared in bewilderment at the departing vehicle. What had happened? She'd never expected to see Paul again. There seemed to have been a fight. But he'd looked unharmed as he got into the car. She noticed someone being escorted down the steps from the garden. 'Steve, have you any idea what's going on? Look, isn't that Paul's "watchdog" over there?'

Steven turned round. 'Good Heavens! It's the Russian in handcuffs. Now this, I must see.' He strode off, leaving Jill little the wiser.

She started to shiver uncontrollably and flopped onto one of the Esplanade benches, where Alan and Sheila found her shortly afterwards.

The doctor's daughter looked at Jill. 'Alan, I think your mum's suffering from shock, we've got to get her warmed up.' Sheila put down her drum, joined Jill on the bench and fanned out her plaid, wrapping it round the shivering woman. 'Come on, get yours off.'

Alan put his damaged pipes beside the drum, unpinned the brooch on his shoulder and hauled off his plaid. Sheila sat back and let him wrap Jill in a double thickness of wool. They both rubbed her arms and back and after a couple of minutes were relieved to see the colour return to her face.

'Thanks,' said Jill when her teeth stopped behaving like castanets. 'I feel a bit better now.'

'Hey! What's happening?' Gregor stood in front of them, almost as white-faced as Jill had been. 'Has Mum been hurt?'

'Not really,' said Alan.

'Sort of,' said Sheila.

'I'm OK,' said Jill, 'but will somebody please tell me what the heck's going on.'

Alan took a deep breath. 'The Russian very nearly did for Paul.'

'Oh my God!' She put her hand over her mouth and stared at him, wide-eyed.

'It's all right Mrs Lindsay,' said Sheila, 'you can relax, he didn't come to any harm.'

Jill huddled into Alan's plaid and slumped against the bench. 'But how did that happen? I thought the band got him away safely.'

'We got him out of the stadium, no problem,' Alan went on, 'but Duncan made a blooper over the pick-up point and Paul had to come the whole way with us.'

'Yes, that's what Brooks told us,' said Jill, 'but what was the stushie in the garden?'

'That was the band giving the Russian their version of a Glasgow kiss!' He grinned at his mother's expression. 'OK, so nobody head-butted him in the face, but Ron gave him a working-over with his drumsticks after I threw my pipes at him.' He chuckled. 'After all, the Great Highland Bagpipe was once proscribed by the English as an instrument of war.'

'But what was he doing there in the first place?'

'Somehow, the Russians spotted Paul was with the band,' said Alan, 'and it wouldn't have taken much for them to find out where the parades end.'

'Just before the caber-tossing started,' said Jill, 'I met Paul with this chap he called Yuri, who mentioned using binoculars… And he had a programme, which includes a map of Dunoon, so he'd easily find a way here avoiding the crowds.'

'But how did you recognise him?' asked Sheila. 'He was wearing dark glasses and a kilt. He looked just like a tourist.'

Alan bared his teeth in an approximation of Koshachin's smile. 'Soviet dentistry. I couldn't help noticing how awful it was while we were in the beer tent. He smiled after Ron nearly bashed him with the bass drum and I recognised that mouthful again… So when his hand came up to hit Paul with something, I threw my pipes at him. No time to get out my *sgian dubh*.'

'Pure dead brilliant!' said Sheila.

Alan gave her an admiring look. 'But it was you who spotted the poisoned dart, or whatever it was.'

Jill said to the youngsters. 'You're both marvellous. You saved Paul's life with your quick thinking.' She glanced over at Steven who waved at her and made a beckoning gesture. She pointed to herself. He shook his head and indicated Alan and Sheila. 'Alan, I think Dad wants the two of you over there.'

They moved off and Gregor sat down beside her. 'Mum, why are you wrapped up in a plaid?'

'Sheila diagnosed I was suffering from shock and this was to warm me up.'

'I'm not surprised after all you've been through since breakfast…and it's chilly hanging around by the sea.' He half got up, rummaged in a pocket and produced the remains of a bar of chocolate. 'Here, you'd better have this. They say sugar's good for shock.'

'Thanks.' She gratefully ate his soggy offering. 'But where have you been? I was getting worried. You did the same thing last year, wandering off without telling anyone where you were going.'

'Sorry…but when I got back to the coach after Mr Brooks stood me an ice cream, you and Dad had disappeared. Mrs Morgan was there with some of her pals and said you'd gone to get something to eat. She asked me if I'd like to go with her and her husband for a bite and stay with them to walk behind the band in the parade, along with family members and local supporters.'

'That was kind of her.'

'We went to a café and I told them about Paul being a double agent and our journey here by helicopter with Mr Brooks 'cos the Russians were after him and why he had to dress up in Sandy's gear so he could escape from the stadium.'

'Well, you certainly sang for your supper,' said his mother dryly. 'It'll be all round the village by tomorrow morning…if Elspeth hasn't already phoned Old Elephant Ears.'

Gregor's face fell. 'Oh, I never thought about that… But does it matter?'

'Not at all.' Jill patted his knee. 'If you hadn't told them, someone else would have. It'll just become another bit of village folklore…and at least you gave them the correct version.' She looked over to the group round the Russian. Duncan and Ron had joined them, along with two more policemen, one with braid on his hat. She nudged Gregor. 'The top brass seems to be getting in on the act.' They sat and watched.

The senior officer appeared to listen attentively, making the occasional pacifying gesture while Steven apparently translated a flood of furious Russian. The officer spoke to each of the band members in turn, then returned to his colleagues for a short discussion. Jill saw the arresting officer produce a small packet and hand it to his superior, after which he went to the Russian and removed the handcuffs. The erstwhile prisoner immediately waved his arms about and shook his fists, but his tirade stopped abruptly when Steven said something to him. Jill stared as the man crumpled into himself like a ruptured balloon.

Steven then had a brief conversation with the police. The senior officer shook his hand and made a dismissive gesture at the Russian. The group dispersed and Steven and the four band members came back to where Jill and Gregor were sitting.

'Well, what was that about?' she said. They all looked at Steven.

‘The cops decided the Russian could go as he hadn’t actually injured anyone.’

Jill stared at him, open-mouthed. ‘But he tried to kill Paul.’

‘Yes, all of us here are agreed on that, but Paul and Brookes have gone and we don’t know what’s on the dart, so we’ve no on-the-spot proof. I get the impression the police have enough to do this weekend with mopping up drunks and the last thing they want is a diplomatic incident.’

‘’S not fair,’ said Gregor, scowling. ‘He’s getting off scot-free.’

There was an angry buzz of agreement.

‘That’s what it looks like, but it’s anything but.’ Steven held up his hands for silence. ‘In view of what I went through, when the so-and-so started to go on about assault and wrongful arrest,’ he gave a self-satisfied grin, ‘it gave me great pleasure to point out he’d cocked up his mission, he’d attracted the attention of the local police and his dart was being sent off for analysis – all of which’ll go down like a lead balloon in Dzerzhinsky Square.’ He looked at the others’ puzzled expressions. ‘That’s where the KGB has its headquarters. You’ve just seen a dead man walking.’

There was a stunned silence, broken by a muttered, ‘Serves the bugger right,’ from Ron.

Steven turned his attention to Jill and repeated Gregor’s question. ‘Why are you wearing a plaid?’

‘I was a bit shivery earlier on.’ She smiled at him. ‘But I’m fine now, love. Sheila and Alan got me warmed up and Gregor gave me some chocolate. They've all been looking after me.'

Her husband leant down, felt her hands and briefly touched her cheek, subconsciously copying Paul's earlier gesture.

Duncan had been watching the passing traffic. 'There's our coach just gone by to the meeting point by the pier.' He turned to Jill. 'Come on Mrs Lindsay, you'll be warmer on board. Mebbe someone'll have a flask of tea or coffee.'

They walked down the Esplanade to where the coach was waiting. There was a general melée with band members stowing their instruments into travelling cases and taking off the outer layers of their uniforms. While this was going on, Jill noticed Duncan, Willie and Neil rounding up anyone who looked as though they were about to go back into town. Some of them didn't seem at all pleased at being told to get onto the coach.

She also noticed Joan, standing on her own, shoulders drooping, staring at a wheel. She went over to the girl. 'Are you OK?'

Joan turned round, tears running down her face. 'I've just realised I'll never see Paul again.'

Jill gave her a quick hug. 'I know how you feel.' She swallowed hard. 'We'll all miss him.'

The other sniffed and wiped her face with the back of her hand. 'He were great fun…and a real gent.'

'He was indeed – and he always said how nice my hair looked after you'd done it.'

Joan brightened up. 'He did?'

Jill nodded. 'Honestly.'

Joan gave her a watery smile and went off to board the coach.

The Lindsays waited till the others got in and found some unoccupied seats next to each other. As Jill settled herself, she looked out and saw the Russian sitting hunched on a bench, staring at the sea.

Steven followed the direction of her gaze. 'Huh! If the sod's got any sense, he'll take a running jump off the end of the pier.'

Jill said nothing, but she couldn't help wondering about a wife who'd probably never receive a silver brooch.

Once everyone was on board, Duncan went round counting heads and called for silence. 'Now, some of ye are no' pleased at leaving so early, when in past years we've stayed for a celebration – or wake.' There was a general mutter of agreement. 'But don't worry folks, ye may not be going off on the rammle round Dunoon this time, but never fear, ye won't have anything to complain about, I've arranged for something special on the way home.'

'It'd bloody well better be!' shouted one of the band's supporters.

'Duncan'll see you OK,' Neil yelled back as the coach set off.

After a short drive, they drew up in a car park. Jill recognised it as the place where the helicopter had landed that morning, which seemed like several lifetimes ago. She looked down from her seat and saw Elspeth and Johnny standing beside their car, waving at the coach.

'Right folks,' announced Duncan. 'This is where we take supplies on board. Any strong-armed volunteers?'

Jill watched in amusement as cases of different sorts of drinks were transferred from the Morgans' car boot into the coach, to the accompaniment of loud cheers and whistles.

'And anyone who's not happy with that lot can walk back to Dunoon,' said Duncan, before the coach doors shut. 'And it's not all. Elspeth's phoned The Village Inn at Arrochar and we'll be stopping there for food later on.' There were more cheers.

As soon as they set off again, Ian opened a bottle of whisky, poured it into the silver cup he'd been nursing and passed it round for everyone to toast the band's success. When it reached Gregor, Jill smiled at him and made a point of looking the other way.

Later on, Duncan walked down the coach, chatting to those still capable of holding a coherent conversation and Jill asked him how he'd organised their celebrations.

'Mr Brooks gave us a very generous thank-you and when we had a breather during the parade, I spotted the Morgans following the band. They'd come in their own car, so I gave them some cash, asked them to buy the drinks and meet us at Sandbank.' He grabbed the back of a seat as the coach swung round a bend and started to climb. 'I knew we'd all be wanting a celebration after our win, so rather than hauling drunks out of pubs later in the evening, I reckoned it'd be easier to provide it on board.' He straightened up and addressed all the passengers. 'We'll soon be stopping at Rest and be Thankful, so if anyone feels like puking, ye can wait till there.'

When the coach drew into the parking bay at the top of the hill, most people got out to stretch their legs, but several staggered away and bent over.

Jill was surprised to see Sandy was not one of them and he was carrying his pipes, having been reunited with them at some stage. He walked over to a promontory and started to play. In the twilight, the music echoed around the steep glen leading down to Loch Long and the hairs rose on Jill's neck. She shivered.

Duncan was standing beside her and noticed her reaction. 'That's the best way to hear the pipes… Ye might not think it, but Sandy's a bonny player when he's more or less sober.' He tapped his foot to the unusual rhythm and cocked his head. 'Hmm… *Glasgow Week in Hamburg*.' He laughed. 'After today, mebbe we should rechristen it: *Cowal Weekend in Dunoon*.' He went back to the coach and tooted the horn. As Jill boarded, he said in an aside, 'Better they get rid of it up here than in front of our next stop, or we might not be allowed back.'

The Morgans were waiting for them in Arrochar and a slightly less raucous coachload enjoyed their meal. Sandy soon had his pipes out again and got feet tapping. Someone said to Elspeth, 'How about some dancing? We can do it on yon bit of grass by the shore,' and there was general agreement, to the delight of the tourists who had been attracted by the music. After a bit of discussion, *Mairi's Wedding* was chosen as there were enough people present who knew the steps.

As Jill whirled round, she remembered the last time she'd danced it at Castle Tullum. She smiled at Joan and received a wistful look back. There were cries of 'More' when they finished so Elspeth suggested *Strip the Willow* as it was a simple dance in which everyone could participate, tourists included, and the pipers took it in turn with the accompaniment.

Duncan finally called a halt to the impromptu ceilidh. 'Time we were off, folks. We've had a long day – and a very successful one.' There were claps and loud cheers. 'Thanks for your company and I hope you all enjoyed yourselves. Goodnight and a safe journey home.'

Had Jill been asked if bagpipes could be played sitting down in a moving coach, she would have said it was impossible, but Sandy hadn't finished for the evening, though his tempo gradually reduced to slow marches.

Once the music stopped, many of the passengers drifted off to sleep, Steven included, his head on Jill's shoulder. He briefly woke up at one point. 'Why was someone playing Dvorak on the pipes?' he said drowsily.

'You know it as the theme from the *New World* Symphony, but to pipers, it's *Going Home*.'

He slipped his arm round her and murmured, 'Going home…to our wee cottage…good…'

As they wound their way along the shores of Loch Lomond, Jill gazed at the moonlight glinting on the water. What a day it had been… She looked around the coach. Alan and Sheila were entwined on a nearby seat and Gregor was sitting in front of them, talking to one of the drummers. She sighed contentedly and snuggled up to Steven. *All* the Lindsays were going home.

EPILOGUE

After Paul's sudden departure, Castle Tullum College had no difficulty in finding a replacement for their modern languages teacher. At the end of Steven's first term in his new job, a letter arrived at Forthview Cottage from Brooks. It enclosed a Christmas card in an unstamped envelope addressed to the Lindsay family. The greeting consisted of a sketch of Wee McGreegor holding a daisy and both were smiling.

ABOUT THE AUTHOR

Susan Miller is an Honorary Vice-President of the Glasgow & West of Scotland Family History Society, for whom she has researched and written several reference books. She has also written numerous articles for genealogical journals. She has four grandchildren and lives in Stirlingshire, where she used to be a member of her local pipe band.

Lightning Source UK Ltd.
Milton Keynes UK
UKHW011604150519
342717UK00001B/54/P